Acclaim for
MORTAL SIGHT

"A unique blend of fantasy and literary elements."
— *School Library Journal*

"An absorbing fantasy about a teenager's struggle to discover her destiny."
— *Foreword Reviews*

"An unabashed piece of Milton fan fiction, *Mortal Sight* concerns a heroine who at critical moments finds prophetic guidance in verses of *Paradise Lost*. It's compulsively readable, especially its fight scenes. I highly recommend it."
— Prof. John Rumrich, University of Texas-Austin

"Delightfully spooky with characters you can care about."
— C.C. Hunter, *New York Times* bestselling author

"*Mortal Sight* is a wonderful achievement. Beautiful writing is joined to a gripping concept. A delight from start to finish. Highly recommended."
— Thomas Locke, bestselling author of *Emissary*

"With frequent references to Milton, *Mortal Sight* is a promising beginning to an intriguing series."
— *Orehaven Magazine*

MORTAL SIGHT

MORTAL SIGHT

THE COLLIDING LINE | BOOK ONE

SANDRA FERNANDEZ RHOADS

ENCLAVE

Escape

*For the ones searching for a place to belong
and to John, who always believed*

1
THE STORM

Some girls want to change the world. Others want to rule it. Me? I'd be happy if fall never came. Weird, I know. Don't get me wrong, there's plenty I'd like to change—a lot of things, in fact, but as soon as the autumn wind blasts through town and the leaves turn aspen yellow, I know what's coming.

I open the front door as quietly as I can so Mom doesn't wake and slip onto the front porch. A sleepy haze lingers in the soggy air the way it does before the sun burns away the morning dew. Not fully awake, but no longer dreaming.

I step over the creaky board, tiptoeing to the front steps. As soon as I reach the splintered rail, a quiet voice greets me. "Hi Cera." Jess, the neighbor kid from the duplex attached to ours, sits on the bottom plank in her school uniform. Her dirty tights stretch at the knees as she crosses her legs. Her windblown ponytail tilts sideways as if she's attempted to braid her own hair. If she wasn't so proud to be seven, and, in her own mind, old enough to take care of herself, I'd offer to smooth it out.

"Hey, Jess." I keep my voice low so the sound doesn't carry through the cracked windows. "Waiting on your aunt to take you to school?"

Jess slumps her shoulders and rests her freckled cheeks in

her hands. "Aunt K is still sleeping. She gets real mad when I wake her. Can you take me?"

"Always." I hold out my hand. Jess's tiny fingers, sticky with day-old syrup, grab mine. She stands and scoops up her tattered backpack. "I'll patch your bag later, if you want." I lift mine to show her the edges sealed with silver duct tape.

Jess gives a big nod. Hand in hand we walk down the sidewalk under a canopy of oak trees. "I'm working on a new art project." Jess hops over tree roots buckling the concrete.

"Yeah? What is it?" I check over my shoulder with the eerie feeling of being watched. Trees sway as the wind picks up, and cars pass along the main road, but there's nothing unusual.

"We rip up tiny pieces of paper and glue them down to make a picture." Jess swings my hand as we turn the corner and walk along the creepy woods with gnarled trees. Ghostly fog hovers three feet above the forest floor. I shiver.

"A mosaic? Nice. What's it gonna be?"

Jess's eyes brighten the way they always do when I ask her about her art. "I wanted to do a dragon, but the boys took all the black paper. I got stuck with light blue and brown. So I took scraps off the floor and tried to make a giant white flower like the ones you showed me in that art book."

"O'Keeffe?" I smile and glance at the overcast sky. "Impressive. I'm sure it'll look amazing."

Jess beams. When the brisk wind kicks up, she wipes a lock of hair out of her face. "I'm naming this piece *The Fate Flower*."

"Ooh. Sounds ominous. Can't wait to see it." Out of the corner of my eye, a lethargic shadow moves through the dense mist hovering in the woods. When I turn to look, it's gone. It's probably a bird, or a squirrel. Or some other random animal. Regardless, I pick up my pace.

Jess skips alongside me and smiles. "You can have my picture when I'm done."

I give her hand a gentle squeeze. "I'd love it."

I slow my pace after we clear the woods and start our way along the ivory fence near a row of old houses converted into eclectic shops. Jess, catching her breath, looks up at me as if something suddenly occurs to her. "Why don't *you* go to school?"

I pull my hand out of hers. "I study at home, remember?"

Jess wrinkles her face, confused. "How do you make friends?"

I don't. And that's exactly why Mom doesn't want me in school anymore. I shrug as we weave around a half-unloaded delivery truck. "I guess I have to make friends in other ways." In fact, Mom would come unhinged if she knew I was talking to Jess even this much.

Jess shakes her head. "I wouldn't want to stay at home." With her belligerent aunt passed out most of the time, I don't blame her.

Swollen, bruise-colored clouds churn in the distance, darkening the sky. A storm is moving in fast.

The school sits halfway down the block. Before we cross the street, I glance over my shoulder with that paranoid feeling. Trucks rush down the road, a mom pushes a jogging stroller while talking on the phone, but as usual, no one notices me.

Jess wiggles her loose front teeth as we reach the sidewalk. I nudge her forward. "Go on. I'll wait here until you get inside." A peal of thunder sounds in the distance. My feet bounce. I want to stop by the market and pick up a few things before Mom wakes up and finds out I'm gone. She needs something besides stale peanut butter toast to eat before working her night shift.

Jess's braid bounces against her backpack as she runs up the steps. When she reaches the school doors, she turns and waves at me before heading inside. Distant thunder shakes the ground, and a sudden gust of wind rustles through the trees, swirling leaves over the road. Great.

Fall is here. According to my annual track record, I've got about a week left in this town—maybe less.

My feet pound the sidewalk a little harder as I pick up my pace. I hate moving. I've been doing it every year around my birthday for the past ten years, and it's gotten old. Mom always makes a big deal out of my panic attacks. I know we can't pay for whatever I need to get better, but moving isn't the answer. For once I want to stop running.

Out of all the places I've lived, Wakefield is the only one that feels like it could be home. Anything goes in this sleepy artist town with painted sidewalks and bright murals on brick walls. Even now as I pass the quaint café on the corner, some shaggy California blond wearing a denim jacket and torn jeans plays guitar while he sings to a growing crowd. I don't know the song, but as the melody rises, so does my resolve to stay.

Before I cross the road, that unsettled, paranoid feeling flares again. I glance over my shoulder and scan the square. Several people enter the café while others stop and listen to California play. Rain drops splat the sidewalk where a few people greet one another and toddlers with saggy diapers squeal as they run through the park, but no one even looks my way. No one, that is, except for two girls with silky hair whipping behind them as they saunter toward the café. I lift my chin and pretend to glance into a store window etched with the name Elysium's Edge as they lock arms and size up my frizzy ponytail and worn-out running shoes against their designer bags and matching boots.

When I look past the dusty haze of my own reflection, my pulse kicks into high gear. A colossal painting is propped up on the back wall of a new gallery. I know this painting from Mom's art books, but I've never seen it up close.

I push the door open without a second thought. An airy chime floats through the vacant space that smells of fresh paint and new construction. I gingerly step over splintery crates sprawled all over the pine floor.

As soon as I pass a set of neon paintings hanging on a

narrow wall, a man's voice echoes through the vaulted room. "Can I help you?"

A lanky guy with intense poise and black-framed glasses steps out from a hallway in back. "The gallery opens at the end of the week."

"Oh," is all I manage to squeak out.

He's probably in his late twenties. Maybe thirty. A red mark circles the base of his neck, half hidden under the collar of his black T-shirt. My stomach twists. I don't know why it strikes me, but I'm pretty sure Dad had a similar birthmark.

He adjusts his glasses. "Did you come about a job?"

I take a deep breath and snap out of my daze. "I saw the painting and wanted a better look." I'm drawn back to the dark canvas displayed behind him.

When the guy steps closer, I get a whiff of some strange chemical. Or maybe a solvent. "That one?" He gives a dismissive look over his shoulder. "You're familiar with it?"

I nod. *The Storm,* by Pierre Auguste Cot. He's a classical Romantic."

He smiles. "So, you find that romantic?"

I'm so mesmerized by the artwork, I don't respond. I know this piece couldn't be the original, housed at the Met—it was shipped in a flimsy pine crate and the suffocating temperature in the tiny space is way too humid for safekeeping—but I'm lured just the same. Up close, the painting of a girl and boy fleeing a raging storm is absolutely gorgeous.

The guy comes up next to me. "My business partner wanted this one displayed. Said it would lure a *select* crowd." His voice is a distant noise as I study each brushstroke.

The sulfuric chemical scent on the guy's clothes gives me a headache. Doing a quick exhale before the next inhale and breath-hold, I say, "It has incredible movement, consistent with Romantic artists." My focus gravitates to the girl wrapped in a gauzy alabaster gown. A clean light glows on her chest. She's angelic, otherworldly, compared to the sinister darkness closing in on her. A shirtless boy with disheveled black hair runs beside her. He's so smitten, he can't keep his eyes off the girl and is completely oblivious to the chaos swirling around them. A heated ache sprouts in me as their bare feet flee over the rocky path in perfect unison. Clutching different ends of an apricot-colored cloth, the fluttering fabric billows over their heads, protecting them like a shield from the coming storm.

"Any idea what she's thinking?" The guy crosses his arms and blankly stares at the canvas. With his spiky brown hair and olive skin, he looks nothing like the boy in the canvas.

I study the girl's face. Looking over her shoulder, she has this look of fascination, determination and . . . there's something else mixed in her concentrated expression that I can't place. It's not fear . . . no. "If I had to guess, I'd say that any moment she'll stop running and face what pursues her head-on."

He tilts his head and examines her closer. "That would be a mistake. Don't you think? She seems frail. Maybe she's better off running." He laughs, lightening the air. "I'm Mark, by the way." He holds out his hand. I take it.

Shaking a guy's hand feels strange—so much so, that my hollow stomach flips a little. "I'm Cera. Marlowe." I release his firm grip and tuck a loose strand of hair behind my ear, wishing I had washed up this morning.

Mark turns to face the gallery. "What do you think of that collection on the north wall?" He motions to the neon display.

I turn my focus to the square canvases perfectly spaced on the wall. The choice of assaulting colors brushed into twisted, crippled trees that bend in agony feels downright disturbing. Either that, or the creep factor comes from the thick, clumpy shadows hovering around the roots. Everything in me wants to rip the artwork down and free the trees from their misery.

"There's a lot of . . ." I search for the right word. According to Mom, I have a verbal filter problem. Thinking before I speak is on the top of my work-in-progress checklist. "Emotion . . ." I say, finding a benign word. "Each tree is a different color. Is that symbolic of transformation? I'd say seasons, but you have five and not four."

"Not a bad read." He gives me a once-over. "I was expressing different personalities."

I look again. Yeah, I totally don't see that. "It's kinda Warhol."

His voice hardens. "Not intentional."

"I meant that as a compliment." My cheeks warm the way they always do when I mess up.

After an eternity of silence and the longest internal debate of whether that's my cue to duck out, he asks, "You an artist?"

"Me? No way." I step back, laughing at the thought.

"Know any? We're new in town, looking to promote local artists. We'll pay good money too. So if you have friends, neighbors or whatnot, I'd be happy to take a look at what they have."

He'll pay for the work? If that's true, then I know of one artist, a really good one. "I do. She sketches. Mainly graphite."

Mark's awkward smile makes him look as if he's in pain. "If she's got what we're looking for, I'll give her a shot."

"Sure, no problem." Why did I say that? Of course it's a problem. Mom won't show her art to anyone. She rarely shows me. Way to go, Cera. You've just bumped number nine on the work-in-progress list to number three—perpetual lying.

His expression turns serious. "Listen . . . do you want the job? You seem to appreciate art, unlike most kids your age." He looks me over. "You about seventeen or eighteen?"

Nice to know he thinks I'm older. I smirk. "About." I will be in a week, anyway.

"Perfect."

I hadn't thought about getting a job. Mom would flip out if

I did—and not in a good way, especially with it getting close to the time we usually pack up and leave. If it weren't for Mark's expression, I'd think he was joking. "Really?" I glance through the window with that feeling of being watched. More leaves fall as the wind picks up. A dark shadow retracts into the treetops. I blink. Then it's gone.

Mark steps in front of me, blocking my view of the window. "We'll pay three times minimum wage."

"Three times?" I can't contain my smile. I've just landed the trifecta of opportunities. Not only could I stay in Wakefield, Mom could be happy drawing again, and I'd finally have a shot at a normal life. We'd even have extra money so I could find answers to heal me. This day couldn't be more perfect. I'll find a way to break the news to Mom later.

"Give me your number." Mark places a piece of paper and a pen on the edge of the desk blocking a short hallway. I rest my bag in the office chair. "I'd be interested in getting your thoughts on a few other pieces of art, and if it's slow, feel free to do homework." He looks down at my messenger bag. My copy of *Paradise Lost* has managed to slide out through the broken clasp.

"Sounds great." I shove Milton back into hiding. "Need me to fill out an application?"

A half smile highlights his stubble. "No need." He glances at the front window. "I'll check with my partner, but with your interests, that shouldn't be a problem." He stares at my bag. "I think you're exactly what we're looking for." I swear there's a knowing glint in his eyes, but I must be imagining things again. He couldn't possibly know about Milton and me. "Bring the sketches this time tomorrow. If they're good, we'll add a nice finder's fee."

"Tomorrow?" I sling my bag over my shoulder. "Yeah, sure." As soon as I agree, unease gnaws inside me. I've got twenty-four hours to either convince my mom about this opportunity or find her sketches behind her back and tell her afterward. I know how protective she is about her art.

I smile and grab the door handle. Pushing my hip against the glass, I say, "Thanks, Mark. See you tomorrow."

"Tomorrow." He nods goodbye.

Thunder rolls across the sky. My smile fades. I'd forgotten about the storm. I better hurry to the store and back home before the downpour unleashes its fury on me. As soon as I step onto the sidewalk, the crisp air slaps my cheeks. I clutch my jacket closed since the zipper is broken and lean into the wind. Despite the cold, fizzing happiness bubbles inside me.

I've just been given an opportunity of a lifetime—a chance to change everything for us. I swear, no matter what, I won't let my panic attacks mess this up. I'm staying in Wakefield, even if it kills me.

2

MORTAL SIGHT

After picking up a few essentials at the store, I hurry home, jogging the few blocks along the edge of the woods before turning down my street. The road is empty except for random leaves crab-walking across the asphalt. A few parked cars litter the far end of the road, giving me a clear view to my house, fourth duplex on the left. It's the faded pastel blue with a broken porch rail.

Yes, I broke the rail. Totally on accident. I didn't know the wood was rotted and I sat on it. End of story—except that I did try to fix it. Mom told me not to. Said the banging would draw too much attention, and it was best to leave it alone. So there it sits.

Another peal of thunder hammers the sky, a few drops fall, but still no drenching downpour. I head up the porch steps, skipping the splintered one. A large black feather rests on the doormat but blows away when I open the front door. The musty wood scent reminds me of my grandmother's house, except hers didn't have the decades-old cigarette smoke embedded in the walls. I don't see Mom. It's not until I accidentally step on that one creaky board in the living room that she calls from her room down the hall. "Cera?"

"Yeah, Mom, it's me." I fluff the pillows on the couch and straighten the rickety coffee table. It takes everything I have not to spill the news about the job—yet. I've decided not to surprise her until after she's selected as an artist for the gallery. She's always making sacrifices for me. It's time I do something nice for her in return.

Mom shuffles down the hall. "Where were you?"

"Ran to the store." I hold up the bag to support my partial truth—it's the least volatile of my morning events. I adjust a picture on the wall and open the blinds, brightening the room, despite the stormy sky.

"You shouldn't be outside." Mom stops at the end of the hall and rests against the frame for support. She frowns at the open blinds. Clutching her robe, she makes her way toward the window. "What brought this on?" She closes the blinds.

"Oh, nothing much." I pick up a water glass and breakfast plate and head to the kitchen. "Just—"

"You were with the neighbor, weren't you?" The room is dark again. "You know better. Don't—"

"Draw attention, I know." I toss my bag on the counter before unloading the soup and bread into the cabinet. "Jess needed help."

Mom follows me to the kitchen and leans against the counter, hemming me in the tight space. "I love your heart, but what's going to happen when we leave? She can't get attached and you can't either."

"Can't we ride it out this time?" I tidy up the ceramic jar of cooking utensils. "This is one of the nicer—and safer—places we've stayed. It's quiet, artsy, and . . . I kinda like it here."

Mom sours at my comment. "That's not possible, and you know it." She coughs. Mom's health hasn't been all that great lately. Moving isn't the best thing for her either.

I work hard to keep the excitement from leaking through my voice. "What if I . . . got a job? I could work part-time so you could go to the doctor for that cough. It's getting worse. And . . ." I look down and pick at my middle nail. "Maybe I could see one too."

Mom works hard to stifle another cough. She takes my hands. Hers are cold but velvety soft. "Cera, a job isn't an option for you. And you know we've tried doctors. They don't help." She cups my cheek with her palm, making me feel like a helpless little girl. "We're a week away from your birthday. Once the attacks are triggered, they won't stop until we move."

She's convinced that my panic disorder, in addition to mold exposure, pollen, or you-name-it, is also tied to trauma triggered from Dad walking out on us ten years ago on my seventh birthday. I pull away from her and wad the grocery sack in my fist before stuffing it in the top drawer. "We've never stayed anywhere long enough to find out if I'll actually have more than one episode. For all I know, I have an attack once around my birthday every fall and that's it. I can handle one attack per year. No big deal."

Mom crosses her arms. "Maybe one day things will be different but for right now . . ." She must see the disappointment in my face because her eyes soften. "It's what works, what keeps—"

"Me safe. Yeah, I know. But I still don't see why." My phone buzzes in my bag. Mom eyes my purse on the counter, raising one suspicious brow. I fish around and yank out my phone. Frankly, I'm just as surprised as Mom. It's a local call. "No one has this number but you." And Mark from the gallery. I shrug. "Probably a misdial." Before she can question me, I scoop up my bag. "I've got a paper due." I swerve around her before heading down the hall. Mom locks her suspicious glance on me. It's not a total lie. Her drawings are on paper, and I told Mark I'd bring them in tomorrow. The phone vibrates in my palm again. When I'm out of Mom's visual range, I glance at my phone. The caller has left a message.

Closing the door to my room, I fumble to play back the message and then press the phone tight against my ear. "Hey, it's Mark. My partner wants to meet you and . . . to see the sketches as soon as possible. Can you come back by later today? Call or text and let me know you got this."

There's just one problem. Two, actually. Mom indirectly vetoed my getting a job, and I'll have to wait until she leaves for work before I can rifle through her room for the sketches.

I text back because Mom's supersonic, echolocation ears will hear me if I make a call: *Hi Mark. Got your message. Getting sketches tonight. Bring them tomorrow a.m.?* My fingers shake as I hit send, hoping that's not a deal breaker.

In less than a blink, he's replied with two thumbs up: *See u then.*

I plop on my bed with a big exhale and stare at the ceiling. What am I thinking? This will never work. But maybe it can. I really want it to. The chance to sketch professionally would be great for Mom. It would be great for the both of us. Of course, the timing couldn't be worse, this close to my birthday when Mom's senses are on high alert, but . . . maybe I can pull it off. And if her sketches aren't chosen, and I have an attack like I always do, then . . . I guess we'll probably move. Again.

I glance over at my closet door where I've taped up one of Jess's crayon drawings. She's colored every inch of the paper with a cerulean sky overlooking a black lake surrounded by lush hills. My chest tightens. Abandoning Jess feels wrong. I'm not my father. I won't walk out on people who depend on me. No matter how things turn out with the sketches, I have to fight to stay.

I slip the copy of *Paradise Lost* out of my bag. The poem helps me feel . . . well, not so crazy and alone. Sure, it's archaic, written roughly five hundred years ago and isn't some scientific article or case study, but strangely enough, the words describe exactly what I'm going through.

Flipping through a few pages, I imagine John Milton standing with quiet authority, patiently waiting for me to pick up on the meaning, the same way my old English teacher would do when I'd stare out the window. I stop on a page where I've circled and highlighted the verses:

Shine inward and the mind through all her powers
Irradiate; there plant eyes; all mist from thence
Purge and disperse, that I may see and tell
Of things invisible to mortal sight.

No doubt, Milton, you describe what happens in my panic attacks in a way that no one else seems to understand. That first line, *Shine inward* is the bright light shining in my mind when the episode hits—and yes, *all mist from thence purge and disperse* is the smoky mist of my mind dissolving so I can see what comes next. *Things invisible to mortal sight.* But this part stumps me. When the mist in my mind disperses, it shows random broken images, not *"things invisible."* Unless you're talking about hallucinations?

I see misty shadows out of the corner of my eye every now and then, but I've only had a hallucination one time. I imagined a black bird the size of a bear perched in the woods, but that was a long time ago. It was right after my first attack and I was seven, so my memory of it is a bit hazy. Even if I'm wrong and the poem doesn't hold the answer that unlocks my cure, just imagining that I'm not alone—that someone understands me—has been a great coping device.

Then, like a slap in the back of the head, Milton hurls a random verse through my brain, as he often does. *"Thou hast seen one world begin and end . . ."* Yes, my world always begins and ends every year when I move to a new town, I know. I flip through the poem to match his voice with the words on the page. I read on, hoping there's something to quell the lingering rawness in my gut. *"Much thou hast yet to see . . ."*

The wind howls through the cracked glass as heavy raindrops splatter on the roof. I peer out the window through the sheets of rain. Seeing. That's the answer isn't it, Milton? My heart races with certainty. But what am I supposed to see?

I spend the rest of the rainy day waiting for Mom to go to work so I can search for the sketches, which isn't easy because I hate waiting. Patience is high on my work-in-progress list. When it gets close to the time Mom usually leaves, I slip out of my room and head to the kitchen to heat up the can of soup I bought for her—the good kind with chunks of real chicken.

As Mom trudges down the hall, I pour the steaming soup in a bowl and slide it across the counter. "Made you dinner."

"Thank you." She eases onto the barstool with a stifled groan. Her face is pale and her eyes dark, but even still, she has this graceful elegance about her I wish I had. As she eats, I execute my rendition of culinary brilliance for my own meal: a toasted cheese sandwich and apple slices with the bruises cut out.

"I hope the rain lets up soon," I say. If the downpour continues, Mom will be drenched by the time she gets to the train.

She lifts the spoon to her lips and blows the steam away. "I think I'll call out sick today." The dull knife slips on the apple skin and grazes the side of my thumb.

"Really?" I work hard to keep my voice even. "You never do that." I run my hand under cold water as I wash the knife so Mom doesn't notice the blood. She must suspect something's up because her hawk eyes don't let up as she takes another sip. I suppose I'm not doing a great job at being subtle. First cleaning up the house, now making her dinner . . . I grip the dishrag, applying pressure on the cut.

"A day of rest might do me some good." As she finishes dinner, the spoon clinks against the bowl, sounding about as hollow as my stomach.

"Rest is good. You can stay here and relax and draw the way

you used to." I pull back the towel and inspect my thumb. The cut looks okay, only throbs a little. "I could grab the sketchbooks from your room." Brilliant plan, Cera. Sometimes, I amaze myself.

Mom shakes her head. "You know I don't draw anymore." She stifles a cough.

I gingerly take the burnt bread from the toaster with a knife. "Would you? If you didn't have to work? You're a great artist. You even studied in Paris." It's where she met Dad, but I know better than to mention that fact.

Mom forces a weak smile as she dabs the corner of her lips with a napkin. "That was a long time ago." She pushes away from the counter. "Thank you for the soup. I'll be in my room."

I slap a piece of hard cheese on the burnt bread. Great. Just great. Now I'll have to ask her outright. I nibble a bit of the apple slice as my mother lumbers toward the hall. "Mom?" My pulse flares. "Can I have one of your drawings?"

Her shoulders stiffen as she makes a half turn and searches me with laser-like scrutiny. "Why this sudden interest in my art?"

I swallow and take another bite of apple, chewing methodically while I fish for an answer she'll believe. "You never show me." I shrug, trying to downplay my desperation. "You have me study classical art, but I'd like to see your work. I want something to hang in my room, that's all."

Her eyes harden. Somehow she always picks up on my insincerity. Surprisingly, she doesn't call me out. "They're not worth showing anyone. Just scribbles." Her voice cracks as she continues making her way down the hall. "Don't stay up late." She closes the door to her room.

Asking her outright didn't work. Rifling through her stuff isn't going to happen. So much for surprises. Now I've got no choice but to come clean and tell her about the opportunity and hope that she'll agree. But I'm not poking the bear tonight. I may be relentless, but I'm not stupid. I'll wait until morning when she feels better.

3

SEEDLINGS

Claws scrape the shingles, jolting me out of bed. I sit up in a cold sweat as soft light cracks through the blinds. Calm down. It's probably a squirrel. As I throw on a T-shirt and my nicest pair of jeans, my copy of *The Prince* falls on the floor. Ah, Machiavelli, my short-lived obsession that ended when I met Milton.

I open the top drawer, push some clothes aside, and tuck Machiavelli near a volume of English Romantic poets. That particular book currently houses the only item I have that belonged to Dad—a small, cracked vinyl record of a Beatles song with the phrase *"ma belle,"* the nickname Dad called me. He used to play that song, singing at the top of his lungs as he swung me in his arms, dancing around the room. If Mom knew I still had the record, she'd make me throw it away, even now that he's dead. All these years I've managed to keep it hidden. Right now it's tucked between the pages of Lord Byron's poetry—another brief obsession. I shut the drawer and swipe Milton out from under my pillow. Mom's door is still closed. I sneak by as quietly as possible, determined to let her sleep, and go outside.

The morning air is crisp, a lot colder than just yesterday. "Hey there, Jess." I jog down the steps. "You ready?"

Jess sits on the bottom step, fidgeting with a plastic container.

"You're trying to break out of the bubble house again." She adjusts the lid of the makeshift terrarium that houses her lima bean family. Over a week ago she came home with a project from school in plastic cups and tried to plant the little guys. I found a two-liter soda bottle, cut the bottom and refit the top to make a protective "bubble" house. Jess named the beans while we planted them. The little vibrant bud is her. The sickly yellow one is Mom, and sure enough mine is the crooked stalk pushing against the crack in the lid.

"Hey, your stalk is looking stronger." I set my bag on the splintered step and kneel beside her. "Look how big it's gotten."

"I guess." She rests her freckled cheeks in her bare hands and stares at the seedlings.

"Did something happen? Want to talk about it?"

"Not really." She scratches a bug bite on her wrist.

An icy breeze sneaks under my jacket. "Then let's head to school so you're not late." I stand up and tuck my hands in my coat pocket, feeling my pair of wadded-up gloves. I can handle the cold but Jess's hands are already flaked and red. The autumn air will be freezing by tomorrow and I doubt she has any gloves. I hand my pair over. "Here, take these for later."

"Thanks." Jess stands up and takes the gloves.

"They're probably too big, but you can grow into them," I say, watching her wiggle her fingers into them. The extra fabric at the end of her tiny fingers flops as she stretches out her hands, inspecting the gift.

"Perfect." She flashes me a grin, holding her smile longer than necessary.

I realize why. "Whoa, did you lose a tooth?"

"Two," she says, but not as proud as I expected, given her grin.

"Two. That's a big deal!" I bend down to get a better look.

"It is when they come out on their own, I guess, but not when someone trips you and you knock them out on a bookcase. Aunt K says the tooth fairy doesn't pay for those."

"Well, maybe she'll make an exception."

She shakes her head. "She didn't." Jess pulls off a glove and digs into her pocket. "See?" She holds out something that looks more like two small pieces of popcorn than teeth.

"Hmm," I say. Her smile disappears as she hides the teeth back inside her pocket. "But . . . there's something you didn't know." I pick up my bag and reach inside for the last of my crumpled money. "The tooth fairy left this at my house. She can't go against your aunt's house rules, so she asked me to make sure you got this."

Her eyes widen at the few dollars sitting in my palm. I unfold her cold fingers and stuff the money in her sticky hand.

"Really?"

I nod because I don't want to verbally lie to her again.

Jess stands as straight as possible. "The gift shop is selling pencils that smell like watermelon."

"By the looks of it, you could get four if you wanted." I tuck my hands under my arms as my teeth begin to chatter. This cold front is moving in fast.

Without warning, Jess wraps her arms around my waist and squeezes. She rests her chin on my stomach and looks up at me, smiling wider than I've ever seen before. "They won't make fun of me at school."

"Why would they?"

"Because the tooth fairy *did* come." She releases her octopus grip. "They say she doesn't come to kids like me."

"Kids like you? You mean beautiful, brave ones?" I smile.

Jess scrunches her nose. "No." She looks down and messes with the floppy tips of the glove. "Kids that can't get new stuff like everyone else."

"Well, they're wrong then, aren't they?" My lies suddenly feel justified. After I start working, I'll be able to buy her a whole box of pencils, better-fitting gloves, and a new coat with a fur-lined hood so she won't have to wear those earmuffs that deaden all sound.

Wiping frizzy hair out of her eyes, Jess smiles and grabs her backpack. "Aunt K is taking me to school today, so I'll go to the gift shop later." Jess wads up the dollars gripped in her hand.

"Want me to walk you there after school?" I glance over my shoulder for signs of her aunt.

Jess stands tall. "No, silly. I know the way."

"Remember to turn right at the white fence." I motion so she gets a visual.

"Right." She mirrors me. Her eyebrows squeeze in concentration, scripting the path to memory. Even so, I'm not so sure she's going to remember.

A car engine knocks and pings as Aunt K's red sedan slowly backs onto the grass, missing the driveway by at least three feet. The windows are fogged making it hard for me to make out her aunt's morning mood.

I kneel down and stuff the money in her pocket. "Keep your money hidden until you need it, okay?"

Jess nods. "What's your favorite color?" she asks, as I help zip up her jacket.

"Honey yellow."

Jess wrinkles her nose. "Carnation pink is better." She flashes that gapped-tooth grin, but it quickly disappears when her aunt lays a long honk on the horn. I cringe. The sound is sure to wake Mom. I tuck my hands under my arms and watch Jess trudge to the car. Not only does she struggle to get into the back seat, but her aunt backs over the curb, knocking over a trash can and bicycle, before Jess has even closed the car door.

I plant my feet into the spongy grass. I can't abandon Jess. I'm taking the job and staying in Wakefield, no matter what.

One of the bearded college students living across the street rushes out his door wearing flannel pajamas, a concert T-shirt, and hair that hasn't been washed in a week. "Dude!" He picks up his mangled bike. He spots me on the other side of the street. "Did you see that idiot?"

At that moment, my hands clench. Tremors coil through my arms. No. No. No. Oh please, not now. Not out in the open and in front of someone, no less. It's one week too soon.

"I . . . I can't . . ." I swallow back a scream and the rest of the words, as stabbing heat streaks down my legs. I stagger, tripping over my feet that I can't feel, and reach for the side rail.

"Need help?" the guy calls. He jogs my way. I shake my head, struggling to get back into my house. With each step, squeezing pain spirals up each vertebra. "Can I call an ambulance?"

"No!" I grit my teeth and pull myself up the steps. My foot slips through the rotted wood. "Please, don't."

He holds his hands out, conceding, and backs away. "Cool." As I lunge for the front door, he turns to go, mumbling, "I'm surrounded by a bunch of mental heads."

I stumble into the house. My bag tugs at my side, a heavy weight. I press my palm against the wall, forcing my legs to keep moving. Get to my bed. If Mom sees me, if she knows, we'll be packed up and gone by sunset. I'm determined to suffer through the attack and prove that I can handle them on my own.

Burning steel feels as if it's being rammed and twisted into my spine. A high-pitched sound in my ears drowns out the steady hum of the refrigerator. The musty scent of aged cigarette smoke ignites a piercing ache in my head. My stomach churns. Don't puke. Fight it. As I take another step, reaching the hall, sharp pain slashes across my back. Standing in front of Mom's door, I stifle a wail. The world spins black, like I'm slowly being sucked into a tunnel. I've got to get to my bed before darkness takes over.

Somehow, I drag myself into my room. My hands shake as I close the door. As soon as I do, my sight vanishes. Everything turns black. All feeling strips from my legs. My knees collapse, hitting the wood floor. I push piles of clothing out of the way, feeling my way to my bed, abandoning my bag in the process. Pain kicks me in the spine. I face-plant into my comforter and bite my tongue to keep from screaming. I taste blood. Hot tears stick my hair against my cheeks. I press my trembling lips together.

Hoisting myself onto the bed, I shove my face into the pillow to stifle my cry. Torturing pain rips through me, taunting me to scream. I pound the mattress, fighting to stay quiet.

More rippling pain tears down my back. I know what comes next. The feeling of hot needles snakes through my eyes, lodging deep into my skull. I press the heel of my palms into my eye sockets, but it does nothing to quell the pain. It never does. Now comes the silvery mist, like a lingering haze after fireworks. It takes over my sight and flashes isolated snapshots of images across the movie screen of my mind.

> *Blinding white light*
> *Splashing mud*
> *A disheveled mouse with a flapping tail*
> *A green kite in the wind.*

My blood turns ice cold. My stomach hardens. I have to run. I have to get away. Escape. Thick air chokes my throat. My legs won't move. I'm trapped, lying paralyzed in my bed.

> *A bird with black wings and the face of a lion swoops down*
> *A piercing screech shatters the air*
> *The mouse lies on wet ground, sliced open.*

Pain sizzles my spine. I writhe. My arms flail. A violent tug yanks somewhere deep inside me, as if my soul was being sucked out. I wish it were and I could die right now. I knock into my nightstand, sending my alarm clock hurtling to the floor. Controlling my own body isn't even possible. All I can do is suffocate in the hot pillow and fight the screams. Hang in there, it's almost over . . .

White flashes again. Everything turns red.
Then swallowed by darkness.

My stomach cramps. Vomit pushes its way up. Oh please, no. Completely blind, I feel the edge of my nightstand and follow the leg down the side and around until I find the plastic trash can. Bringing it close to the edge of my bed, I lean over and heave. Hanging there, limp and cold, a raw terror settles over me. Those birds sounded as if they were right outside my window, ready to destroy me. The silver haze fades to black. The attack is over, but the lingering sense of danger remains.

Mom's door creaks open across the hall. She heard me? With every ounce of strength left, I shove the trashcan back in its place—or at least I think I do—and pull myself back into bed to hide under my blanket.

My door clicks open. Somehow I manage to lie still under the covers as the door hits the wall. "Cera?" Mom's worried whisper cuts through my throbbing head. Acid burns my throat as I swallow. Her voice tells me she knows. The acrid smell of bile doesn't help my case.

It takes every last bit of strength to make myself lie still with the sheet pulled over my head. I steady my breathing and keep my trembling hands tucked against my chest. Boards creak as she comes to the edge of my bed, kicking into something. Probably the alarm clock. Every nerve feels raw, but I have to be strong. Breathe slow, rhythmic.

I know it's juvenile, but I pretend to be asleep. No such luck. She pulls the blanket off, not fooled. A sweet draft, smelling of lavender and pencil lead replaces the hot, stuffy air. Her trembling fingers rub against my clammy cheek, pulling my sweaty hair off my face. "Honey, I'm right here." Her voice sounds weak. "Everything will be okay." A knot swells my throat shut. All I want to do is sit up and tell her the image I had was the worst ever, and that I felt every bit of the pain as if it were happening to me. But I keep quiet.

Mom sniffles. Is she crying? I want to open my eyes, but I don't dare move, not when I can feel her hovering over me. If my eyes meet hers, I'll fall apart. After a few seconds of waiting for me to respond, she rummages for something on the floor.

I crack open one eye. The blinding haze is gone. Through my lashes, I catch her setting the alarm clock on my nightstand. The floorboard creaks again as she quietly goes out with my trash can and shuts the door. After I'm sure she's gone, I unleash silent sobs, drenching my pillow.

I've just ruined everything.

4
FIGHT TO STAY

It's late afternoon when I finally wake up. I sit up, my body stiff and sore. I roll my shoulders and push myself out of bed to change my puke-stained clothes. After slipping into a pair of jeans, I carefully navigate a light blue T-shirt over the bruise that's starting to form on my wrist from where I busted my hand against the alarm clock.

My head throbs when I bend down to pick up my bag as it vibrates. I check my phone. A missed call and text messages. All from Mark. I rub my temple to quell the ache. I promised him the sketches this morning and was supposed to meet the other owner. I sit on the edge of my bed and read the messages, all saying roughly the same thing: *Come by whenever you can. Bring the sketches. We're waiting.* I'm thrilled that I didn't blow the opportunity. I suppose girls with knowledge of classical art are in short supply. I send a quick text back: *Couldn't make it this a.m. Don't have sketches yet.*

I open my door and search for Mom. Her door is closed, but I can hear the bathroom sink running. My phone vibrates with Mark's response: *Come anyway. Partner here.*

With Mom occupied, I can slip out, secure my job, and then come back ready to stand my ground about not leaving Wakefield. I grab my jacket and bag and step lightly through the living room. I send Mark a quick reply: *Headed your way now.* I stuff the phone in my back pocket.

A chipped mug of cold tea sits on the coffee table with a few of Mom's art books. Tucked underneath that pile is her old sketchbook. Maybe she's drawing again. Last night's conversation must have made an impact. Not only that, if I can dig out a sketch, I can take her work to Mark after all. She'll notice if I take the whole book, but not if I take one drawing.

A folded paper pokes out of the sketchbook. It's practically begging me to look. How can I not? Excitement floods through my veins as I slide out the aged paper.

Before I can unfold it, Mom's door creaks open.

I stuff the drawing inside my bag between the pages of *Paradise Lost*. Stacking her art books just as they were, I jump up from the couch and slip on the jacket to cover the bruise on my arm. I rush to open the front door before she spots me.

"Stop right there." Mom's voice drops low. Too low. I swallow. I'm positive she knows about the attack, but did she also see me take the sketch? I take a deep breath and turn to face her.

She stands at end of the hall looking ghostly pale with tired, bloodshot eyes. "Shut that door." Mom stifles a shiver at the exposing cold creeping through the room. I quickly close the door. "We're leaving. There's no time for anything else. I've already made the arrangements and picked up the rental car." It takes her effort just to get to the coffee table. She scoops up the books and sketchpad with a quiet grunt. Her fingers are smeared with pencil lead. "There's a town in the Northeast with a manufacturing company that needs someone in their shipping department. It will be a little cooler, but we'll manage." She clutches the books to her chest. The last thing Mom needs is colder weather. "Start packing your room, then help me with the kitchen."

I shift, repositioning my bag strap on my shoulder. "Mom, you're not well."

"Are you trying to deny you had an episode? You were screaming this morning, Cera. Did you think I wouldn't know?"

"I'm not denying it. I'm saying I can handle it."

The dark circles under Mom's eyes intensify her stare. "Go, pack your room. It's best we leave within the hour."

"Within the hour?" I follow after her as she heads to her room, walking her hand along the wall for support.

"Mom, that's insane. You need rest. Not only that, instead of spending money on a new deposit or rental car, you need to get treatment for that cough—it's draining all your energy."

She sits heavily on the edge of her bed. "It's not me I'm worried about." She places her sketchbook in the unsealed box at the foot of her bed. Neatly stacked moving boxes line the wall near the door. "If you aren't willing to pack your room, then I'll just assume you plan on leaving everything behind."

It's a passive threat. I don't have many belongings, but Mom knows I hang on to what little I have. What she doesn't know is that this time, I will fight to stay. My pulse punches the inside of my throat as I dig my feet in the dingy brown carpet and cross my arms. "Things are good here. We should stay and make it work."

Mom puckers her lips and stacks the box in line with the others. "Your attacks will only get worse if we stay, and then you'll start hallucinating again and claim you're seeing strange creatures walking around. I won't risk someone finding out and putting you in some institution because of it. It's my job to protect you, whether you like it or not."

"No one's going to take me, or lock me up, or whatever. In fact—" My phone buzzes in my back pocket. When Mom's back is turned, I check the number. It's Mark again.

As Mom turns to face me, I hit the button, sending the call to voicemail.

"It's what's best for you." She puts her hands on her hips. "You don't have a choice in the matter. End of discussion."

Heat boils inside me. She's flat-out wrong. "Having a normal life, *that's* what's best for me. Maybe you don't care to find out what's wrong with me, but I do. I need to find answers as to why I'm this freak—"

"You're not—"

"Yes, I am, Mom, and you know it. Look at me. You won't even let me go to school anymore. I don't have friends, or a pet, or anything else normal kids my age have. *You* certainly don't even have a normal life. You're acting totally irrational because I've had an episode—"

My phone pings with a voice message. Mom stiffens. Her wrinkles contort into that all-too-familiar scowl. "Who's calling you?" She puts her hand out. "Give me your phone."

I pull away. "It's no one."

Mom's face blanches with absolute terror. "Who have you been talking to?" She rips the phone from my hands as another text message comes through.

"Mom—" I try to get my phone back as Mom silently reads the message.

Her expression hardens. "Grab only what you need—we're leaving right now."

I expected a fight, not a full-blown freak-out. "What's gotten into you? Why are you acting like I'm some murderer who needs to skip town before the police arrive? Is it because I talked to someone or that I had an attack? People have epilepsy and they don't skip town. Besides, I got through it just fine."

She abandons the phone fight and, with a renewed strength that comes out of nowhere, hurries past me in a frenzy. She hustles down the hall toward the kitchen. "It's not fine. You don't understand."

I charge after her. "Understand what? That you're totally overreacting because of a few bad dreams and one phone call? I have panic attacks. So what?"

She scours the room before heading straight for her purse sitting on the kitchen counter. I don't know if she even heard me.

"Seriously Mom, for the last ten years we've always packed up and moved like we're fugitives. I'd like to know what it's like to have a normal birthday. Instead of a party or cake, I get bubble wrap and a stack of cardboard boxes from whatever shipping company you're working for. Can't we stop running for once?"

My mother's eyes glisten with hurt, but she doesn't defend herself. One thing about Mom, when she's determined, she's a total bulldozer and doesn't lose focus. "Get your things, and get in the car."

I stand by the couch, blocking her way to the front door. "You're going off the same way you did when I had that first attack ten years ago. It's not like it's new. I'm telling you, I can handle these episodes."

"Lonicera Eleanor Marlowe, I said get in the car."

I plant my feet. "No."

She arches one eyebrow and her jaw tightens. I know that look. It's the one that says my open defiance has just waged war. She's even used my full name. My pulse drums in my head with warning, but I can't cave. If I do, something inside me will die. I lock my knees, holding firm. Mom has no idea how hard I'm willing to fight.

"Don't argue. Get in—"

"I won't run from my problems anymore. From now on, I'm facing them head-on. I'll find out what's wrong with me and change it. I'll walk Jess to school and let her know she's not alone. In fact, she's probably shivering in front of the school waiting for me right now. I'll stop hiding in the shadows. I'll make friends and fix the stupid porch rail. I won't let a few attacks ruin my life. Not anymore. This time, I'm staying!" I kick the particleboard coffee table, sending Mom's ceramic mug flying. It shatters against the wall.

Mom clutches her keys, turning her knuckles white as she speaks slowly, deliberately. "Moving has kept us safe—kept *you* safe. Facing your issue is the *worst* thing you could do. Do you hear me? Don't ever—it will destroy you and everyone around you. Now get in the car."

"So I should just listen to you because—"

"Because you're acting like your father! These attacks destroyed him. I won't let that happen to you!" She tosses her purse to the floor and goes into a coughing fit. Her face turns red and her hair, usually smooth and perfectly placed, hangs in her face.

Her heated words are a final kick in the gut. She's never compared me to my dead father. She never talks about him, doesn't even have a picture of him. It all makes sense now—why we move. I'm the burden on her slumped shoulders, the monster she's trying to hide. I can't even control my own anger. The broken mug and cold tea splattered on the wall are proof.

I back away and stare down at the puffy spot on the carpet where the coffee table once sat. "You're ashamed of me. I get it."

"Cera, no." Mom reaches out, but I dodge her and swipe my bag off the chair. Her voice chokes. "Please don't ever think that."

It's too late. I head to the front door. I've got nothing left to say.

"Cera, you can't go out that door." Mom presses her hand against her lungs and takes a deep breath. I can't tell if she's mustering the strength or if she's laying the drama on super thick so I'll feel guilty and cave.

"What's to stop me? I can take care of myself from now on, so go ahead and move on your own. I took a job at a gallery paying more than what you make. I could have changed things for you too. That call was the curator looking to pay for local art. I was going to bring him a sample of your sketches and surprise you with the news." I reach into my bag.

Mom's mouth hardens. In fact, her whole body turns rigid. "You didn't—"

When I pull out the sketch, her face turns into an expression of absolute fear.

"Is that—" Her eyes are desperate as she steps toward me. "Dear God, no. You saw it?"

"I don't care to." I toss the sketch at her, but the paper floats back, landing near my feet. Despite my comment, curiosity gets the better of me. I glance down.

It can't be. I blink and look again. Right in front of me, drawn in violent graphite streaks, is the deformed bird from my hallucination. How is it possible? My hands shake . . . this sketch . . . it's the same grotesque bird I saw in my attack this morning, but . . . the image isn't the same . . . no. The picture in my hand shows the image from my first attack—ten years ago.

5

BITTER MEMORY

"Cera, give that to me." Mom's panicked voice is nothing but distant noise. My hands tremble as I pick up the paper. Like looking at a photograph, the sketch from ten years ago resurrects the image in my mind as if I'd experienced this attack this morning. Except it's different from the one I just had. This sketch has two birds, not one. The creatures' oil-slick wings are extended, covering the sky. Their lion jaws hang open with black saliva dripping from their fangs. Falling through the air, a raggedy doll screams. She has three scratch marks raked across her leg. A smaller bird with narrow, snakelike eyes perches on a building and waits with mouth open, ready to swallow her whole.

Fear wraps around me like a tourniquet, just like it did this morning and all those years ago. At that moment, it's as if a cloudy film peels off my eyes. Everything seems clear. The pointed nose on the doll . . . looks like Marcy's—the girl who died the day after I saw this image in my mind.

"Cera, please!" Mom yanks the paper out of my hands. "We have to leave."

I step back. "How did you know what to draw? Why would you . . . I never gave you details about the scratch marks on the doll's legs . . . or the birds."

Trembling, Mom crumples the drawing. "I will tell you everything after we leave—"

"Tell me what? That I saw Marcy's death play out the night before it happened? That I'm not crazy? That somehow the monsters I see during the attacks are real? Or that all these years you've been lying to me!"

Mom sinks on the couch. "Cera, it's not like that. Listen—"

"So you can lie again?" My throat chokes with a fist-sized knot as tears push through, blurring my vision. I blink them back. "You said I imagined birds pushing my only friend off the bleachers because I was trying to cope with her death. I argued with you, telling you—begging you to believe—that I saw the image *before* she died. You convinced me I was wrong. But I remember the night of my first attack so clearly now. You grabbed my hand and squeezed it tight. You leaned close and asked me to imagine we were looking at the scene together. Is that how you knew? Why have you never once said you understood?"

"You were so little—"

"You've had this sketch for ten years!"

"I will show you all the drawings after we leave—"

"*All* the drawings? You drew out *every* image from each attack I've ever had?" Then it hits me. "Did someone die each time?"

Mom wipes back her tears. She presses her trembling hands to her knees and doesn't speak. She doesn't have to. The answer is written in her eyes.

I can't find air to breathe. This can't be true. "Where are the other sketches?"

Mom lowers her head. "Seeing them won't change anything. Please, honey, we need to leave now."

"I need answers, and if people died, I have to know who." Without a second thought I race down the hall to her room. I know exactly which box to grab. I rip the top open and dump out the contents before she tries to stop me. Books thump to the floor. Two sketchpads fall, releasing a confetti bomb of yellow-tinted paper all over the brown carpet.

As the pages settle, one sheet lands near me. It's a sketch of a tiny frog drowning in a sea of black mist. I sink to my knees to get a better look. The deep-set eyes on the frog remind me of the boy from my third-grade class. His name was Alan. I remember because he was the only kid in that town who wanted to be my friend. I'm not sure how the details seem so clear just by looking at the sketch, but I can tell the shadow emerging from the black mist is a hand from the deformed, sallow man from my nightmares. The creature reaches up, choking the tiny frog. I never told Mom about this one and we moved right after I had the attack. At the bottom left corner of the sketch, she's written the date. Nine years ago. And next to the date she's written the word "confirmed."

I flip the page over.

A newspaper clipping stapled to the back reads: "Boy, eight, drowns in local pond. Alan Watkins, a third-grader at . . ." My heart nearly stops beating.

I slide another sketch in front of me. The gorilla creature, the one with the pointed tail, breathes out fire. Flames consume a thin-necked bird, a crane, with curly hair—reminding me of a girl in sixth grade.

The words "confirmed" are scrawled at the bottom of this sketch too. Another article, stapled to the back, says: "Middle school cheerleader, Sylvia Reynolds dies in tragic house fire."

I turn over each page. Slumped on the floor, a stab twists in my gut as I stare at my horrific world drawn out with meticulous charcoal strokes. Did I cause this? My chest caves in. I can't breathe. All this time, Mom moved us to keep the bodies from piling up. Gravity presses down, weighting the air. The moving boxes, now coffins surrounding me. Adding salt to the wound, Milton punctures my thoughts with the verse:

Now conscience wakes despair
That slumbered, wakes the bitter memory
Of what he was, what is, and what must be
Worse; of worse deeds worse sufferings must ensue.

Worse sufferings? How can anything be worse than this?

"Cera, I'm so sorry." Mom leans against the doorpost. Her skin looks paler than death as tears stream down her face. "I was only trying to protect you."

I clutch the drawing and rise to my knees. "How can you see what's in my head?" She stares at the carpet and doesn't answer. "All this time you've known. Somehow you can see what I do, and you drew it out and kept them secret. Pretended none of this was true."

"You were seven, eight, nine. You wouldn't have understood."

"But how could you just let people die?" Milton's verse boomerangs back in my head: *worse deeds worse sufferings.* "Did I . . . kill them somehow?"

"No." With painful effort Mom kneels beside me. "You have visions. They're prophetic."

"Who else knows about this? And why didn't we save all these people?"

"We can't."

"Why not? Marcy's accident happened less than a day after I had my attack, which means the visions come true in less than twenty-four hours, don't they? That's why you're in such a rush to leave. No one would believe that I can see what I do. You're afraid they'll lock me up, so you're willing to let people die? That's no different from killing them ourselves, Mom!" I pull away from her, nauseated.

She removes the paper from my hand. "Don't say such horrible things. We couldn't stop it from happening."

"If you knew who it was—"

Mom shakes her head. "I didn't. Not until I found the articles weeks, sometimes months, after we left." When she looks at me, I read the terror in her eyes.

"But I can tell who it is just by looking at the sketch, like I did just now. If I had seen the drawings back then, I would have known. I could have saved them." Then it hits me. "You drew the images from this morning, didn't you?" I glance at her hands. Graphite is smeared in the crevasses.

I scramble to my feet. "If the incidents from my vision happen in less than twenty-four hours, then I'm running out of time."

Mom stands. "Cera, there's nothing you can do. We have to leave before—"

"Before someone else dies?" I grab a box. "No, Mom. You talked me out of believing in my visions once before and I let a girl die, along with all the others across an entire decade. I won't let someone else die if I can stop it."

I rip open the top, tossing out musty shoes and yanking out sweaters smelling of lavender. I tear the next cardboard box apart. "All these years you let me believe I was crazy." I take another carton and dump out shampoo, hairbrushes, makeup, and her entire bathroom drawer. "You lied. Again and again. Made me feel alone when all along you *knew*."

"Cera, stop!" Mom grabs my arm, sobbing, begging as she gasps for breath.

I pull away from her and tear open a box filled with art books. I whip each one out and hold it in the air before hurtling it on the floor. "You pretended none of this was true." I toss a book against the wall. "People died needlessly." I send another book hurling against the bed. "More people will die unless you tell me where the last sketch is!" I grip the final book from the box, ready to throw it across the room. Mom's eyes grow wide. I'm holding another sketchbook. It's the one I gave her for her birthday that she uses for to-do lists.

"Cera, give that to me." She tries to grab the notebook. "Trust me when I say you can't stop it from happening."

More than half my life she's kept secrets, and now she's asking me to trust her? I turn my back, moving away, and flip through the pages of scratched-out lists. No drawings. I try to recall the pictures from my mind. There was a green kite, but I can't for the life of me figure out what a green kite means. Papers flying? No that's not right. Once I see the image drawn out, I'll know. I'm sure of it. I flip through the last few pages. Then I see it.

"Cera!" Mom grips the edge of her bed and stumbles my way.

I ignore her and focus on the sketch. In light strokes, almost invisible, is that same deformed bird. My skin turns cold. She's drawn him with a greedy look of death in his eye. His talons are extended. Sceptered claws *"besmeared with blood / Of human sacrifice and parents' tears."* It's the demon, Moloch, in *Paradise Lost.* The way he puffs out his chest, as if waging *"open war"* is just as Milton describes. And the small mouse running across the road . . . it's Jess. The braided tail flapping in the wind, the two teeth missing on the mouse as she screams while she's being sliced open. The green kite is a dollar flying in the air. Jess is going to die, and it's all my fault. I gave her money to buy those pencils. I begin to shake.

"No matter what you think you see, you can't do anything to stop it from happening."

"I have to try!" I drop the sketchbook and race out of the room.

"Cera, don't! They'll find you," she pleads through her tears as I run out the front door.

I sprint down the shabby patch of crabgrass and race down the street, toward the row of bushes. My breath streams out in front of me as I search for Jess down streets tunneled with oak trees, and then the woods. Icy wind blows cold against my cheeks as I take the reverse path from her school to the gift shop, hoping to intercept her on the way. My eyes water but I keep looking for

Jess's messy braid. She isn't anywhere in sight. My frozen lungs scream, pleading me to stop, but I have to press on.

Random drops of cold rain pelt my face as a large shadow moves across the road. I push against time and race over the buckled pavement. I turn corners and weave through parked cars. I dodge irritated shoppers. "Jess!" I cry out, hoping my cracked voice will carry on the arctic wind and find her before my vision comes true. A gust of wind pushes against me, freezing my lips. Steel-blue clouds creep across the sky, snuffing out the sun's rays. Thunder rumbles.

Then I hear a sound that makes my skin prickle: a shrill cry, like a pig squealing for mercy in a slaughterhouse, only ten times louder. Even over the pulse pounding in my ears, that shriek is undeniable. I'd know it anywhere.

It's the horrific call of that demon bird.

6

MOLOCH

"Jess!" I scream and dash around blocked-off areas of road construction. I had the vision less than nine hours ago, but don't know if that's enough time to keep it from coming true. I push myself harder to reach the main road in time. Please let her be alive. Let me see her flash that toothless smile when I run around the corner. Let her be walking safely down the sidewalk. Please don't let her be dead.

I turn the corner and skid to a stop. It's not Jess I see, but the predator bird, Moloch. He dips out of the clouds and flies over the open road. My heart slams hard against my lungs. The beast that only lived in my head is alive, right in front of me. He's not drawn on paper or flashed in snippets from an image. The massive creature is soaring a good three stories above me. The black beast—with the body of a raven and six razor-sharp talons on each finger-like toe—is the size of a grizzly bear. His terrifying head has fangs and the slit yellow eyes of a rabid lion. This isn't a hallucination. That horrifying creature is real; and somehow he will kill Jess, even though everyone around me acts oblivious to his hideous existence.

As he flaps his wings, the wind whips, kicking up whirling dust tornados on the road. Everything inside me is screaming to run, but I'm rooted in the sidewalk, unable to move.

The beast circles around. I get the feeling this has all happened before—that I've been here, watching every detail play out—but I know I haven't. It's all been in my head. But now the creature puffs out his chest and spreads his wings, casting a dark shadow over the sloping road. He prowls the cloudy sky ready for attack. But where's Jess?

Moloch swoops down over the road. His head smoothly tilts from side to side, but he doesn't see me because his beady eyes are locked on a truck coming down the road. This truck has slanted metal bars—or ladders—strapped on both sides. There wasn't a truck in my vision or the drawing. Was I wrong?

The truck gets closer. Those aren't ladders. The silver frame is a thin metal crate that carries giant sheets of frosted glass. I weave around a parked car. Moloch circles above the buildings before swooping down. Digging his talons into the top of the truck, he jerks the vehicle back like some play toy. The driver slams on the brakes to get control. A silent scream gets caught in my chest. Moloch spins the truck faster. Black smoke rises from the tires. The smell of burnt rubber invades the air.

Why is Moloch attacking the truck? And where is Jess? I still don't see her. Maybe I've got this all wrong. Maybe the driver is the one in trouble. Regardless, how do I keep anyone from getting hurt? I don't know what will work; I only know I have to do *something*.

The beast shrieks, sounding delighted, as he bangs his oversized wings against the crates. It only takes one hit before cracks spread through the glass and pieces start to wiggle loose. If Moloch doesn't stop battering the truck, those pieces of glass will start flying all over the road.

Sliced open. So that's what he's doing. My image, or at least what I deciphered from Mom's sketch, showed Jess cut open on the road. If Moloch cracks the sheets of glass and spins the truck so the shards break free and find their target, then Jess has to be close by.

I scan the area. There, several blocks down, Jess darts into the road. My heart practically stops. She is chasing something caught in a violent wind. *A dollar bill.*

I run into the street. A car honks. Another screeches. Someone shouts at me. I ignore them and push fast in her direction.

"Leave it, Jess!" She's wearing the earmuffs and doesn't hear me. She tackles the dollar to the ground in the middle of the street, caging the flapping paper between her oversized gloves.

I force every fiber of my being to propel me faster down the road. Moloch launches the truck closer to Jess. The vision flashes in my mind: the little mouse screams. My heart feels ready to explode. I'm still too far away.

I shout helplessly. My voice is smothered by the sound of cracking thunder and shattered glass. Jess rises to her knees as glass blades sail through the air. Jess lets out a piercing scream and shields her face with her arms.

I'm so close. I can make it. I can save her.

I'm one body length away. I leap and reach out. My fingertips scrape the hem of her sleeve and grab—nothing but a fistful of air. Jagged glass stabs her in the chest, knocking her away. Her terrified scream turns silent.

I land hard on the asphalt. My stomach, elbows, and hands scrape against the gritty road as glass spears rain down. I shield my head, but get nicked on my left side below my ribs.

For a moment, everything is eerily quiet. Tires stop squealing. The mangled truck creaks to a stop in the middle of the intersection. Jess is crumpled on the pavement several feet away.

I crawl toward her, my hands and elbows scraping over glass shards, but I don't feel the pain. "Jess." Her name gets caught in my throat. "Can you hear me?" Her usually vibrant eyes are vacant, staring past the thick clouds. Her chapped lips turn blue and her mouth hangs open with her abandoned cry. "Jess, I'm here. It's me, Cera." She doesn't answer. When I grab her hand, two sparkling pencils roll out of those oversized gloves. One is pink. The other is honey yellow. One of the dollars I should never have given her lays at her side, steeped in blood.

Thunder cracks through the sky. I sink next to her.

Tires screech, and then a deafening crash follows. The ground shakes beneath me. I glance up. As if in slow motion, the mangled truck flips high into the air, spinning directly above. I scramble to my feet, even though it's too late to run. The underbelly of the truck will come crashing down on me any second. I'll die alongside Jess. And I should . . .

Out of nowhere, a figure attacks me from the side, smashing against my ribs and knocking all wind out of me. Caught in an iron grip, we're airborne. Everything's a blur as we crash and then roll onto a patch of grass just beyond the sidewalk. Whoever holds me takes most of the hit. I fight. Kicking. Punching. Screaming to break free. The ground shakes as the truck craters into the road a few yards away, crushing Jess.

I lay stunned. I've been saved, but Jess . . . I can't abandon her. I shove away and scramble to my feet.

"We have to get out of here, now!" a guy's voice shouts over the hissing radiator as I'm grabbed from behind.

"Let go!" I surge every bit of strength and deliver a hard elbow to what proves to be a solid stomach.

He loosens his grip but takes hold of me again. "You can't go back."

I break loose. A mix of adrenaline, panic, and shock numbs the burning in my hands as I claw through the heated debris desperate to find what's left of my little friend. Part of me knows she's not alive and there won't be a trace of her in that fire. The other part can't accept it.

The guy takes a hold of my arm and drags me back.

I kick and wrestle out of my shredded jacket. "I said, let go!"

"If we don't get out of here, we'll die." His voice grinds

against my ear. The frenetic crackles and sizzles of the radiator underscore his urgent plea. Something sputters. Then I hear a faint click. He iron-grips my wrist and yells, "Run!"

The truck erupts into a fireball. I'm thrown, midstride. Searing heat laps at my heels. I dive through spearing glass and flying metal. I smash onto the sidewalk several car lengths from the wreckage and hit an electrical box bolted to the concrete.

I lay on the cold cement, dazed and battered, with a deep throb pulsing in my side. Large drops of cold rain pelt my head and gashed shoulder. Flames creep through the intersection but remain a good distance away. I push up on my elbows and drag myself behind the electrical box and take cover. The stench of burnt oil and the sweltering heat reaches even here. Plumes of black smoke rise from the wreckage. Moloch lands, hiding somewhere in the smolder, and squawks as if he's proud of the mayhem and relishing his kill.

Jess's tiny body is trapped and alone somewhere under that pyre. The vision came true—all of it except for the fire. Why didn't I see the fire? Not that it matters. Jess was killed just how I imagined she would be; everything was detailed in Mom's drawing. Mom will have one more article to clip. She will write *confirmed* on the bottom corner of the paper the same way she's done with all the others. If Mom hadn't lied to me, I would have had more time to save Jess. She'd still be alive.

Hurried footsteps crunch over broken glass somewhere behind me. "Are you okay?" The guy kneels beside me. "You've been hurt something bad." He has no idea how right he is on so many levels, but he's probably talking about the bright red smudge bleeding through my T-shirt. Seeing the blood makes everything real. "Can you stand? If not, I'll carry you." He puts a hand on my arm, ready to scoop me up.

"I'm fine." A total lie, but I brush his hands off. My dad was the last person to carry me, and I was seven. There's no way I'm letting some random stranger carry me now. I force myself to sit up, looking at his face for the first time.

His crystal-blue eyes stare through shaggy white-blond hair as they study my wounded shoulder. It's the guy who was playing guitar in the square, the one who looks like a surfer from Southern California.

"Let's get you help." He scans the road for a solution with a determined look chiseled across his face. His eyes narrow, and I follow his gaze back to the fire. Moloch holds what's left of my charred jacket between his sharp teeth. The beast, about fifty feet away, looks as if he's about to toss my jacket in the air and devour the fabric. He doesn't. Instead he lays the fabric at his side like some souvenir and flaps his wings, shooing away the smoke. A blistering heat wave billows in my direction and burns my eyes.

"We have to go," California whispers, but I'm too focused on Moloch to respond. As sirens approach, the creature rummages through the debris, searching with fierce intensity after Jess. My chest tightens. She's already dead. Leave her alone. Does that vile monster want to rip her apart as well so they won't find a trace of her? I'll stab the beast through the heart, gouge out its eyes. Split apart every shred of feathery skin so he won't hurt anyone ever again.

I grab a twisted piece of metal lying near me. Fire doesn't kill him, but a skewer into the chest might. I push my knees underneath me and grip the hot metal in my fist. Before I can stand, California presses his hand on my good shoulder.

"What are you doing?" he asks, sounding shocked. "Nuh-uh. You can't go after it. You can't let it see you."

"I couldn't care less if . . ." I freeze. *It?* What does he mean by *it*? We're all alone on the narrow side street. The voices that carry through the wreckage come from the main road, on the other side of flames. The only thing I can see besides the burning truck is Moloch. "*It* will see me?" The word sticks to my throat.

"The Cormorant." California lowers his voice. "It thinks you're caught under the truck. It won't be long before the beast figures out you got away. Good thing you dropped the jacket. It'll buy us some time. C'mon, hurry."

An icy chill runs through my veins. I can't be hearing right. "Wait." I'm light-headed. "You can see that demon?"

California doesn't flinch. Through those shaggy bangs, his tense eyes lock on Moloch's every move. "Yeah, and if we don't find a way out of here soon, that demon's gonna see us too."

7

AWAKENED

I gawk at California in disbelief. Kneeling beside me, he is staring at the disfigured bird-beast as it walks through the fire. He can see Moloch? My heart pumps fast, knocking out all my breath. Someone else sees this warped creature wandering the earth?

Moloch's back is turned. The creature flaps his silken wings, stirring up the flames. Before I can peel myself off the sidewalk, California slips his arms under mine and lifts me to my feet.

"I got it," I say. "I'm fine." I'm really not. My head spins. I'm light-headed and I'm leaning to the left, but the last thing I want is to be treated like an invalid or worse, a patient.

"Let's go, then. But be quiet."

"I won't abandon Jess . . ." I'm hyperventilating.

"You knew that girl." He never takes his eyes off the Cormorant. "I'm sorry. But there's nothing you can do for her now. We need to get away while we still can." He glances at my side. "I know someone who can look at that wound. We gotta go now or the EMTs will take you to a hospital."

He's right, and the set look on his face tells me he knows it. Almost on cue, an approaching ambulance siren wails a few blocks away.

I nod, even though any step away from the scene, away from Jess, will thrust a dagger deeper into my soul.

"C'mon." California raises his black denim jacket, creating a canopy to shield us from random raindrops and floating cinder. As he hovers over me, a warm ocean scent invades the space. He's a little too close. I grab a corner of our makeshift shelter and shift, giving him room.

As California steers me away from the fire, I look back over my shoulder at Moloch. About ten yards away, the beast squawks and sifts through the flames. There's not a scratch on him. "How can we kill it?" I again look for something that might do the trick. When I let go of the jacket, Moloch tilts his head in my direction. His yellow snake eyes narrow as he stares right at me. My blood turns cold. He's seen us.

Moloch lets out a piercing cry—one that's so loud, my eardrums might split. "Go, go, go!" California drags me as he runs. Smoky wind burns my eyes. As if that's not enough to blind me, the violent flap of Moloch's wings whipping my hair in my face does. My feet somehow manage to stay underneath me as California hauls me down the street. He grips my wrist so tight, I can barely feel my fingers. He needs to let go. I can run faster if he does.

Moloch's shadow flies right over us as we reach the corner. I yank my hand out of California's grip just as sulfur-scented wind whooshes against my arm. I gasp. Moloch almost sliced my arm off! I peer through gritty strands of my hair. The slimy tip of Moloch's talon, oozing black blood, tilts down, ready for another swipe. Run. Faster!

"This way." California grabs a fistful of my T-shirt and pulls me around a white contractor van. We weave around the truck parked at the end of an alley and leap over a pile of trash. Moloch stays on our heels until we enter a back lane latticed with metal balconies and dangling fire escape ladders. Moloch isn't entering the narrow pathway. He's suspended in midair at the entrance, beating his wings. Smart move, California. Moloch's wingspan is too wide for the cluttered path. He can't get through—or so I think.

Using his bird legs, the stealthy creature lands on the van and tries to jump down. Luckily he hits the fire escape ladders, which slows him down and puts more distance between us. I speed up, but our lead is cut short when we hit a cluster of air conditioning units blocking our path.

"We'll have to climb over." California looks over his shoulder. Moloch is writhing himself between the brick and the truck and still can't get through. He backs up. For a brief moment, I think he's given up—that we might be safe—until, with one swipe of his talon, he yanks the van back and tosses it aside. He's found a way in.

When I reach to pull myself up, a stabbing pain streaks through my abdomen. I yelp.

"What's wrong?" California asks.

My knees buckle. I lean against the cold metal and suck in the deepest breath I can muster as my skin turns clammy. "Just keep going." I grip a handle near the top of the air unit, despite the throbbing in my side. One look back at Moloch, at the hate brewing in his fiery eyes, tells me we're out of time. He's knocking away bits from the fire escape like they're nothing but paper straws.

In a matter of seconds, California is on top of the rusted air units, reaching down to help me, but I've already managed to tuck the tip of my tennis shoe in a groove and pull myself up on my own. Moloch screeches. His squawk is so loud, I can feel the metal vibrate. He's gaining on us.

Lightning flashes, brightening the alley. Out of habit, and so I don't get caught off guard, I count the seconds before the thunder cracks while I hopscotch on top of the rickety air conditioners, following California's path. *One one thousand . . . Two one thousand . . . Three one thousand . . . Four one thousand . . . Five.* Thunder explodes. California startles but he doesn't slow down.

He swiftly navigates the rusted units, careful not to get his foot caught in the tangled wires. I try to do the same, but I'm not nearly as quick.

A brisk wind whips around me, kicking up the smell of tangy metal mixed with rotting flesh. I take another quick glance behind me. Moloch moves down the alley, shrieking as he juts his neck forward. He's getting too close.

California jumps down first. He reaches up for my hands. I take them. With my bleeding side, jumping seven feet to the ground on my own isn't an option, and sliding off the rusty metal will only slow me down.

We're not two steps removed from the rusty A/C units when a pole harpoons from the sky, whooshing behind my back. For a second, I think it's Moloch, until I take a quick look. A three-foot metal pipe impales the pavement behind me, but Moloch is still ripping through fire escape ladders behind us. That pole came from overhead, which means . . . I look up. Another demon bird. My whole body tenses. This bird is sleeker. His head is pointier than Moloch's, but he's just as vicious.

"Why are they trying to kill us?" I gasp, running beside California.

"That beast is a predator. Hunts the Awakened. You're about seventeen, right?" He shoots a quick glance my way. I nod. I will be at the end of the week, anyway. "Newly Awakened," he says in a hoarse whisper. "It's their favorite target."

I don't have time to ask what he means by Awakened. The second bird rips metal poles from the wall, sifting and searching for the best iron bar to harpoon right at us. And he's found one. California is focused on knocking crates and trash out of our way as we run. He doesn't see the second beast calculating our every step. We're too open. Nothing covers us. We'll have to change course, or the monster will have a clear shot at us.

My tennis shoes slap against the concrete as I will my legs to run faster. "Look out!" I yank at California, but even then, I'm not able to pull him completely out of the way.

The iron bar whizzes down and slices across his forearm. California grunts in pain and grabs his arm as he sees the bird overhead for the first time.

This time I'm the one asking. "Are you—"

"I'm fine." He ducks around a corner with his arm tucked against his side. "Get to that last door."

We run, zigzagging through the alley. Another spear launches down but misses us by a good two feet and instead stabs a trash bag California threw aside. With only dim amber lights over back-alley doors, Moloch and the second bird are harder to see. Rats scatter into the shadows. My lack of sight only amplifies the sound of scraping metal coming from somewhere overhead.

California skids to a stop. "In here." We duck under a flimsy balcony, taking cover as California tries to pry a rusty door open with a bent pipe. "We can't outrun two of them."

The second bird sends down another metal spear, puncturing our metal roof with a deafening clang. *Belial.* The name comes to mind. Oh, you're so full of it, Milton. You described Belial as a wicked, cunning debater, casually floating on a lake of fire. This bird is actively fighting to kill us.

"As when a prowling wolf, / Whom hunger drives to seek new haunt for prey." Yeah, you've got that part right, Milton. We're definitely prey.

Another flash of lightning gives me a clear shot of where they are. *One one thousand.* Belial tries to swoop down the ladders but can't fit. He squawks—short, staccato sounds, working his way down. *Two one thousand.* Moloch rips coils from the air units then caws back to Belial as if planning a coordinated attack. *Three.* Thunder cracks through the sky.

"Come on. Come on!" California urges through gritted teeth as he wedges the pipe in the door.

My eyes stay trained on Moloch. The beast rolls his neck and leans forward to sniff the air. He lets out a series of purrs and squawks. Both creatures slow their pursuit. Every drop of blood in me turns cold. They're communicating to one another while hemming us in. They watch our every move and creep closer. We're caged animals—and there's no way out. An image flashes through my mind from a memory—a vision long ago. These are the same birds that attacked Marcy. The ones that sliced her leg and waited to swallow her whole.

My body trembles. All my life these beasts have been destroying everyone around without my knowing. I refuse to be their prey. *They're* the ones that need to be destroyed. California didn't ever say whether or not they can be killed, but I'd rather die trying than run away and let them live. A skewer right through each of their black hearts might do the trick. My throat tightens as I grab a torn iron handrail off the asphalt. The weight pulls against my scraped shoulder, but I clutch tight anyway.

"Got it!" California says, as the metal door opens, scraping against the pavement. Blood drips down the back of his palm, and there's a tear in his jacket. "Get inside."

The door leads to nothing but echoing darkness. "No, they're trying to trap us."

Belial is perched overhead, picking apart beams and poles, trying to wiggle himself back up through a tangle of ladders and twisted metal. Moloch sways, focused and ready to pounce any minute, as if he's waiting. But waiting for what?

Suddenly, Moloch springs into the air. Launching right at us. No—at California. I grip the pole and yell. I race toward the beast, hurling the spear directly for its heart.

The javelin bounces off of Moloch's chest and rebounds across the cold pavement with a hollow clank. My futile weapon did nothing to stop Moloch's attack. His curled serpent tongue unravels as he sails toward us. California swings a metal pipe, striking Moloch in the jaw, knocking the creature back. Moloch staggers.

He bashes the pipe against Moloch's head again while swiftly dodging the vicious swipe of his talons. California gets knocked on his back. Moloch crouches, ready to pounce. I scream over the clashing thunder and swipe another metal pole off the ground before running toward Moloch. The demon bird locks eyes with me. In that moment, California digs his weapon through the beast's shoulder. Moloch shrieks and California wastes no time. He scrambles to his feet, yanking me with him.

"Go!" He heads back into the deep recess of the alley. Where? My eyes adjust to the rain-soaked curtain of fog. With one kick, California punches a hole through a rotted red fence and crawls through. Lightning flashes. *One.* Moloch shakes his head as if trying to recover. *Two.*

Thunder cracks. California pulls me through the opening. A cold raindrop drips down my back. Where is Belial?

"This way." California picks up speed as he races out of the alley and around the corner to a main road. "The train isn't far."

A car honks, slamming on the brakes as we dart across the street. Dusk deepens as we weave around parked cars and humming light poles into another alley. Another alley, is he serious? But this one is shorter and opens to a backstreet. A chain-link fence holds back the woods. Overgrown tree limbs hang over the metal fence, banging branches in the frantic wind, urging us to run faster.

Moloch's screech blasts from all directions. If they're scouring the area from the sky, there's no way we can outrun them. We need a distraction so we can get away.

California leads the way, leaving dots of blood on the pavement. Not only that, the metallic smell from either his cut or my bloody shirt lingers.

"Do they have a sharp sense of smell?" I ask, running beside him.

"That, plus laser sight."

"Then we need to wrap your arm or cover it somehow. You're leaving a trail." In this light, against the pale pavement, his blood won't be hard to spot.

He stops near the stucco wall and pulls his jacket sleeve up to inspect his arm. The cut looks gaping and deep. I stifle a gasp. Without pressure, he'll be in serious trouble. "Here." I rip the clean hem of my torn shirt. "Give me your arm." I tie the fabric around the wound on his forearm.

He breathes between his clenched teeth. "Thanks." He bites on the end to pull the tourniquet tighter. A thought hits me. The back of this building has a few exit doors with lamps overhead. We tried going in once before. Maybe we can buy ourselves some time if we get the birds to think this time, we *did* enter the building.

I tear another piece of my shirt. This time I rip off the bloodstained part, feeling cold air brush against my bare stomach. "We need to throw them off our scent." I jiggle the door handle. It's locked.

"We've got to keep running." California catches his breath as he checks the sky. "You're right about them trapping us. They already know we're somewhere close."

"That's exactly what we want them to think." I stuff the torn piece of my blood-soaked shirt in the crevice of the door jamb near the handle. "You said it yourself—we can't outrun two of them."

"That's genius . . . at least, I hope it is." He pulls on the door to help me tuck the fabric deep enough to stay put.

"If Moloch isn't smart enough to notice that my shirt is pushed in and not caught in the door, then it might work." I will my fingers to stop shaking as I finish the crude job.

"Moloch?"

"The Cormorant." I ignore his confused look and smear the door handle with the excess blood on my fingers.

An earsplitting screech blasts through the damp air.

"Over here." California runs around the shipping container. He pulls back a loose part of the chain-link fence and slips into the woods, holding it open for me to follow. As I squeeze through, my feet sink into soft, wet mud. Good thinking. Without the sound of our shoes on the pavement, not only will we be harder to hear, but the wet earth and heavy pine might hide our scent as well. Or at least I hope so.

Hidden under the canopy of swaying tree branches, we navigate farther along the dirt path, getting as far away from the bloodied door as possible. But I feel uneasy.

"We should go deeper into the woods," I say. California's sun-bleached hair will be too easy to spot against the murky trees.

"We'll make too much noise rustling through there. We need to stay along the fence, follow the path back to the main road."

"But we're exposed. They can spot us," I whisper, staying close at his heels.

"Not if we keep under cover. Duck behind tree trunks. If we need to, we can hide behind that trash bin down there."

The branches block my view of the sky. I'm almost afraid to breathe, afraid my own breath will drown out the sound of these stealthy birds swooping in for the kill.

California crouches behind the large trash bin. It reeks of onions and rotting potatoes that will hopefully hide our scent. My knees sink into the wet earth next to him. A rat scampers over my lap. I swallow my scream. Along the back side of the buildings, clicking nails softly tap along the pavement. They're here. Walking. My hands tremble and my feet twitch. I'm ready to run.

California presses his warm hand on my knee and gives me a small shake of his head. Against every fiber in me, I force myself to stay still. I swallow hard, straining to listen for the tapping nails over the sounds of a skittering rat in the dumpster, incessant crickets in the woods, and a rumbling train in the distance. The steady nail tapping continues, but it sounds as if there's only one bird. Where's the other one?

An icy gust blows over us. As soon as I smell rotting flesh blended with sulfur, I freeze.

Lightning flashes. I start counting. *One one thousand.* I glance up. *Two . . .* My insides turn to liquid. Belial's black talons perch on a gnarled branch two stories above. He hops to a smaller bough closer to the building, which groans and buckles under his weight. Luckily, he's no longer above us and hasn't seen us yet. Thunder roars through the sky, shaking the earth. Any breath, any movement, and we're dead. My resolve for revenge melts. I'm back to being hunted.

California watches through bangs that stick to his sweaty face. Shadows from the dim lights highlight his tense jaw and tight lips. Moloch lets out a shrill shriek. Is he calling more vile creatures?

My feet tingle, turning numb beneath me. My trap with the door didn't work. Now we're caught. With Belial overhead and Moloch somewhere in the alley, there's no way we'll make it out alive.

Crouching low, California gently leans into me, pressing his arm against mine. I realize my body is shivering, whether from cold or shock. He is too. Maybe he can't keep his balance perched down for this long, or maybe he needs to feel that he's not alone before we die. I press back, my shoulder against his arm, affirming that we're dead together. I still don't even know his name.

Moloch lets out a series of caws mixed with strange purrs. Belial, perched near us, squawks back and then takes off. Through a break in the branches I watch Belial flying over the roof of the building where I left my bloody shirt.

The sound of scraping metal competes with the hard rain bulleting through the trees.

California shifts to peer around the trash bin. So do I, but I stay behind him, looking over his shoulder. Moloch pops the door off its hinges with his talon as if he's opened a soda can. As soon as Moloch shoves his head in the building and starts squirming his body through the back door, the skies open, pouring down rain. California turns his head to me and nods.

Without hesitating, I run. Drenched, I take off along the wire barrier, my feet sinking into the mud, faster than ever before. I don't slow down until the fence ends at the street intersection. Somewhere over the row of shops across the street, a train rumbles. I'm so disoriented, I have no clue where we are or which way to go.

California sprints up alongside me. "Train's this way." He slows to a jog, following the tree line. "Two blocks down. Then left."

Moloch's and Belial's shrieking cries ride on the frantic wind as we turn the corner. Lightning flashes. Thunder cracks. I don't even have time to count. We dodge idling cars with rapid windshield wipers and frantic deliverymen unloading boxes from a truck.

Cold rain dumps over us. Just ahead, the amber lights from the train platform glow, signaling we're close. Through the blurry rain, the train hisses, holding its doors wide open.

8

EAST RIDGE

I sit on the train in a numb, autopilot mode as we rocket through town, leaving the Cormorants behind in the pouring rain. California sits beside me. Exhausted, I rest my head against the window. City lights streak through the dark as the glass vibrates. The day is past, and Jess's cindered body slips further away. Hot tears run down my cheeks, but I don't wipe them away.

My side throbs, my shoulder burns, and the stinging pain from each scrape, magnified. My breath fogs the window, but it doesn't matter. I can't see anything on account of the tears. I couldn't save Jess. Her wide eyes trusted me, believed me, when I handed her the money. It's no wonder Mom wanted to move every year. I'm exactly what Dad said I was before he walked out the door ten years ago. No self-improvement list can fix what I really am: "a monster that will cause more destruction than good." Mom's drawings showed it. Jess's death proves it. I sink my head in my hands. The pain digging in my side is nothing compared to the ripping inside my heart.

My whole life has been a lie. Move after move, attack after attack, Mom knew. She knew I wasn't crazy but let me believe it. She probably knew the horrible creatures were real and that there were others like me who could see them, but she would never let me have enough friends to find out. I've wanted answers for ten years, and she withheld them from me. Why? The door of my life suddenly feels thrown wide open to hell, and there's no way to go back and close it.

California drapes his heavy denim jacket over my shoulders. "Hey . . . everything will be okay."

I bristle. His words are exactly what Mom says after I have an attack. Words that are a complete lie.

I press my back against the window and choke out the words, "Nothing is okay. Nothing has ever been okay. So don't sit there and say everything is okay when it's not. Jess died. I couldn't save her. Freakin' demon birds are out there killing people and hunting us down. I'm on a train headed to who knows where, and for all I know, that beast will be waiting as soon as we stop!"

California looks surprised, but he doesn't take offense at my outburst. He leans back. "The Cormorants won't be waiting for us." His voice is calm. "We lost them for now." He searches my face, for what, I don't know. "There's this place in East Ridge—"

"Is that where this train goes?" I've heard the rumors of murders and drug deals in East Ridge. It's the last place you'd want to be when the sun goes down—but then again, most of those rumors came from Mom. But not all of them. I grip the cold rail in front of me. "I'll just ride it out till I get back to Wakefield."

The windows rattle as the train sways. California glances over his shoulder. "They'll be waiting for us in Wakefield. Better to get you patched up in East Ridge. There's a safe house there—"

"How could any place be safe now, *especially* in East Ridge?" The train lurches and I stifle a wince when pain jabs my side. "You saw how those creatures tore into anything that got in their way."

"Hesperian is safe. Trust me. Plus, we'll get you help for that cut."

Hesperian? "The only help I need is in knowing what those evil creatures are, why they're killing people, and how to annihilate them." As far as trusting this guy, he won't look me directly in the eyes. Not a good sign. I can't read him unless he does.

"Hold up." He looks confused. "You mean, you don't know?"

"Know *what*?" My side throbs as the train vibrates over rough tracks. "I don't even know your name."

California shakes his head in disbelief. His wet hair sticks to his jaw. All this time I thought he was older, but looking at him now, I'm guessing he's about my age. "I'm sorry, I really thought you knew . . ." He finally looks right at me. When our eyes meet, I'm jolted with a paralyzing flutter. He quickly looks away.

I swallow. What was *that*? He's left me feeling wobbly and exposed. I press up against the window, putting as much space between us as possible in this cramped seat.

He exhales and rubs his hand over his face. "Listen." His voice drops low as his gaze sweeps over the empty train. "I know what we just went through seems unreal."

"You think?"

"The reason you see those creatures—the Cormorants—is because you've got a special ability to see this second realm where the beasts wander. You're an Awakened. Normally we get this 'second sight' when we turn seventeen or sometimes as late as eighteen. Being an Awakened also comes with a Bent—"

"Stop right there." I hold up my hand because he's slinging way too much bizarre information at me all at once. "Back up a second. So this is all *real*?"

At that moment Milton barges in with the verse: *"Millions of spiritual creatures walk the earth / Unseen, both when we wake and when we sleep,"* confirming California's words. I can't concentrate with two people talking to me at once. I press my fingers against my temples, hoping to quiet Milton.

California nods. "By realm I mean a layer over our own physical reality. The Awakened have the ability to see what everyone else can't. Not everyone is an Awakened. We don't know why. We call the ones that aren't 'Commons.' Usually Awakened are artistic types, but that's not always the case."

I sit in silence for a second and process what he's told me. As crazy as this news sounds, for the first time, the answer doesn't feel like a lie. "Do I see into this other realm all the time? 'Cause I don't always see those beasts everywhere I go." But then again Mom would move me after each attack and maybe that's why. I look out the window. Dim lights in the distance grow closer, but nothing looks unusual, and the only disturbing sound is loose siding rattling somewhere in the rhythmic train.

California reaches over and wipes the fog off the window. "You won't see anything right now because the creatures aren't around. When they are, we can see the destruction they cause. They'll do anything to stop us."

My mind races, leaping ten paces ahead. "You called them predators a while back. They hunt us because they know we can see them. If that's the case, we can stop them, right?" As I speak, Mom's warning flashes through my head. She had said not to face "them." I have a strong feeling this is what she meant. I sit up. "Tell me how to kill them. I'll do whatever it takes to stop those beasts from hurting anyone else."

"So would I." He glances at me for a quick second, but avoids eye contact. Then, suddenly aware that his leg is touching mine, he straightens. He's so tall, his knees hit the seat in front of us. "And I'm Maddox, by the way."

I glance at our warped reflections wrapped around the metal bar in front of me. My head spins, trying to process—and believe—everything he's just told me. "I'm Cera."

"When we get to East Ridge, we'll patch your side. You can meet the others, and I'll hook you up with Devon. I'm sure you've got a ton of questions, and he knows more than anyone, except Gladys, who runs the place, but she's usually not around this late."

There are others? My mind can hardly wrap around the

concept that intuitively I know is true. Something thumps against the outside of the train. I recoil, pushing away from the window.

California—I mean, Maddox—stiffens and glances out. "We're just entering the tunnel." His shoulders relax as he leans back in the seat.

My whole world feels upside down as this random guy talks about beasts, creatures, and other realms as if it's perfectly normal. If it weren't for the throb in my side, I'd think I was dreaming. "You seriously mean . . . you have answers as to why I see what I do and what's wrong with me? I'm not really . . ."

"Losing it?" He shakes his head. "There's nothing wrong with you. You're Awakened, just like the rest of us."

The rest of us. As far as I've ever known, there's never been anyone else like me before. I blink at the insanity of it all. "So, what am I . . . ? Besides being awake, or whatever. You said something about being broken?"

"It's called a Bent. You're a Guardian or possibly a Blade. I can't tell for sure. Devon will know."

"Is Devon some guru who slaps these lovely tags on people?"

"No." Maddox laughs slightly. "He's a Caretaker. Part of his Bent, besides shepherding our group, is identifying Bents so he can pair you with a mentor."

"Will this mentor teach me how to kill the beasts?"

"If you're a Blade, then sure. Blades are warriors that attack the beasts. Guardians like me, and possibly you, we're supposed to protect the Awakened from the beasts. Not really attack them."

I cross my arms. "Then I want to be a Blade."

A smile curls in the corner of his mouth. I'm not sure if he's smirking at my ignorance, thinks I'm joking, or what, but either way, I'm not insulted. He's the only one willing to tell me the truth. "You don't get to choose. You're stuck with whatever you're born with. Although the Bent doesn't show up in its full form till you're about seventeen or so."

I frown. "You don't get a choice? That's not encouraging." I debate mentioning the visions to see if that makes a difference, but as the train slows, I decide against it. I know better than to spill stuff about myself, especially to a total stranger. I search for my bag. It's not here. Panic flashes through me. Oh, that's right. I left everything at home when I ran out the door. I've got nothing but the clothes I'm wearing, and they're in pretty rough shape at the moment.

"This is it." Maddox sits up and glances out the window as the train lurches to a stop. I stay put as he stands. Sure, I want answers, but I'm not totally sold on the idea of walking around East Ridge.

"Come on." Maddox stands in the aisle, waiting. "Follow me."

As I clutch the jacket closed and glance out the window, Milton intrudes with the verse: "...*follow me, / And I will bring thee where no shadow stays.*"

I take a breath. Fine, Milton. I shut you up once already. If bringing me "*where no shadow stays*" means getting the answers I need to bring clarity through the lies and avenging Jess's death, then I'll get off this train and follow some guy I just met, even though the idea seems totally insane. I'm pretty sure Milton's not using Adam's pick-up line to compare me to Eve. When she looked at her reflection in the pond, she was so stunning she couldn't tear herself away. Me? I look as attractive as a drenched alley cat.

As the train chimes, signaling the end of the stop, Maddox leans over. "You okay?" he asks, ready to help me out of my seat, but I'm already on my feet.

"Yeah, I'm fine." Even though I'm light-headed, I push my shoulders back and don't let on how bad my side hurts. With Milton as my North Star, I refuse to let pain stop me from getting the answers I need.

Cold air blasts over me as I exit the safety of the train.

My eyes adjust to the dark as I search for the bird beasts, but he's right. No creatures await us. We walk the abandoned streets of East Ridge, drenched, cold, and hungry. Maddox shoves his hands in his pockets, keeping his bandaged arm tucked against his side. Red scrapes from our battle with Moloch decorate his arm like infected tattoos.

This whole area is run-down. Puddles glisten in the pot-holed street. Windows are boarded up. The ones that aren't cast dim light over the sidewalk. I almost trip over someone huddled on the ground near a doorway that smells of rat urine. Sure, the place might be free of any beasts, but that doesn't mean it's safe. My skin prickles with warning as I walk. I suddenly regret my decision to get off the train, because something tells me that the rumors about East Ridge are all true.

9

HESPERIAN

Bickering voices, followed by crude jesting and drunken laughter, float down as we turn the corner. The shadows of two or three people sit on a roof with feet dangling over the ledge. They choke back long swigs from glass bottles. I draw closer to Maddox's side. "You sure this is a good idea?" To keep up with his long stride, I have to work twice as hard—which does nothing to ease the throbbing in my side, not to mention the wet denim jacket rubbing against the burning road rash on my shoulder. I take in a deep breath of cold air and focus on the flickering streetlamp halfway down the narrow road. A whiff of fried food wafts through the damp air, either from a restaurant or someone's apartment. My stomach rumbles. I'm *so* freakin' hungry.

"Trust me, your chances of being hidden are much better out here." He walks around a muddy puddle. "If the creatures come anywhere close, we'll know in plenty of time to get out or hide. Blades and Guardians are on lookout all over the place."

I glance over my shoulder. On the opposite side of the street, a dark figure wearing a hooded sweatshirt follows. Although it's a person, not one of the creatures, the brisk, cocky stride says he's looking for trouble. Uneasiness sweeps over me. "Is that one of your Blades?"

Maddox stops under the streetlamp in front of a storefront with blacked-out windows. As he peers across the dark street, he stands tall with fight written across his shoulders. He couldn't take anyone down right now, not with his arm all banged up. The best I can do is run.

Maddox relaxes. "Yeah, he's with us." He acknowledges the guy with a chin nod.

Thankfully, the guy's stride doesn't slow. He nods back and continues walking, keeping his hands tucked in the front pocket of his sweatshirt. "C'mon. Let's talk inside. It's warmer."

Maddox presses a call button on the brick building that spans the entire block. Under the dim glow of the streetlight, I can make out the etched letters of the name *Hesperian* on the glass, but that's about it. I can't see anything inside.

"In *there*?" I step back. Going in that run-down building is crossing the sanity line by at least a mile. I don't know what I was expecting, but it certainly wasn't heading into a dilapidated and abandoned motel that's probably infested with diseased rats.

"I think you'll like it." Maddox stands with the door open, waiting. A bell chimes down a dark corridor. Warmth smelling of vanilla coffee and cinnamon scones spills out of the doorway. I inhale the air, hoping a deep breath can somehow satisfy my hunger.

He glances down as I clutch the jacket closed. "We need to get your cut checked out, and I'm guessing you're probably hungry."

Am I ever. My stomach growls in agreement. Forget sanity. Food wins. Lured by the intoxicating promise of food, I walk in the building, following the aroma.

"Through here." Maddox steps down a few stairs. My eyes adjust to the dim light. At least there aren't any rats, as far as I can tell. "Watch your step. The floor slants a little."

I follow behind him, feeling my way down the paneled hallway. French fries. I definitely smell fries. My mouth doesn't just water—I honestly drool. I wipe my lips with the back of my hand. "Is this a restaurant?"

"Sort of." Maddox stops when he gets to a sturdy mahogany counter. I stay in the shadow behind him and peek through the brick archway that spills a soft light into the corridor. A few tables with mosaic tabletops and vinyl diner chairs are scattered around the room, and stone columns line the back wall, separating out sunken alcoves with wooden tables and benches. Acoustic guitars and a few voices fill the air, but the music isn't consistent. The strumming stops and starts again as if we've entered a preshow sound check.

"Maddox?" A girl's smiling voice flutters across the counter through the dark, and with it comes a faint scent of potter's clay. She carries over a basket of silverware.

"Hey, Claire," Maddox says, sounding sheepish. Nothing like he did earlier. He is blocking my full view of the girl as she rolls utensils in napkins.

"Where'd you go? The whole place was worried about you. Gladys was a nervous wreck. Devon was about to send someone out just to calm her down. And Harper's been—"

"I've . . . I was just—busy." He tucks his hands in his pockets, shifting his weight. I doubt he's still cold. The sweet air is as warm as a blanket right out of the dryer. I'm surprised she doesn't see me, but then again, I'm hidden in the dark.

"Oh, sure . . . well . . . I'm glad you're back." She polishes the tip of a knife before setting it on the napkin. "And hey, I'm working on a new project. Want to see it?"

"Your last one was amazing. Maybe later?" As Maddox steps aside, I get a clear shot of Claire, a cropped redhead in a flowing lime-green shirt. She's naturally pretty. Her beaming smile fizzles a little when I come out of his shadow. And as soon as she sees me wearing Maddox's jacket, she switches her attention back to him.

"So that's where you've been. Found another one, huh? Another girl." She mutters that last part.

I cross my arms. "I'm Cera." Not some unwanted stray Maddox pulled in off the street. Claire narrows her eyes. The heat from her glare sends a sharp zap through my hollow stomach, about as strong as a punch in my gut. I try to hold her stare even though I feel wobbly and transparent.

Luckily, when Maddox rests his hands on the counter, Claire switches her focus to the scraps of my T-shirt wrapped around his forearm. "You got hurt? How'd that happen?" Her eyes widen. "You know Harper's gonna flip out."

"I'm not hurt." Maddox drops his arm below the counter. "Just a couple of scratches, that's all."

He's such a liar. I want to call him out, but Claire's it's-your-fault-he's-hurt expression makes me tense, so I keep my mouth shut. "What's her Bent?"

"Guardian, I think." Maddox glances over his shoulder to look at me. Yeah, right. If I am supposed to guard others, then I'm awful at it. I couldn't even protect Jess. I want to ask Maddox why he thinks so, but one look at Claire's probing death stare and I swallow my question.

"You better talk with Devon."

"That's the plan. He around?" Maddox leans against the counter, looking about as beat and worn as I feel.

Claire transfers her stack of rolled silverware back into the basket. "He's in the back."

"Tell him to meet me in the alcove." Maddox messes with the bandage on his arm but keeps it hidden below the counter.

"Sure thing, and I'll send Harper back there too. She left her kit in your space anyway." Claire picks up the basket and shifts her glance my way. As if I've passed some test, if only by the skin of my teeth, she adds, "Oh, and welcome, Cera." I doubt she means it, but I force a smile anyway.

Before Claire leaves, Maddox reaches across the counter and grabs her arm. In a low whisper he says, "Hey, do me a favor.

Don't say anything to Harper about my arm, will you?"

Claire nods. A knowing smirk is plastered on her face. I have no idea what that's all about, and I don't care. All I know is that when Claire steps through the archway, disappearing around the corner, she takes the tense, clay-scented air away with her.

"What's up with her?" I exhale. "Her hate glare sizzled through me like an X-ray laser."

Maddox half smiles at my comment as he walks toward the archway. "Claire is a Blade. She's still training on detecting and destroying threats and sometimes gets a little . . . intense."

"A *little*? More like a lot. I guess I should feel lucky I passed her test, huh?"

"You're fine. Trust me."

I want to trust him, but my stomach is knotted up, and not just because I'm starving or because of the constant throbbing in my side. "Why didn't you tell her about the Cormorants and what happened? Because your arm isn't just scratched up."

"She doesn't need to know." He walks off into the café.

I follow right behind, ready to badger him about his lame answer, but stop as soon as I enter the room. From the hallway, I thought it was only a small café, but the place opens up into this large space under a domed, stained glass ceiling. My eyes lift, taking it all in. It's as if I've stepped into the pages of Mom's Italian art books, and I can hardly breathe.

I stand there, soaking up the converted church. Goosebumps rise on my skin. The sound of frothing milk underscores murmuring voices. Occasional laughter floats through the coffee-scented air. A wooden staircase hugs the wall as it climbs up to a second story. Hundreds of paintings in various sizes, some framed, others just tacked up, wallpaper every inch of the plaster that rises to the ceiling. Some modern art, some classical reproductions, but way too many to take in. There might be a replica of Blake's *Temptation and Fall,* though I can't tell from this far away and in this light. Red vinyl booths, all filled with students drawing or writing, line the wall to my right. In every corner, vibrant voices churn with creative energy. As I breathe in the warm air, the uneasy feeling thaws. A strange sense of belonging takes its place. For the first time ever, I think I might have found a home.

Almost.

10

WAR WOUNDS

A guitar strums, pulsing through the air. I turn to look. Behind the wall, a group of guys sits with guitars, congas, and a slew of other instruments. They play a few notes in the alcove, laugh, and then take sips of coffee. A wiry boy with shiny black hair and tanned skin takes the pencil gripped between his teeth and writes something down.

An artistic force pours through every crevice in the room. It's hard to believe a place like this exists. "This isn't a normal coffee shop."

"You could say that," Maddox says, searching for someone in the room. His cheeks are wind burned, and that intense look on his face has melted away. "Hesperian is the only place like this, so we come hang out." He smiles for the first time, revealing small dimples.

"We?"

"Other Awakened. Like us. Like you." He glances down at me for a brief moment. "It's nice to have a place, you know, to belong. Especially when you feel alone." He says this so quiet, I wonder if he's speaking to me at all.

"Maddox!" the wiry guy with the black hair calls out. "Come spin a few." He holds up a guitar. "I'm working on a new one. Check this."

The guy plucks out a few notes, then looks up, pleased. Maddox tucks his injured arm behind him. "Sounds cool. But I'll catch you later, Amide. I've gotta talk to Devon."

Amide flashes a radiant smile when he sees me. "Do you play?"

"Me?" I step back. "Uh . . . no."

"Shame. I needed a good drummer." Amide pounds a few beats on the conga. "Bring me a drummer, Maddox!" Amide doesn't sound like he needs much help. He's doing an amazing job on his own.

"Doesn't work that way," Maddox says. "But if you really need someone, ask Tanji. You know she'll do it."

Amide shakes his head with a mocking frown. "That's cold, man. Very cold."

Maddox grins in response. "Come on, Cera. Let's go."

No one stares as we straggle across the room looking ragged and weary. As we pass a corner of wingback chairs filled with a few girls on laptops, none of them look our way. They're all deep in their work.

Maddox walks over to a glass case stocked with cupcakes, cookies, and all kinds of breads. Behind the counter a metal door swings back and forth revealing a blur of Claire's lime-green shirt on the other side. I'm glad she doesn't turn around and give me that hate glare again. As dishes clang in the kitchen, Maddox swipes something off the glass case and then weaves through tables strewn with half-eaten burgers and fries and a stray pickle here and there. I follow, trying my hardest not to reach out and garbage-mouth someone's leftover fries. The throbbing in my side intensifies as we make our way across the café.

"I'll get you a burger after you get cleaned up, but take this for now." He hands me a chocolate cookie wrapped in a napkin.

"Thanks." I devour the cookie in one bite. It's soft, and the creamy chocolate melts on my tongue. I wish I had another, but at least the sweetness quells the hollow ache in my stomach. I swallow the last bit and glance around for a drink of water. No water fountain, but I spot a girl painting a detailed copy of Lord Leighton's *The Garden of Hesperides*. I know that picture from Mom's art book. The girl painting the replica has a long brown braid. I must be starving because all I can think is that her hair looks the color of a fresh-baked pretzel.

"We'll meet Devon over here." Maddox heads to a cozy alcove under the staircase.

I wipe my lips with the napkin and then drop it in the trash. "Is Devon anything like Claire? 'Cause if he is, then a little notice would be nice."

"Nah." Maddox jogs down a few steps into a sunken room. "He's a whole lot worse." He grins and heads to the long wooden table in the middle of the space.

A shiny red medical box—or makeup kit—sits on the edge of the table, not far from a pile of sketchbooks and a few tin cans filled with black pencils. In the back corner, an acoustic guitar leans against the wall near a pile of clothes and a black backpack. Maddox flips the latch, opening the box. The air fills with the smell of rose-scented rubbing alcohol and bandages. While Maddox is pulling out supplies, I head over to check out a sketch pinned on the stucco wall near the guitar. It's a charcoal drawing of a tightly knotted band of thick twine or rope. The detail of each fiber is incredible. Each strand is a different shade and thickness.

Whoever drew this is an even better artist than Mom. "Amazing," I say under my breath. I follow the twisting fury of each cord, wrapping around the others, fighting to stay together.

Five. The number comes to me. Five what? Lines? Threads? I stare at the sketch, counting the twisting ropes.

"That's, uh . . . mine." Maddox pulls the picture off the wall. "I don't know who keeps coming in here putting that up . . ." He tucks the drawing into one of the sketchbooks sitting on the table.

"It's really good," I say as he kicks aside a pallet of blankets near the back wall.

"Thanks." He picks up some clothes off the floor and stuffs them in the backpack before heading back to the medical box. "I'm not as good an artist as my . . . uh . . ." He rifles through the box, pulling out a plastic spray bottle. "And I'm not a Healer, but I can at least get some of your minor cuts cleaned up until Harper gets here. This is her stuff. She's got a mad Bent for healing and is still training." He motions for me to sit on top of the table. It's not lost on me that he changed the subject, but I let it go and climb up, feeling a sharp burn dig in my side. I wince, almost doubling over, but Maddox holds my arm.

"I got it," I say automatically, even though I let him help me up. Now that the adrenaline has worn off, the pulsing throb makes it hard to breathe. I don't have bandages and medical gear like this at home. The last thing I want is my gash or any of my other cuts to get infected.

Maddox stands a little too close beside me with the antiseptic spray in hand. He squirts a cloth with the solution, then takes my hand, turning my palms over, and lightly dabs the scrapes. The solution smells of pollen and stings a little. It's the throbbing pain in my side that hurts the worst. In order to tune out the pain, I study him closer. His sun-bleached bangs hang in his face. His smooth lips tighten while he concentrates on cleaning my scraped palms. Even though he's not looking directly at me, I get a good look at his cerulean eyes. They're deeper than the clearest ocean. He even smells like ocean air. I'm suddenly aware of each breath and how fast my heart is beating. I swallow, hoping he can't feel my pulse racing.

The air separating the inches between us thickens when he glances at me. "Does that hurt?"

I shake my head, and pull my hand out of his. "Can this spray be used on my shoulder?" The denim rubs over the wound as I slide off the jacket. Maddox gets another cloth from the medical box. The scrape isn't awful. My side hurts much worse. I grit my teeth and lean back to inspect that wound. The edges of the punctured cut are red and oozing thick blood over a slit of white skin. "My cut's really not that bad. Just nicked," I lie, dabbing my shoulder with the clean cloth Maddox hands me.

He tries to keep his focus away from the skin exposed by my ripped-up shirt. I tore a third of the bloody part off in order to get away from the birds and used another third to wrap up his arm.

I take the spray bottle out of his hands. "Thanks, I've got this."

"Uh . . . yeah. I mean . . . you sure?" He clears his throat as he runs his hand through his hair. A thick scar runs from the edge of his left eye down his jaw near his hairline. I involuntarily shudder at the pain of getting a scar like that. When he catches me looking, he turns his face away and shakes his hair loose. "Yeah, well . . . too much of that stuff bites back, so be careful." He steps back and picks up a cloth.

"I can handle it." I put all my attention back to my pulsing side and squeeze the nozzle. I gasp as cold spray freezes my skin. It's really not so bad. I give another big squeeze, foaming the entire wound. Then the sizzle starts. My eyes water. What have I done? I hold my breath and dig my nails into the wooden table, locking my legs together so I don't kick Maddox as he cleans up his own wounds. I freeze, waiting for the pain to pass.

Maddox returns to my side and grabs my hand. "Breathe, or you'll pass out." All I can do is close my eyes. The pain traveling under my skin is so bad, tears squeeze out and race down my cheeks. The pain isn't as bad as one of my attacks, but close enough. It takes everything I have not to bawl right in front of him—or punch him, for that matter. "It's Harper's special mix."

"Whatever it is, it's pure evil." I exhale, keeping my eyes closed as spots dance inside my eyelids.

"It hurts, I know, but I promise you'll heal ten times faster."

"After everything that's happened today . . ." I open my eyes, breathe in and sputter, "I can't believe that the thing that hurts the most . . . is a stupid can of spray that's supposed to make me feel . . . better."

"The irony." Maddox shakes his head as his lips spread into a slight smile. "For the record, I wouldn't have sprayed that much on you . . . just so you know," he says with a lighthearted grin. His eyes meet mine for a brief moment. My stupid heart races a million beats per minute as that electric shock zings through me again.

I look away and stare down at the gash. Considering that every friend I've ever had is dead, I'd probably end up hurting him somehow too. Until I know more, it's probably best to keep my distance. "Thanks for the warning." The burn burrows deeper into the wound. I want to collapse on the table, but any movement feels unbearable. "How long does this take before I stop feeling like someone's twisting a heated knife in my side?"

"A while. Sorry." He presses a cool bandage against my cut. When his fingers brush against my skin, a small flutter swirls in my stomach.

"I've got it." I choke back a wince and put my hand on the bandage, taking over. "I take it you do this a lot, fight off the birds and such."

He shakes his head while ripping open a new gauze packet.

"You don't randomly tackle people in the street and whack demon birds across the face? I figured that's a norm for you."

"Not really." He smiles faintly. "I usually find the Awakened alone. They think no one understands what they're going through."

Another pain wave radiates through the cut, making my skin clammy. Don't pass out. Deep breath in. Then exhale. I lift the oozy cloth. Oh, that's so disgusting. My stomach turns, sloshing what's left of that sweet cookie. Come on, Cera. Hold it together.

"Here." Maddox hands me the clean cloth then picks up a roll of surgical tape, tearing off a piece. "Part of being a Guardian means you can spot Awakened pretty easily. I've been able to find them before the Cormorants do. Most of them anyway."

"What happens to the ones you don't find?" I tense as Maddox's fingers softly rub the tape on my skin, outlining the bandage.

His downcast eyes hide behind those shaggy bangs as he rips another piece of tape. I wish I could take back my question because I'm pretty sure I know the answer. "So you've fought them before?" I backtrack. He gives a subtle nod. Is that how he got the scar? "Have you ever killed one?" He gives a small head shake, but it's not enough to show me whether his scar matches the hook of a Cormorant's talon. He's done a great job keeping the gash hidden under all that hair. "How can they be destroyed? Do you know?"

"You really want to stop them, don't you?" He shoots me a curious glance as he holds out another strip of tape, but for whatever reason, he won't look directly into my eyes for very long.

"Of course I do. Don't you?" I rip the tape off his finger and finish sealing my wound that's reduced to a dull throb. Nothing I can't handle. "After what we just experienced, who wouldn't? That freak-of-nature killed Jess. I swear I'll do everything I can to make sure it never hurts anyone ever again."

"Destroying Cormorants—"

"Isn't what a Guardian does," a commanding voice booms through the tiny space.

A well-built quarterback of a guy stands at the top of the steps with his arms crossed and a hard look chiseled on his face. Solid muscle bulges under every part of this guy's rich, dark skin.

Not only does his confidence make its way into the room well before he even takes a step, but he clearly wouldn't have any problem snapping a Cormorant's neck—or anyone else's, for that matter. "Just what do you think you're doing?"

The guy looks at the bandages strewn all over the table. My stomach sinks. I suddenly feel as if I've been caught doing something terribly wrong.

11

ALLIANCE

"I was just patching up a few scratches, Devon." Maddox casually tosses the medical tape back in the box before facing the combat-clad guy standing at the top of the steps. Devon looks to be about twenty-one, maybe older.

Devon glares at us. "You think you're a Healer now? Is that it? Or were you trying to torture the poor girl? She looks downright terrified." He glides swiftly down the steps. "Did you get her anything to eat?"

Maddox intercepts the guy before he reaches me, keeping his wounded arm behind his back. "She's hurt—"

"Then get her a Healer." Devon's biceps flex as he crosses his bulky arms in front of his chest. When Maddox said Devon was the group's Caretaker, I imagined him to be doting and rail thin. This guy is pure muscle. There's not a single thing wimpy about him. "Cleaning up your own cuts is one thing. You know not to patch up someone else if Healers are around."

A tightness coils inside me as Devon chews out Maddox. Before I know it, my voice cracks through my dry throat. "It was my fault." I force myself to sit tall. "I was the one who sprayed that stuff on my cut. Maddox . . . he just tried to keep me from passing out." Cold air brushes over my exposed stomach as I slide off the table. A sharp pain cuts through my side. I release a silent gasp but manage to suck up the pain. Maddox tries to help me down but my feet have already found the floor.

Devon's expression softens. "You all right?"

As I stand, I don't know whether my arms should cross in front of me, rest on my hips, or cover up my midriff. I end up holding my arms low in front of me and acting as if nothing's wrong. I lift my chin and square my shoulders. "I'm just a little scratched up. Maddox said I should talk to you. That you know about . . . my Bent? I need you to put me with someone who can tell me how to take down those warped bird creatures."

I must have said something wrong, because as soon as Devon frowns, Maddox throws his hands out. "Devon, listen—"

"No, *you* listen. First healing and now talking about destroying the beasts? You're a Guardian. Act like one."

"Is that a message from you? Or Gray? 'Cause you're sounding a whole lot like him right now." A slight edge cuts through Maddox's voice.

Devon rests his hands on top of his head and releases a long exhale. He smells musky and earthy. "All I'm saying is that you can't go rogue and head out alone on some crazy unauthorized mission without telling anyone. You do that and you're asking for trouble." Devon steps closer and pats Maddox on the shoulder. "Looks like you found it, anyhow." He motions to Maddox's arm. "What happened out there?"

"Nothing much." Maddox shifts, folding his arms against his stomach. He looks relaxed, but there's a subtle lilt in his voice. He's lying.

Devon's eyes flicker to the bandage on my side. "Nothing much? What were the two of you doing out there?"

"Nothing—"

"Fighting Cormorants," I blurt. Maddox stiffens. I couldn't care less as to why he won't confess, but I'm tired of the lies.

Ironic coming from me, I know.

Devon scowls at Maddox. "You tried killing one, didn't you?"

"It was in defense. Only while were trying to get away, I swear."

"Great, Maddox." Devon paces the tiny alcove and runs his hand over his shorn hair. "You blatantly disregarded your rank. There's no way the Alliance will overlook that—"

"They don't need to know." When Maddox steps away from me, coldness fills the space. Alliance? Maddox didn't say anything about an Alliance.

"Oh yeah?" Devon spins around. "Then how are you going to explain your injury to Gray? He was in here earlier looking for you."

"Thought so." Maddox sits on the edge of the table. "I'll deal with my brother later and take the fallout then. I'll tell him to back off and leave you alone. But right now, Cera needs your help." He glances my way. "What's her Bent? I'm thinking Guardian, maybe a Blade. I can't tell for sure."

Devon stops and looks me over as if I'm some enigma. He's got a strong jaw, full lips, and striking caramel eyes. "Cera, I need to confirm that you're one of us. That okay?" He moves closer, keeping his voice soft and even. Confirm. I hate that word. After seeing it written on Mom's sketches, that word can't mean anything good.

"Depends." I strain to keep my voice cool.

"Maddox, go grab her something to eat."

Maddox doesn't budge. "She's an Awakened, I promise. I don't think she knows about the Current. I didn't get a chance to tell her."

"What Current?" I ask.

Devon lifts his chin, studying me with a wary expression, but he must sense that I'm nervous, because he keeps his distance, the same way someone assesses an injured animal before coaxing it to safety. "It will only take a quick second or two. I just need you to look right at me. That's all." He taps his index finger at the corner of his eye.

"That's it?" I ask, using the most casual tone I can muster, because I never look anyone in the eyes for long. When I do, I know better than to show any weakness. I steady myself and look him straight in the—

As I meet Devon's eyes, a zing races through me. It's the same feeling I had when Maddox looked directly at me while we were on the train. I'm being read like an open book. I desperately want to look away but I can't. Devon's eyes are soft, not prowling. He's processing, but not judgmental.

Maddox tries to interrupt the thick silence. "I told you she was one of us—"

"Feel that?" Devon says to me, overriding Maddox's voice. "That Current is how we recognize one another—how we know for sure you've been Awakened." As if he's extracted whatever information he wanted, he turns to Maddox. "She's a Legacy. She might have a dual Bent. Maybe that's why you can't tell."

He's sized me up with one look? "Legacy? What does that mean?"

"Means your Bent's been passed down from your parents," Maddox says.

"My parents?"

Devon nods. "Recognize that feeling and remember it," he tells me. "We've had a problem with some girls around here confusing that Current with something else. Especially with this one here." Devon pats Maddox on the shoulder.

"That's not true." Maddox snatches his jacket off the table and slides it on as he makes his way to the back of the room. He should be taking off that bloody bandage and cleaning up the cut, not covering the wound.

"Did your parents tell you about the Current? About what it means to be Awakened?" Devon asks curiously.

"No. Maddox was the first . . ." My voice sounds weak.

Devon looks at me in disbelief. "You really don't know about being Awakened? That's not possible. You've got Legacy written all over you." He rubs one hand over his mouth as if working something out in his mind.

"That's what I thought at first." Maddox takes a pencil from the tin can on the table and spins it between his fingers. "But then I thought maybe she was a new line."

"I'm a what?"

"Which division of the Alliance are you with?" Devon ignores my question. "You're not from the Mid-region. Are you from the Southern or Western?"

"With the what?" Devon might as well be speaking Mandarin. "I have no idea what you're talking about. Maddox didn't say anything about joining some alliance." Although he promised me a burger.

Devon shoots a disapproving glance at Maddox and says, "The Alliance is the organized group of Awakened."

"I couldn't explain it all earlier. We were a little busy trying to stay alive, Devon." Maddox rips a sheet of paper from one of the sketchpads and pulls out the bench to sit down. "It's easier if I draw it out." As soon as he draws a loose oval in the middle of the page, his shoulders loosen. He turns the paper slightly in my direction, inviting me to come closer. "Awakened like you—like us—live all over the world."

I stay on the opposite side of the table and inch closer as he outlines perfect continents with quick, short strokes. He didn't have to draw an explanation, but with each pencil mark, his hands relax, brushing over the paper as if releasing the day's crazy onto the page.

"The Global Alliance Council oversees six divisions around the world," Devon says, making his way to Maddox. "We're in the Northern U.S. Region, here." Devon taps his finger on Maddox's map, then inspects me again. I get the feeling he's trying to figure out where I fit—if at all. "Each Region has formal training centers that operate under and report to a Region Council."

Maddox shades the oval with short, rapid strokes. "Yeah, but Hesperian is different. We're more of a safe house. We cultivate and strengthen our Bent through our art—the way the Alliance used to be. We're not just focused on structured training and inflexible rules, like now." He continues drawing. "All you really need to know about the Alliance is that each Region has different ranks, depending on the strength of your Bent."

"Strength is secondary." Devon's tone is corrective. "Ranks depend solely on compliance *and* training."

Maddox keeps his head down. When he stops drawing, his shoulders tense again.

I hold my hands up. "I'm not interested in structure or regions or joining any Alliance or whatever you've got going on here. I only want to know how to—"

"Hey there, stranger," a girl's raspy voice purrs through the room. At the top of the steps, a tall, gorgeous blonde with straight bangs, dramatic charcoaled eyes, and sweeping lashes leans against the wall. She's clearly not talking to me. In her tight raglan T-shirt and even tighter jeans, she runs her finger along the wall as she parades down the steps. A perfumed rose scent smothers the air as she saunters across the room, zeroing in on Maddox. "Where've you been?"

"Hey, Harper." Maddox doesn't turn around to greet her. Instead he rips out a new sheet of paper and starts drawing something else. I raise an eyebrow. This is Harper? Figures.

Devon, on the other hand, is beaming. "Harper Grace Weatherly." He stands tall as he moves in her direction. "You're just what we need."

Oh, I bet.

"Yeah?" Harper drops her chin and bats her fake lashes with

a playful smile. Devon pulls out the bench near me, inviting her to sit down. Harper's eyes flicker over me for a brief second like I'm merely another light fixture on the wall, which is fine by me. Instead of accepting Devon's offer to sit near him, she straddles Maddox's bench.

"Cera just came in. She has a few cuts and scrapes." Devon's bright smile dims as Harper runs her fingers through the back of Maddox's hair while she watches him draw. Maddox doesn't seem to mind the attention. He continues drawing without pulling away. Devon, on the other hand, takes a deep breath then clears his throat. "Make sure they're cleaned up properly, will you?"

Harper narrows her smoky eyes and measures me with a full body scan. Great. Another stare down.

"I can fix that," Harper says flatly, almost condescending. I doubt she's talking about my wounds. She's scowling with disgust at what's left of my T-shirt.

"I'm fine, but thanks anyway." There's no way her blood-red fingernails are getting anywhere near my side or shoulder. With the look she's giving me, she'll probably pour a gallon of boiling alcohol all over my cuts. I get her message about Maddox loud and clear: territory marked. Not that it was even a possibility. In fact, it's laughable that I could be a threat, especially to someone as striking as her.

Maddox sets the pencil down and looks at me, concerned. "Even though you sprayed it to death, you should at least let Harper make sure your cut was cleaned out."

"You touched my stuff?" Harper reaches over and pulls the box toward her. "What's her Bent? Is she a Healer?" Harper flips the latch and checks her inventory. "Devon, did you know about this?"

Maddox picks up his pencil and lowers his head. Under his breath he says, "She's not a Healer. Don't worry."

If he thinks I didn't see his eyebrows rise under all that shaggy hair as he made that comment, he's sorely mistaken. "What's that supposed to mean? You think it's funny that I was in pain while you bandaged me up?" I want to chuck a sketchbook at him as he tucks a paper in his back pocket, but I cross my arms instead.

Maddox sits up. "What? No! I didn't mean—"

"*You* tried healing her?" Harper's eyes practically shoot fire at Maddox. "I swear—"

"Cool it. All of you." Devon's booming voice shuts all conversation down. "Harper, I already talked to Maddox about crossing the line, and Cera didn't know better."

Harper slams the lid of her medical box. "That doesn't give them the right—"

"Check her wounds and get her a blanket or something. Maddox, come with me. We're getting food."

Nope. Don't think so. There's no way Harper is putting those flawlessly manicured hands on me. "I don't—"

"Harper's the best Healer in this place." Maddox cuts off my protest as he pushes away from the table. "Let her take a look." He says this last bit with that same protective attitude he had back on the street when we were running from the Cormorants. What about his injuries festering under that jacket?

"If that's the case, then you should let her look at your arm first, seeing that it was sliced open and all. I'll head out with Devon."

Harper gasps. "What?" Her full, red lips drop wide open. "You're hurt?"

"Nah, I'm fine."

"Take off the jacket." Harper stands and pulls at his sleeve.

He winces. "I said I'm fine."

"Look at your hands." They're bright red with cuts and scrapes. "You are *not* fine." Her voice raises an octave with each comment. "Were you going to fix this on your own? Why didn't you tell me?"

"I'm okay, really." Maddox protests, but Harper manages to strip off the jacket. She frowns at my blood-soaked T-shirt wrapped around his forearm. "What did you do?"

"Wrestled a metal pole. It got too close, that's all." Maddox gives her a wry smile, playing down our near-death experience.

That's such a lie. "It was more than that. We almost died." I look at him. "I get that you're a super tough guy, and all, but you've been bleeding out way too long."

Harper's eyes widen. "Get into my room right now. My medical kit can't fix this. You're going to need antibiotics, stitches, and who knows what else. I could kill you myself, Maddox Carver." She grabs her kit in one hand and him by the other. Maddox frowns and shoots me a disapproving look, but I couldn't care less. He needs help for that wound. He's clearly lying about how much pain he's in, and the idiot wasn't going to say anything, so I had to.

"Take Cera with you and clean her up as well," Devon says as Harper leads Maddox up the steps. "I'll be there in a few."

Harper glances over her shoulder, irritated at my presence. "Sure. Whatever."

"I've already bandaged my cuts. I'm good." As I plant my feet on the stone floor, a dull pain throbs in my side. Okay, maybe I'm not good, but at least I'm stable and not actively bleeding like Maddox. "Devon, I'll go with you. The only thing I really need—besides food—is to find out how to destroy the Cormorants."

Devon doesn't even entertain my idea. "Get your wounds checked, and then we'll talk." Before I can add a final protest, he jogs up the steps and heads toward the kitchen.

I exhale. Fine. I'll let Harper look at my side, and then I'll hunt down Devon and corner him until I get the answers I need. But I swear, if Harper tries to hurt me, I'll kick those perfectly straight teeth into the back of her throat. I hobble up the steps after Harper as she drags Maddox toward a narrow archway under the staircase. I maintain a ten-stone distance behind them. If I'm supposed to belong, then why do I feel as if every step down the hall is like walking straight into a viper's nest?

12
LISTENING

The minute I reach the sliding barn door halfway down the hall, the stringent smell of a nurse's office assaults me. However, the sterile scent in no way matches Harper's whimsical decor. A giant sunburst chandelier hangs in the center of the room, funky colorful throw rugs separate the two medical cots set against opposite walls on the right, and the rattan partition blocking off a room in the back gives the space a warm, Middle Eastern feel. Harper's room is cozy and not at all as ascetic and heartless as I imagined. Even still, I won't let my guard down, despite the look of her pseudo-dorm room—complete with a hand-stitched quilt neatly folded in a basket and a mini-fridge that's probably stocked with fresh-squeezed cactus juice.

"Lie down." Harper guides Maddox by the shoulders, pushing him onto the cot—or massage table—set against the wall near the doorway. Between the cots—or beds, or whatever they call them—a gauzy, scarlet curtain on the brick wall tents a cedar shelf arranged with flickering candles in yellow glass canisters.

She lets out a loud, annoyed breath as she sees me in the doorway. "Sit on the opposite bed and wait your turn." She pulls a metal cart to her side and slams her medical kit on top.

I'm not liking her bossy attitude. In fact, I hesitate crossing the threshold and reconsider entering her mystical lab. Maddox brushes Harper's hands off of his shoulder. "Take care of Cera first. She needs it more than me."

"I'll be the judge of that after I look at your arm." She plants her hands on her hips and stares him down, daring him to defy her again. As much as I want to stay rooted at the doorway just to spite her, Devon won't talk to me until I get my side checked out, so I've got no choice but to comply. I make my way to the empty bed and plop down—a bad move because now my side throbs even worse.

Maddox leans back and swings his feet up on the table. "You'll see my cut isn't so bad." He tries to stifle a groan, but Harper's quick to pick up on his pain.

"What? Don't tell me you broke a rib too?" Harper lifts his shirt. She frowns at the nasty bruise forming on his side. "How did this happen?"

"Can't remember." With a straight face, Maddox glances at me, then my elbow. Harper presses his ribs. Maddox winces. "Ouch. Okay. Yeah, that hurts."

I lean forward and stare at my shoes as I swing them over the polished concrete. His injury is my fault. I elbowed him when we were on the street. I didn't mean to hit him that hard. Well, actually, that's a lie. At the time I did mean it, but that was before . . . I take a deep breath and press my scuffed palms on the cool sheet.

"What were you doing out there? Wait, no. Don't answer." Harper lifts her long fingers in the air to stop him from speaking. "I don't want to know. It will just drive me crazy. I'll look at the cut on your arm first, then I'll deal with your side."

She gently unties my shirt scrap from around his forearm. "This thing is filthy." She removes the makeshift bandage and sets it on the hammered metal cart. I can't see the cut because

Harper blocks my view as she sits next to him. She closes her eyes and takes a deep breath, resting one hand on his shoulder and the other on his bicep. Her fingertips curl as her hands rest on his bare skin. I shift on the cot and look away.

Harper opens her eyes and glares at me. "I can't feel what's going on while you're gawking at me. Stop moving and stay quiet." She focuses her attention back to Maddox. "And you . . . stop withholding."

I'm not sure what Harper means about withholding, and I don't care to know. The room is dead quiet except for the hum of the light bulbs in the chandelier, a few distant voices floating in from the café, and the whir of the mini-fridge. The door near the fridge is cracked open enough for me to see a few wooden tables and glass lab equipment in the room next to this one. I wait as quietly as possible while Harper places her palms on Maddox's bare stomach for what seems an eternity.

"One broken rib. No internal bleeding and you didn't lose that much blood. That's good." Harper lets go of Maddox. "Your arm, on the other hand, is starting to get an infection. I'll need to start a drip." Harper sways through the room, gathering supplies from a cabinet near the mini-fridge. "You're lucky I caught this when I did. Any longer and the infection could have gotten into your blood."

I sit back. "Wait, you can diagnose someone by placing your hands on them and . . . listening? How?"

Harper's haughty smirk makes me regret blurting out my question.

"Told you Harper's got mad gifting." Maddox props himself up on one elbow as Harper sits on the rolling stool next to him.

"That's totally insane." And downright terrifying. Although I don't want picture-perfect Harper to know that the mere fact she can touch someone and know what's going on inside freaks me out. "So you can touch my side and tell me I'm all good?" I lean back, letting my legs dangle. My side pulses with a splintering throb from where I was cut by shattered glass during the truck accident. I know I'm not good, but I'm tired of sitting around. "If not, how much longer before I can go talk to Devon?"

"Not long." Devon stands at the doorway. "How bad is his wound?" He watches as Harper assesses Maddox's arm. His stance is casual, but he isn't looking at Maddox or the gash on his arm.

"Pretty deep, but luckily I caught the infection early." Harper opens her medical box and whips out a few jars of green ointment, slathering a row of each on his arm, then sprays on the foam cleanser before pressing down with a bandage. I cringe, vicariously feeling the burn.

Maddox watches as Harper wraps his arm. How is he not flinching? Maybe Harper really is that good at healing. Either that, or Maddox is a whole lot stronger than I am to endure the pain. "Told you it wasn't bad. But even if it was, I've seen you patch up a lot worse."

His comment—and his grin—makes Harper twist her lips with a flirty smile. She stands up. "Hang tight. I'm not done with you. If the ointment doesn't seal the wound, then you'll need stitches."

Devon leans against the doorframe, his glance lingering on Harper. When she puts on gloves and preps Maddox's arm for an IV, Devon pulls his eyes away and steps into the room. "And what about Cera?"

"She's next." Harper glances over her shoulder at me. "She's a little more complicated."

Story of my life. But how would she know just by looking at me? I thought she needed to "listen," or whatever.

"She's a tough read, for sure." Devon looks away when Harper pricks Maddox's arm with the needle. Maddox stares at the ceiling and doesn't flinch. "Cera." Devon focuses his attention back to me. "I'm going to have you test for all Bents. That way we can see which one—or two—show up the strongest."

"You want her to practice being a Healer?" Harper sounds ultraoffended. I'm not after her spotlight, if that's what she thinks. I can't diagnose anyone by laying my hands on them the way she can, that's for sure.

"That would be a waste of time. If healing doesn't kill the creatures, then I don't really want any part of it." I sit up. "Can't you just tell me how it's done so I can get out of here?"

Devon comes my way. "You've never brought one in that's wanted to leave as soon as she got here, Maddox. Usually they're desperate to stay."

I'm not going to lie, there is a tiny part of me warring to stay cloistered in their community, but . . . "There are horrible beast-birds out there that need to be stopped—"

"Killing any creature isn't going to happen unless you know the realm you're dealing with and you have the Bent to do it." Devon's voice is firm. If I'm reading his stern expression right, he wants me to stop pushing the issue. I open my mouth to badger him when he holds out something wrapped in tinfoil. "Brought you my favorite."

Harper snatches the gift from his hands before I can. "She doesn't eat until I listen to her. I don't want her puking your cranberry turkey wrap all over me if I've got to work on her."

I frown. Now I really wish I could eat the turkey.

Harper places the sandwich on the shelf next to the candles. The flames cower with the sudden draft but quickly rebound, growing tall and steady again. After removing her gloves, Harper checks the fluid dripping through the tube and into Maddox's arm. "Stay put for ten minutes, will you?" She crosses to the rattan screen and faces me. "Back here." Again with the bossy attitude? Harper moves the screen aside enough for me to go into the dimly lit room.

I stay planted on the cot, but Devon nods, telling me to obey. Fine. I slide off the bed and shuffle into the cramped space. The weighted air tastes of damp wool doused in antiseptic. Lovely.

"Strip off that shirt and those jeans and wait for me on the table." Harper closes the partition most of the way but leaves it open enough for me to see her back at Maddox's side. She urges him to sit up, and then she picks an elastic bandage out of her medical box. I shut the partition all the way and move to the back corner near the oxygen tank and blood pressure monitor and kick off my tennis shoes.

As I bend over to peel off my jeans, splintering pain shoots through my side. I gasp. My skin turns clammy. I lean on the corner of the bed for support and hope I don't pass out.

"You okay?" Maddox calls out.

My pulse races and I kick off the jeans. "Totally fine." Totally a lie, but I don't want anyone rushing in here while I'm half dressed.

"Harper, go check on her." Devon sounds concerned but still far enough away from the partition. "I need to talk to Maddox for a minute."

I slip the shirt over my head as Harper's flats patter against the concrete in my direction.

Whatever is wrong with me is bad—like see-a-doctor bad. I know Maddox trusts Harper, but she's only a year or two older than me. There's no way she's gone through medical school.

"On the table. Sit." Harper slides into the room, fully closing the screen behind her, and flips on the light switch.

"Can you make this quick? It's super cold in here." I try not to fidget as I sit on the table in complete embarrassment. Without a cover-up, my lack of curves is apparent, especially compared to her.

She gives me a quick once-over and hands me a stiff white towel that barely covers my thighs. This is Harper's version of a blanket? "Lie down." She turns her back and heads to a cart near the partition, then pulls out a few supplies, including a headlamp. "And turn to the side, if you can."

Maybe I do what she tells me because I want this over with so I can talk to Devon, or maybe it's because of the daunting surgical tweezers Harper holds between her fingers. The more attitude I give her, the more pain she might inflict. I lie down and do what she asks without putting up a fight.

She gets to work tugging at the bandage on my side. I half expected her fingers to be as cold as the stare she shot me earlier, but they're surprisingly warm. Removing the medical tape doesn't hurt, but the cold air brushing against my exposed wound does.

As soon as Harper sees my injury, her haughty snarl transforms into a concentrated expression. I tense up when her fingers brush lightly against my skin near the wound. Unlike the way she leaned in close with Maddox, Harper stands straight and stares down at me before taking a deep breath and closing her eyes.

I focus on the stucco ceiling, trying not to shiver, and more than a little worried about what she might find. What if she can read thoughts when she's listening? Is that even possible? I don't chance it. I search for random images on the textured ceiling and try not to think about how super awkward and vulnerable it is to lie here in my underwear with the tiny towel draped over me while her fingers press near my wound. I stay still even though the cut itches with tiny electrical pulses. A million seconds later, Harper opens her eyes.

"What did you find?" The words croak through my dry throat.

Harper frowns and doesn't answer me. Instead she reaches up and turns on the medical lamp. I cover my eyes with my arm at the blinding burst of light. Her fingers tap along the edge of the cut. I hold my breath, ready to bring my knee to her pixie nose if she does anything to hurt me. "There's the nasty sucker," she mumbles under her breath.

"What?" I lift my head.

Again, Harper ignores me. She presses her painted red lips together and takes out a purple vial from her pocket. "You're going to need a sip of this." She pours a small amount into a plastic top.

The liquid smells like hard liquor. "I don't drink."

"It's not alcohol. Don't be stupid. Take it." Harper holds the cap near my lips. "Unless you want to pass out from the pain."

Devon shuffles to the partition. "You all right back there?" I'm not sure if he's talking to me or Harper.

Harper eyes me, lying exposed on the table. To my surprise she says, "We're fine. I'll be done in a few minutes. Just waiting on the serum to numb the pain so I can get a piece of glass out of her side."

Glass? No wonder my wound hurts so much. Harper holds out the tiny cup again, this time raising her perfectly sculpted eyebrows, waiting. I know my small window of her grace is closing fast. I take the cap and swallow the cherry liquid in one sip. It burns going down my throat. She's right. It's not liquor. The thick syrup is something else entirely.

"I'm right here if you need help." Devon sounds a little too close to the rattan screen.

"We're finishing up." Harper takes the empty cap and counts under her breath. With each number, her gaze shifts as if she's tracking the serum's path through my body. "Nine . . . and ten. Should be good by now. Now, take a deep breath and don't move." After putting on some gloves, Harper picks up the medical tweezers. I concentrate on Devon's footsteps stomping away and how Harper's fingers pull my skin. I hold my breath. My foot twitches, telling me to run, but I can't. All I can do is lie here and trust that Harper knows what she's doing. I squeeze my eyes shut and curl my fists at my side.

"You can tell, can't you?" Maddox's low whisper carries through the partition and burrows into my ears.

"She's a Legacy, for sure." Devon also whispers, but he's not as quiet. "You'd know that if you got to Council every once in a while and finished training."

"I'm not wasting my time in some protective huddle just to rank up like Gray wants me to. Not when Council isn't doing anything to find new Awakened and let them know they're not alone."

I open my eyes. Harper adjusts the headlamp and glances at the partition before taking a deep breath.

Devon raises his voice. "Let someone else—"

"Who, Devon? I'm doing exactly what a Guardian is supposed to be doing."

Harper zeros the light from her headlamp on the wound and grips the tweezers so tight her fingertips turn white.

"When you're on active duty—after you've completed your training—sure. But not when you're still ranked a second-class apprentice that barely started the program. I can't keep covering for you while you disappear for days without checking in. Not to mention that stunt you tried with the Cormorants."

I lift my head. "Should we tell them to be quiet? I mean, if you need—"

"I can do it." Harper frowns and turns off the headlamp. "I just need a few extra supplies, that's all."

I prop myself up on my elbow. Bad idea because pain digs at my side. I lower myself back down. "You sure—"

"Don't flatter yourself." Her eyes are more piercing than the cut on my side. "I've fixed worse, trust me." She stands and marches to the bathroom door.

Good going, Cera. I've made her mad. Who knows what she'll do to me now.

Harper rummages through a cabinet and turns on a faucet, but the running water doesn't drown out Maddox's voice. "I'll check in with Gray and clear things up, but talk to me about Cera. She reads like a Legacy with a dual Bent. But she didn't even know what a Cormorant was. She called it something else."

Moloch. "When the Cormorants attacked, she tried to fight back."

"She didn't run?" Devon's voice lilts, surprised.

Despite the pain, I push up on my elbows again and stare at

the folds in the screen. They either don't know I can hear them, or they don't care if I do.

"Yeah, but she ran toward it. I had to pull her away. It was like she wasn't afraid of that giant crow beast." Maddox is wrong. I *was* afraid. Terrified. The only reason I fought back was because I was so angry. Not angry, furious. At Moloch, at what that evil predator did . . . "That's why I thought she had a dual Bent—Blade and Guardian, but something's different, and I know you can tell."

The faucet turns off. Harper heads my way with a clean rag and a blue bowl of steaming herbal water that smells of grapefruit. She sets the bowl next to me and turns on the headlamp with a determined look on her face. "Take a deep breath."

I lie back down. "You sure you can—"

As soon as the hot cloth touches my skin, I shut my mouth. The pulsing wound bubbles under the heat. I lie there for what feels like an eternity before Harper takes off the towel. When she does, I feel a slight pinch. A thin glass shard covered in bright red blood clinks into the tiny metal bowl Harper holds at my side. "Got it. You'll feel a whole lot better after I stitch you up. Ointment won't seal a cut that deep." She irrigates the wound with the herbal water and a syringe.

I'm grateful but can't speak. Not because of the serum or the dull pinch of the needle against my skin. Words evade me because, not only am I indebted to Harper, but the truth of Maddox's words weighs heavy. I'm something different. And not in a good way. Unless I rid myself of these visions, I'll never belong anywhere—even here.

"You know you're nothing special, right?" Harper slathers cold ointment on the wound before applying a thin bandage.

"What?" My eyes widen. Please don't tell me she reads minds.

Harper gathers up her supplies. "It's what he does."

"Who are you talking about?" I lift my head and look at the perfect bandage hugging my side.

No longer in her hyper-medic mode, Harper rolls her eyes. "Maddox. He finds the Awakened and brings them here. He has this knack for making everyone feel special, like they're one of a kind. This place practically exists because of him. It was his idea after he met Gladys." She snaps off her gloves. "He found me, and I owe him everything for it."

Why is she telling me this when she should be telling me how long I wear the bandage and how to care for the stitches?

After dropping the gloves in the trash, she picks up a small mirror. "Just thought I'd give you some friendly advice since you're new, and all." She adjusts her bangs in her reflection before checking her lipstick. "I wouldn't want you getting any wrong ideas."

"Don't worry. You've been pretty clear." I sit up, and swing my legs over the side of the table, feeling no pain. Pretty amazing, but I won't tell her so.

Harper opens a drawer to a tall dresser. "Leave your ragged clothes in the corner. I'll probably have to burn them. Here . . ." She tosses me a gray sweatshirt and some black leggings. "Throw on something clean."

I catch the clothes, to my surprise, considering how groggy I am. The oversized shirt is made for someone as bulky as Devon and will probably fit me like a dress, but I'm not complaining. I'm thankful to have something warm to wear.

She slides the partition open. "Oh, and you can take the bandage off tomorrow. Stitches should dissolve by then."

Wow. Turbo healing. "Thanks," I say as my stomach growls. I'm ready for that cranberry wrap now.

Instead of acknowledging my gratitude, Harper tosses her silky hair over her shoulder. "Maddox, you ready?"

I meant my thanks. I really did. But if that's the case, then why do I want to claw that haughty smirk off her face?

I slide off the table. Forget it. She's not worth a fight. Now that I'm healed, I need to corner Devon and get answers.

13

BENT

After getting dressed, I push the partition aside, expecting to find Maddox sitting on the cot with the IV drip leeched to his arm, but he's not in the room. Neither is Devon, Harper, or even the turkey sandwich, for that matter. They've left me alone. Abandoned me in Harper's lair. With heavy feet, I make my way down the hall toward the café to find Devon. I'll call Mom and let her know I'm all right after I talk to him.

Lively voices, laughter, and peppy drum beats fill the café. I have no clue what time it is. If I had to guess, it must be close to nine, maybe even ten o'clock at night. I search the room for Devon before stepping fully in. It's not hard to spot him through the crowd. He's almost a head taller than most everyone else, and his hearty laugh warms the room.

He's talking to a bowlegged guy with wavy brown hair, a flannel shirt, and vested jacket. I make my way to meet him at the counter and pass the alcove under the staircase. Surrounded by a small crowd, Maddox sits on the table with his feet propped on a bench and a guitar in his lap. Harper is glued to his side.

I keep walking and head straight for Devon. "Can I have that turkey wrap now?"

I can't help but notice that, as I walk up, he studies my

collarbone a little too intently. "I'll do one better. Burger, fries, and a milkshake for the girl who was walking around with a glass spear in her side."

The skinny, bowlegged guy turns to me. His pale, freckled face is somewhat boy-next-door, and he smells of leather mixed with too much spicy cologne. "That had to hurt. How long did you walk around before ya knew?" When he looks at me, the Current zips right through me. He gives a subtle nod. I'm guessing that's a sign he feels it too.

I nod back. "I didn't know it was there. Harper found it."

Devon grips the guy's shoulder and gives a hearty shake. "Kellan, this is Cera. I'm thinking she might be a Blade, but I need to talk a few things over with her first. I'll send her your way if that's the case."

Kellan stuffs his hands in his pockets and looks me over, this time with a little more scrutiny. I match his long, hard look, analyzing him just the same. He seems ordinary, but not afraid to take risks—a cowboy, but not.

I feel smug. I'm getting pretty good at handling these stare downs. He doesn't smile, but when he drawls, "Welcome," he's sincere.

"Thanks." For the first time since I've arrived, someone isn't questioning my belonging.

"I'm headed to the roof," Kellan says. "Tanji and I are on watch tonight. Catch ya later." He tips his head to me and then ducks out of the room. All he's missing is the cowboy hat.

Devon looks at me. "How are you feeling?"

"A little groggy, but I'm good." I glance at my side where the bandage hides under my bulky sweatshirt dress.

Devon's eyes gleam. "Harper's one of a kind. She can fix just about anything."

"Oh, I bet she can." I can't hide my sarcasm.

He raises an eyebrow. "She didn't hurt you, did she?"

I shake my head. "No." But she's not exactly rolling out the welcome mat.

"Good." He pulls out a chair at a nearby table and motions for me to sit. "Let's talk about you."

I take his offer and lower myself into the seat. "There's not much to talk about. But learning why everything's happening and how I can defeat the creatures . . . that's another story."

Devon sits across from me. "Slow down. Talking about that is like putting a roof on a house when the foundation hasn't been poured. You've got to have a good understanding of what's happening before you run out of here trying to destroy something that can kill you in a matter of seconds."

That's true. I've had one on my tail a good part of the day. It's only thanks to Maddox that I'm sitting here right now. I lean back. "Fine. Then tell me what I need to know. 'Cause so far all I know about this world is that there's a second realm that only Awakened can see where these creatures roam. They attack us because we can see the damage they do, and apparently there's an Alliance with a Council that trains Awakened, but not in a place like Hesperian. Is that right?"

"Mostly right." Devon waves someone over. The girl with the pretzel-looking braid sets down a basket of golden fries, a steaming burger in a buttery bun with melted cheese and fresh lettuce, as well as a frosted glass topped with whipped cream and a decorative swirl of hardened chocolate. Devon nods his appreciation. I don't even get a chance to tell her thanks because the shy girl lowers her head and walks away without saying a word. Devon pushes the basket my way. "You eat. I'll talk."

"Sounds like a deal to me." My mouth waters as I pick up a crispy fry, blowing on it so I don't burn my tongue, but I can't wait any longer. I shove the salty potato in my mouth. Food. Tastes. So. Good.

Devon's eyes smile as he watches me eat. "I'm sure you

have a lot of questions." I sure do, but I'm too busy stuffing my face with fries to say more. "I know that being Awakened feels overwhelming." He looks directly at me and the electric Current from before feels nothing more than a faint hum. "Let's start there." He points across the room near the brick. "There's a verse painted on the wall."

I squint, trying to make out the calligraphy. Devon has obviously memorized the verses because he recites the words without even glancing at the wall.

> *I oft remember, when from sleep*
> *I first awaked . . .*
> *Much wond'ring where*
> *And what I was.*

Energy rushes through my veins. I sit up. "Milton? That's from *Paradise Lost.* Eve's monologue to Adam about what she felt when she first woke in the garden."

"Very good." Devon looks genuinely surprised. "You took advanced studies, I take it." No. Not even close, but if he thinks I'm smart, I won't correct him. Devon rests his elbows on the table and leans in. "You've probably felt something. Seen things. Maybe even been searching for answers?"

My breath catches in my throat. "Yes. When I first read Milton, something about what he wrote . . ."

"Triggered something?"

Definitely, yes. I lick salt off my finger. "I know this sounds crazy, but every time I read through the poem, it's like Milton is . . . writing more than a story about the fall of humanity or his opposition to the British government. It's like there's another layer with something else hidden in the verses, something he didn't feel open about sharing, but I could see it." Hearing my confession pour out to a total stranger feels odd, but I can't hide my excitement. "I thought it was just my way of coping. I didn't think what I was reading was . . . real."

"You're not crazy. Milton was part of the Alliance back in the 1600s. So are many of other famous artists from the past. Michelangelo. Delacroix. Edvard Munch. Keats, to name a few."

Emotions swirl. "This is totally surreal. I mean, sometimes I even feel like Milton sends me verses out of nowhere, and I can hear him in my head—" It hits me. I'm not crazy. *I'm not crazy.* Milton *has* been talking to me all along. He led me here with his verses. He told me to follow Maddox . . .

"You connect with Milton. With his verses?" Devon seems concerned but adds, "Normally, we connect with artists from previous generations who have our same Bent."

"I'm not an artist." I shove more fries into my mouth, because I get the feeling I might have said something wrong. Best thing to do now is redirect the conversation and hope he doesn't notice. "So, these Bents—are they like talents?"

My question does the trick. "More like an innate strength or skill." Devon explains, "Awakened all have a Bent. We've identified that most fall into five groups: Healers, like Harper; Guardians who find and protect the Awakened, like Maddox; Blades who fight the creatures the same way soldiers might, like Kellan, who you just met; and Caretakers like me, who keep everyone in balance, since there seems to be ongoing enmity between Blades and Guardians."

I swallow a bite of the juicy burger and wipe my chin with the paper napkin. I want to ask why there's strife between groups, but Devon forgot to mention the fifth group. "What's the last Bent? You only explained four." I wash the burger down with a sip of the milkshake.

"Seers."

"As in . . . they see the future?" I try to still my features. This has to be what I am.

"Not always. We're not entirely clear on all aspects of their Bent because they are so rare. If someone was a Seer, we'd cease all other training and send them to Council for extra protection." Devon watches me closely as he says, "Milton was a Seer."

"Milton was blind." I laugh.

"They make the best kind."

I rearrange my spoon, lining it up next to the fork, and stare at my warped reflection in the shiny metal. "So someone couldn't be a Seer and fight the creatures?"

"No, they'd be far too vulnerable."

"Well, that's insulting." I slide the knife up and arrange the trio in a straight line.

Devon gives a quick grin. "In a good way. Seers' visions show us what's to come, tidbits about who we are, our power, and our essence. That's information we can't let get into enemy hands."

"Enemy, like the creatures?" I think about how Mom hides her drawings, even from me. "How would they get information?" They're creatures, not people.

"If a Seer hasn't been properly trained to harness the vision, the image can be intercepted by the enemy. If that happens, we lose the ability to decipher the vision, giving the enemy an advantage."

I stir the shake with the straw. Mom must have been intercepting my visions and drawing them out. That's how she knew what I saw.

"What do you mean by 'stolen'?" I choose my words carefully. I can't give away how much I know, or Devon will ship me to Council—the CIA of the second realm—without telling me how to fight the creatures.

"Think of a vision like a printed photograph without a negative. Only one of its kind. If the image gets into the wrong hands before a copy is made, no one else can see what the picture is. That picture gives us information we need to create strategies to keep everyone safe."

"How do you make a copy, or harness a vision?" I'm certain I know the answer, but Devon can't know.

"When a Seer has a vision, the image must be transferred onto an external medium. Transferring the image comes in different forms: sketches, painting, sculpting, poetry—depends on the harnesser's talent. Once the image is duplicated, the image can't be siphoned—or stolen."

"That makes sense, but why are they the weakest of your group?"

"They're not the weakest. In fact, the opposite is true. We keep Seers under tight protection because, out of all the Awakened, they seem to have a 'direct line' in revealing and explaining our powers. And for our survival, that's something we can't let the enemy get a hold of."

I crumple my napkin, dropping it into the empty basket. "So they don't fight, because if they have a vision when they're in a battle, the enemy can intercept the vision and steal the knowledge?"

"Precisely." Devon looks searchingly. "Have you ever had an image in your mind that foretold the future or showed something you couldn't explain, like you thought you were dreaming, but you weren't?"

Acting as nonchalant as possible, I pick a charred fry crumb out of the basket and pop it in my mouth before taking a long sip of the milkshake. How do I answer? Yes, Devon. I've been foretelling deaths since I was ten? Yeah, right. There's no way I'm telling him that I'm a Seer so they can lock me up the same way Mom kept me sheltered and ignorant. My visions always foretold someone's death, not Alliance trade secrets—at least, not that I know of. If I have another vision, I'll draw out the image best I can so it can't be stolen—or siphoned or whatever. Problem solved. 'Cause one thing's for sure: regardless of their rules, I'll do whatever it takes to fight and avenge Jess's death, and I'm not above lying.

I bite on the straw and pretend I'm thinking. I've got to come up with something close in case Devon can read through my lies the way Mom can. "I imagine things I want to happen, but it rarely pans out. Does that count?" Definitely not a lie.

"Unfortunately, no." He looks me over again. After a long, awkward silence he says, "Have you ever heard your parents use the word Dissenter?"

"No. Never." And that's the honest truth. I squirm when he studies my collarbone again, as though he's expecting something to appear.

I brush the sweatshirt collar. "Is something on me?"

Devon shakes his head. "I'm not sure why you're so tough to figure out. It's best if you test out all disciplines. Your Bent will become clear."

"It's pretty clear I'm a Blade, don't you think?"

"We can't go throwing people onto the front lines. Being a Blade isn't just learning to fight. A Blade has an innate ability to detect threats and can sense when someone is about to attack seconds before it happens. It may appear like great reflexes, but it's an added level of protection that keeps them alive. You throw someone into the battle who's not a Blade and they'll be dead in a matter of minutes."

"Guardians don't have that gift?"

"No. They've been given the ability to seek other Awakened, and instead of sensing an attack on themselves, they can sense potential destruction for others and protect them from it. Not fight the beasts."

"So they're basically bodyguards."

"It's more important than you make it sound. It's how most of the kids in Hesperian got here."

"I know, Maddox brought them here." My face warms at my insult. I didn't mean to knock his Bent. It sure makes sense. He could tell what was about to happen in time to pull me out of danger, which only highlights how bad a Guardian I would be, because I couldn't protect Jess.

"There's a slim chance you might be a Caretaker." Devon's mouth quirks. "They fight too. Sometimes."

I sit up. "Seriously?"

"Mainly we keep harmony between the groups and pull everyone together. We only fight when necessary, and that's usually out of a need for protection."

"Let me guess, you also have some higher knowledge?"

"You're not too far off. We pick up things quicker than most. We don't have the same abilities as a Blade, but we can quickly read a situation and act swiftly. As far as our connection with other Awakened, we know what's truly happening beneath the surface, regardless of what's being said."

I catalog every comment I've said to him since I got here. It's a wonder he hasn't called me out. "You mean you have a built-in lie detector."

Devon laughs. "If that's what you want to call it." He reaches over and unfurls my napkin from my empty burger basket.

"Caretakers work a little like this." He looks around to find a pen. Leaning back in his chair, he takes one off of the table behind him. "Think of Caretakers like a circle that holds everyone together." He draws a loopy diagram on the wrinkled napkin. "The next layer inside the circle is the Blade, or the fighter. Then add the Guardian, or the protector, as another layer inside that one." He adds two additional circles, one inside the other. "Those three create an outer layer of protection for the most vulnerable. First, are Healers." He draws a diamond in the middle, intersecting the lines so they touch all the circles. "They connect with each of the three groups and also create an internal protective layer for the Seer, in the center—who is our most vulnerable." He draws a mark in the middle of the diagram and then adds several lines that shoot out from the center mark and stop when they reach the diamond.

"Your group's symbol is either a wonky solar system with a diamond portal in the middle that blasts lasers, or a bad geometry lesson."

Devon laughs again and sets down the pen. His warm smile beams against his skin. "I don't draw that great, but you get the picture."

I do get the picture—in more ways than one. I doubt I'm a Caretaker. I don't bring people together—if anything, I end up destroying them—but if Devon thinks I could be one and they're fighters, then I won't correct him.

"Caretaker, huh? So I get to help slay the creatures?"

"You're relentless, you know that?" He looks at me, almost amused.

I fold my arms on the table and smile. "Yeah, pretty much."

The music stops, turning the room quiet. "I want you to meet with Gladys in the morning. She's a Guardian," Devon tells me. "We'll start exploring each Bent, beginning with her. After Gladys, if Kellan says you show strength as a Blade, *then* you'll learn how to 'slay the creatures.'"

"What?" I frown. "No. Let me work with Kellan tonight. You'll see—"

"Right now the Bent that shows up strongest is Guardian, so we're starting there. That's the plan. Plus, we're shutting down for tonight." On cue, lights turn off in the kitchen, and the sconces on the walls dim. "Get some rest. You've been through a lot, and the serum will probably knock you out soon. Head back to Harper's space. You'll sleep on one of the cots, and we'll start back up in the morning."

Devon stands and waits for me to do the same. I'm frustrated with his decision, but he's got one thing right—I'm exhausted, and with my full stomach, I'm super sleepy. I should probably let Mom know I'm not coming home, but I'll call her in the morning, after I meet with the Blades. Otherwise she'll demand I come home tonight. I push away from the table, feeling groggy. "In the morning, first thing, I'll be out here ready to go. I'm a Blade, Devon. I'm telling you." I stifle my yawn and head back toward the hall, passing Maddox's alcove.

Everyone around him except Harper has left. She twists the ends of her hair as she lingers, watching Maddox put his guitar away. I slink into the hall. I need time alone, anyway. Time to process the day, the news, and the pain twisting inside my chest. Part of me wonders if this crazy reality isn't some horrible nightmare. In the morning I'll wake from the dream, start my new job, and walk Jess to school . . . but I know that's not true. I'll never see her freckled face again, and my life will never be the same.

14

GLADYS SMOCKEL

The smell of fresh coffee and the gentle clinking of breakfast dishes somewhere down the hall stirs me awake. I wrap myself in the warm blanket and curl in a fetal position. Then the reality of where I am sinks in. I push up to my elbows, expecting to feel like I've been hit by a truck—which I almost was—but instead, I feel . . . not so bad. There's a neat pile of clean clothes and a travel kit on the edge of the bed. The other cot is empty. I'm alone. I take the clothes and travel kit off the bed and make my way to the bathroom in back.

I'm not sure if I can shower with this bandage, so I wipe off the grime as best I can, brush my teeth, and comb out my hair. I borrow one of Harper's rubber bands on the counter and pull my hair into a high ponytail. I slip on fitted jeans and a black, oversized button-down shirt. Wearing someone else's clothes feels strange, as though I'm not really me, but at least the outfit is easy to move in. After putting on my shoes, I make my way down the hall to the café.

Morning sun from the stained glass fills the space with warm, sacred light. Guitars lie abandoned on the area rugs near the entrance. A few early risers scattered throughout the café sit in hushed quiet that rivals a library—Maddox being one of them. He's slouched in a booth with his head down, drawing. I look for Devon, but he's not in sight. He might be in the kitchen. As soon as I walk toward the counter, Maddox sees me. "Cera, over here." I do a quick check for Harper. She's not around, so I head his way. Maddox closes his sketchbook when I reach the table. "You doing okay?"

"I'm great. In fact, my side doesn't hurt at all. How's your arm?"

He shrugs. "Better."

"Hey look, I'm sorry I said something about it." I lower myself into the booth across from him. "But I could tell you were in pain and—"

"Don't worry about it. It's all good. That's kinda what Guardians do for each other. Apparently the cut was worse than I thought." He slides a handcrafted mug aside. "Want breakfast? I'll get you some if you want, before everyone gets here."

"I'm meeting with Gladys this morning. I guess she's going to figure out whether or not I'm a Guardian—"

"Good morning, sunshines!" A cheery operatic voice floats through the kitchen doors as they swing open and reveal a stout, middle-aged woman. "I've got crisp waffles in the iron and sizzling bacon on the grill." She cheerfully wipes a spot off the glass counter with a dishrag. Her frosted, over-teased updo could nest a family of birds, and she'd probably never know.

When she spots Maddox, her apple cheeks spread into a smile. She tucks the dishrag in her sunflower apron and bustles our way. "Mornin', dearies." She reaches our table. "You're a new one, aren't you?" Her eyes are warm as she acknowledges me. She turns to Maddox. "Is that where you've been?" she asks, her voice stern.

"Hey, Gladys." Maddox rests his arm across the back of the booth. His bandaged arm, however, he keeps under the table. "We came in last night, but you were already gone."

Gladys pulls the dish towel out of her apron. For a moment I
think she's about to wipe down the tabletop, but instead she rolls
up the cloth and snaps Maddox on the back of the head. "Next
time you plan on being out for more than three days, you let me
know you're still alive. You hear me?"

I try hard to suppress a laugh. Maddox frowns. "Yes, ma'am."
He rubs out the back of his head. "This is Cera, by the way. She's
a Guardian too. I think."

Gladys looks me over. Her face softens. "That so?" She slides
in the booth, scooting me over with a bump of her plump hip.
She smells of vanilla and warm peaches. "Been a long time since
we've had a new female Guardian around here." She sandwiches
my hand between her meaty fingers and squeezes with a death
grip. "You need anything at all, you don't hesitate to ask. All I ask
is that if you're coming or going, I know about it. Need to keep
tabs on you kids and make sure you're all right."

"Thank you." I feel dwarfed in her presence. "Devon said he
wanted me to work with you. Did he tell you?"

Maddox curls his fingers around the coffee mug. "He thinks
she might be a Legacy with a dual Bent. She shows strength in a
couple of areas. He can't pin her down."

The way Gladys perks up, you'd think Maddox called me
royalty. "Were your parents Legacies or new lines?"

I manage to slide my hand out of her warm hold.
"What's a new line?"

She adjusts her apron. "Kids who are the first in their family
to be Awakened. No one is around to explain what they see
and they often think they're hallucinating or have some type of
disorder. Their poor parents, being Commons, don't know what
to do. Some kids get institutionalized, others put on medication.
Or they turn to drugs and some, poor souls, can't go on living."

I get every word Gladys speaks, but I know I'm not a new
line because my mom knew about this world, even drew out my

visions. "Until yesterday, I didn't think there was anyone else like me. Maddox found me, told me he could see the Cormorants the way I could, and brought me here."

Gladys touches my arm compassionately. "Oh, hon, I'm so sorry. I suppose you lost both of your parents? Your fosters were probably Commons and didn't know."

"I'm not a foster child, if that's what you mean. I lost my dad when I was seven but I live with my mom. She . . ." I stop myself. I can't tell them specifics, like she knew about my visions. I'll be tagged a Seer and get locked up.

"She knew?" Gladys asks gently.

My reply is guarded. "Maybe she did, but she didn't tell me."

Her lips tighten the same way Mom's do when I've said something wrong. Maybe I've said too much.

"Have you talked to your mama since you got here?"

I shake my head. "Not yet."

"She's probably worried sick about you." Gladys adjusts the collar on my shirt, smoothing out the neckline. "There's a phone right behind the counter. Give her a call and let her know you're all right, and then we'll chat. Maddox, don't go wandering." She points at him. "I'm not finished with you yet. And I can tell you haven't eaten well in days."

Gladys wiggles out of the booth and then helps me out. "Come, dearie. I'll show you to the phone, and then I'll get you a hot breakfast. Looks like you could use a little something to stick to those bones."

I follow Gladys as she heads to the kitchen.

"Phone's right there." She points behind the counter before pushing the double doors aside, shouting, "I need two hot breakfast platters with extra bacon."

I slip behind the pastry counter and pick up the phone, dialing the number. The phone rings once. My chest tightens. Mom won't pick up if she doesn't know the number. I'll have to leave a message. For all I know, she's skipped town and left me behind. If that's the case, calling her won't do any good. I pull the phone away from my ear and almost hang up, when her voicemail kicks on. I don't have a clue what to say. *Thanks, Mom. Jess died because you wouldn't tell me about my visions and those evil creatures? Have a nice time wherever you're living now?* Forget it. I hang up.

Gladys emerges from the kitchen with a platter of waffles in each hand and two smaller plates filled with crisp bacon and scrambled eggs perfectly balanced on her thick forearms. "Grab those, would you dear?" She gestures at two glasses of juice and a container of warm syrup on the counter.

I follow her back to Maddox with the drinks and syrup. "I've got a few things to finish," Gladys says as she lowers the steaming plates onto the table.

"Thanks, Gladys." I slide into the seat opposite Maddox and trade him juice for a plate of vanilla waffles. "This smells amazing."

Gladys smiles. "Enjoy it, dear, and come find me when you're done." She wipes her hands on the dish towel and then hurries back to the kitchen.

The food practically dissolves in my mouth. I force myself to take small bites and chew slowly, because more than anything, I want to lick every bite off the plate—a far cry from my usual peanut butter and burnt toast.

Maddox downs his bacon and eggs. "What kind of artist are you?"

My mouth is full of a giant chunk of waffle drenched in warm syrup. I swallow in one bite. "I'm not an artist."

"Sure you are." He cuts his waffle along the grid, separating it into tiny squares before filling each one with syrup. "Maybe you haven't explored all options. Do you sing?"

As Maddox eats, I wipe my mouth and sit back, feeling my stomach expand. "No, and I don't dance, paint, or draw either.

I'm a runner. That's about the only thing I do well." Besides destroying stuff.

"I seriously doubt running is your only gift." Maddox stabs a few squares on his fork, stacking them in line. "I'm going to hook you up with a few people and see if we can't find your other, non-running talent. Art helps strengthen your Bent." He won't look directly at me. I bet he's afraid I'll misinterpret the Current like all the other girls around here.

I push my plate aside, place my arms on the table, and stare, daring him to look at me so I can prove his charm has no effect on me. His gaze flickers up for a quick moment, then rests back on his waffle grid. "Ax throwing, perhaps?" He smiles but won't lift those blue eyes to meet mine.

"Possibly." I laugh and sit back. "Thanks for being concerned, but sitting around all day trying to discover my talent isn't what I'm after. I'm more interested in learning how to help take down the big, filthy black monster who killed Jess and sliced up your arm. In fact . . ." I shimmy out of the booth and pick the empty plates off of the table. Groggy voices buzz through the café as the room starts to fill. "I'm going to meet Gladys. The faster I get this test over with, the faster I can work with a Blade."

"You're training as a Blade?" Maddox sets his fork down.

"Yep, with Kellan."

Maddox frowns. "He's—"

"I met the guy. He's cool. I know Guardians and Blades don't typically get along, or whatever, but I'm not interested in taking sides." I've got bigger problems to solve. I balance the plates in my hands. "Thanks for breakfast." I leave Maddox at the table and zigzag through the café, dodging sleepy-faced kids waiting at the counter with empty coffee mugs in hand.

I slip around the counter, push the door open with my hip, and step inside the kitchen. I pass industrial metal shelves stacked with canned goods and plastic containers of flours, sugars, and grains. Behind the shelves is a long wooden table dusted in flour and a wall lined with gas burners and a long iron griddle. A thin guy in jeans, a gray T-shirt, and blue apron works several waffle irons at the far end of the burners near the ovens. He glances over his shoulder. "Take a bucket if you're bussing. It's easier."

I glance at the plates in my hands. "Oh. I'm not. I'm looking for Gladys."

He transfers golden waffles onto a plate with one hand and pours batter into the iron with the other. "Check around the corner." He motions to the wall with the burners. "If she's not there, she's in the cellar." He picks up on my confused expression and says, "Out the door and down the stairs," while pointing to a door behind me near a set of large refrigerators. "You can drop the plates in the sink on your way."

He slides a finished order down a line. A girl with curly hair tied back with a floral bandana dashes into the kitchen and grabs a few filled plates before rushing back out.

"Hey, breakfast tasted great, by the way. Thanks," I say. He smiles, surprised. I go around the corner as he instructed and find an empty washroom with a sudsy sink. Setting the plates in the foaming bubbles, I head for the door to the cellar in search of Gladys.

15

THE CURRENT

I step into the dim hall and go down the steps to my left, leaving the café behind me. As I descend, the sound of moving furniture scraping across the floor grows louder. I follow the sound down the damp hall to a storage room of spare furniture. Stacked barstools tower behind Gladys as she arranges shiny beads and broken glass shards on a bistro table. "I've got a few things needing repair. We can talk while we work."

I don't need to sit around and talk. I need training—or testing—or whatever. "I thought you were going to test me out as a Guardian?"

"We'll get to that." She pats the empty chair next to her. "We need a few more pieces of furniture upstairs. I thought we'd work on this one—isn't she a beauty? The top of this old table is scarred beyond repair, so I thought it'd be fun to echo some of that allure from the stained glass windows upstairs onto here." She makes a circular motion over the bistro table. "I have a few minutes before needing to get started in the kitchen. Do you mind handing me some pieces?"

I try hard not to let my frustration come through as I plop down by her.

"Gently lay out several pieces on the table so you can see

them, get a feel for how they might fit together." Gladys hands me plastic containers filled with broken pieces.

I glance at the rainbow of shattered glass. "How will I know which piece you'll need?" I pick out a few blue angular pieces and set them on the table in no particular order.

"Go with your gut." Gladys picks up a small trowel and dips the tip in a thick paste before picking up one of the tiles I've set down. "Do you know much about the Current?"

I sift through the container of cobalt-blue and jade-green glass and set a few more jagged tiles on the table. "Devon told me it's the way Awakened identify each other, but that's about it." I pick out a spear-shaped piece, the same midnight-blue as Jess's jacket. As I press my finger against the pointed tip, a knot rises in my throat. Gladys's warm hand takes the piece from mine. She lightly pastes the tile before pressing it near the middle of the table. I sift through the container, laying down broken pieces in a swirling pattern. Adding a carnation-pink piece, Jess's favorite color, in the center.

"The Current flows through this world. It's all around us, but we can't see it. Some say it comes from a puncture in the universe. Others say it bubbles up from deep within the earth, connecting from someplace else. It's unknown, and you can't see it with your eyes."

I rub my thumb across the surface of a glass piece and study the pattern taking shape of those already inlaid. I hand her an ivory piece.

"It's an ebb and flow in the world surrounding the Awakened. A slight hum that underscores everything around us, and if we slow down to listen, we might be able to dance in its rhythm." She sets the various pieces I hand her at the center of the table, following the swirl pattern I started.

"So often we're rushing, in our own heads, or just not slowing down enough to realize that it's all around us. We fight and wrestle and fail to see that our predecessors, with their simple way of life, were much more in tune than we are today. So we look to them to help us see what we can't see for ourselves."

I pick up a long, lavender shard and hold it up to my eye to look through it. "So we study the past?" If that's the case, then it makes total sense why Mom made me study classical art.

Gladys takes the lavender sliver, even though I was about to put it back. "Some say our predecessors embedded messages in their art. Others say it's a natural response to being open and sensitive to their calling, but yes. We do believe that there are 'messages' from previous artists that help guide us today."

"Like Milton." I give her a deep purple, almost black spear.

"I suppose. Seers tend to feel the Current more than the others, but we can all feel it in some way or another. It's a force in the realm that feeds our Bent. It's how Guardians are led to other Awakened, and it gives us insight that seems second nature, connecting us. Maddox cultivates art because he understands that tapping into our creative self opens our Bent in ways that simply training could never do. It reaches deep and allows our Bent to flow freely and speak to others, bringing them to awareness of who they are."

She sets the lavender piece on the edge of the table. The sharp edge sticks out too far and could easily cut someone. While she sets a plum piece near the sea of blues, I reach over and guide the lavender shard back within the bounds of the circle.

"The Current holds us together. An invisible bond that, whether we like it or not, keeps us connected." Gladys adjusts the tiles in the center. I set more shards on the table, filling the gaps, and then pick up a tray of shiny tiles. I hand her a few golden-yellow pieces. "We have our differences, that's a given," she says. "But when it comes to using our Bent for one another, we put all that aside." She trims the edge with yellow tiles, pushing the lavender inside the circle. "We're a completely different kind of family. As an Awakened, you'll always have a home right here with all of us, no matter what."

My throat swells. Hesperian is the closest to family I've ever felt. I want to do whatever it takes to keep them safe. No matter the cost.

Gladys completes the circle with the last of the yellow tiles. "That'll do for now." She stands and wipes her hands on her apron, even though the table is far from finished. "Did you talk to your mama?"

I shake my head. "She didn't answer."

"Write down the number. I'll speak with her. We mamas have a way of connecting." She pulls a pen from behind her ear and tears a piece of paper from a small notebook in her apron pocket. My stomach churns as I write the number. I'm not so sure I want Gladys calling. What if Mom tells her I'm a Seer? I change the last number and give Gladys the paper before we head back upstairs.

"I'm curious as to why she never told you."

I shrug. "I don't know." That's the truth.

She wanders back through the kitchen to wash her hands and motions for me to do the same. "Maybe she was waiting till your Bent manifested. I've heard of some Awakened in rural areas doing that, but it's not advisable. Too easy for you kids to become Dissenters."

There's that word again. *Dissenter.* "What is that?" I dry my hands with a clean dish towel.

Gladys's congenial face turns sour. "The worst offense for an Awakened. Irrevocable." I follow as she takes dough from the refrigerator before dusting the surface of the chopping block counter with flour. She tears it in half and hands me a clump before plopping down the baseball-sized dough. "Dissenters were once Awakened who have betrayed what they should be, allowed their power to be taken with the promise of something greater. They allow the Current within them to be siphoned and their essence replaced with elements of the second realm. They become immortal and, eventually, inhuman."

Gladys leans in and rolls her piece from the middle to the outer edge, creating a smooth circle.

I pick up a wooden roller, intending to do the same. "That sounds awful. Why would anyone want that?"

Gladys flattens the dough to a perfect 1/8-inch thick and deftly lifts it in one smooth motion over the roller, setting it in a pan. "Fame. Power." Gladys dusts the table with more flour before squeezing another clump of dough in a tight ball and then kneading it out. "A deep desire to gain something that couldn't be acquired any other way. It's hard to say what motivates people to give up the most precious part of who they were meant to be. The enemy targets newly Awakened, and new lines, because no one is there to explain what is happening. He is able to convert them easily, and they become part of his army. Pawns in the war."

I peel a cluster of sticky goo off the rolling pin. Gladys made it look easy, but I am really bad at this. "I thought the only enemy were those bird creatures. Is someone orchestrating the destruction?"

Gladys kneads the dough harder. "It would be a stretch to call him a person."

I smash the dough back into a ball and try again, but it sticks to my fingers. "Who is it?"

Gladys watches me struggle but doesn't intervene. "Over the generations he's had several names. At the moment, he's known as Sage Marrok LaSalle. Do you recognize the name?"

"No . . . not really." As I wipe goo from my fingers, Milton prods me, as though I should know better.

"Sage he stood / With Atlantean shoulders fit to bear / The weight of mightiest monarchies."

"Wait—is Sage the Arch-fiend who was *'hurled headlong flaming from th' ethereal sky'* with red lightning?"

"Milton described him that way so he could teach the Awakened of things unseen. The poem is only a guide." She stares at me a little too intently. I might have just given myself away.

"What is he after?" I ask, hoping to shift her focus off of me. I work the dough, but it hugs the roller and refuses to cooperate.

Gladys glances at my pastry disaster and picks up a handful of flour. "Our destruction." She slams the dough down on the board.

"Why? Because we can see his realm?"

"We have what he desires."

"Which is?"

I watch her transform my glob into another beautiful crust. "The Current. Because he's not Awakened, he doesn't get a direct feed the way we do, so he takes a little from each Awakened he's able to convert, eventually turning them into his army of souls." She pinches the dough around the edge of the pie pan and sighs. "We've been at war for hundreds of years. It's been said he's a wanderer. A king with no kingdom. Others say he's seeking a way home, back into the first realm from where he came. But one thing is clear. He wants our complete destruction. In fact, no one has come face-to-face with him and hasn't become a Dissenter."

That's alarming. "If he's that powerful, wouldn't he have taken over by now?"

"He is powerful when we're isolated and ignorant of who we are. When we are together, our power grows."

She watches me as I wash and dry my hands and then changes the subject. "Devon's right about you being a Legacy. Seems to me you might even be Elite."

"Elite sounds like royalty." I make light of her comment as I follow her to the refrigerator.

She takes out a few shiny green apples. "Not exactly." She chuckles, handing me the unblemished fruit. "Take these, would you, dear?" I bring the fruit to the table as she gathers a bowl and various spices. Gladys picks up a paring knife and skins the apple with the skill of a hunter. "Elites come from an unbroken line of Legacies. Everyone in the line married Awakened. No Commons." She chops up the apple and adds it to the bowl with a spoonful of sugar. "Like Maddox. His parents come from a long line of Guardians and Blades. All of them, every single one." She hands me an apple to peel.

"So I guess he's kind of a big deal?" I use her paring knife and cut tiny flakes of skin off the apple.

"When you come from an unbroken line, your Bent is often stronger than most."

I massacre the apple but manage to get most of the skin off. "If that's the case," I say, chopping around the core. The knife slips. I'm lucky I move my finger in time. "Then shouldn't he have a dual Bent of Guardian and Blade?"

Gladys sighs. She scoops up the hacked apple bits and adds them to the bowl. After pouring a syrupy mixture that's been simmering on the stove, she trades my knife for a wooden spoon.

"Should be, but not in his case. He's all Guardian, and I prefer it that way. Keeps him out of trouble . . . and alive." As she skillfully peels another apple, I can't help but feel like a failure.

I do my best to at least mix the apples until they're coated evenly. "Are you and him . . . related?"

Gladys laughs. "Oh, no, darling. Not by blood. He doesn't have a mama looking after him anymore." In a matter of seconds, she's poured the filling and sliced up long strips of dough. "I don't care what these boys say or how tough they act, they need their mamas, even though not a single one will admit it. I'm not much into fighting, and with this old body, my days of protecting out in the field are over. Now I consider myself a Guardian of these young hearts. We've seen a lot of loss. A lot of pain. They need someone to pull them through, and above all, keep their hearts pliable to loving others."

I stand in silence, listening to Gladys's soliloquy as she weaves a lattice of dough over the cinnamon-sugar apples in the pie pan.

"I've given you more than an earful this morning. Sometimes my mouth gets running and I can't stop."

I know the feeling. At least what comes out of Gladys's mouth is encouraging. What I blurt often hurts people more than anything else. "Can I ask you something?"

"What's that, dear?"

"Has there ever been someone who had a dual Bent of Seer and Blade? I mean, how would that work?"

"Their Bent as a Seer would outweigh any other gift they had. It's far too important." That's what I was afraid she'd say.

"Has Devon asked you to train as a Seer?" she asks curiously.

I force myself to remain calm. With a casual shrug, I say, "He only said I should test all Bents."

Gladys tosses me a glance. "Have you met Edward? I think you should."

My head spins trying to remember everyone I've met so far, but the name doesn't sound familiar. "No."

"He's Devon's grandfather. Everyone around here calls him Pop. He hasn't received a vision in quite some time and spends most of his time nowadays transferring his previous images into metal printing plates."

"Does he hang out here?"

Gladys gives a layered smile. "At times, but the kids around here aren't very fond of him."

"Why is that?"

She places the pies in the oven. "He seems to read their minds."

"Thanks for the warning."

Gladys laughs out loud and dusts the excess flour from her hands. "We're done here. Thank you for the help, darling." She wraps her flour-coated arms around me and pulls me to her chest. "I'm so glad you're with us." She hugs me tight, her full arms swallowing me in a way Mom's never did. I feel safe in her embrace.

By the time I reach around to hug her back, she's already let go. "We'll work on your pastry skills later." She wipes the flour off my black shirt the best she can. "Go on now."

Gladys picks up a warm muffin out of a pan and drops it on a plate before pushing the kitchen door open. "That boy won't eat unless food is shoved in front of him. Not only that, he's horrible in the kitchen." Gladys places the dish in my hands. "Do me the favor, would you?" She nods at Maddox. He's still in the booth, drawing.

"Sure, but . . . don't I need to train with you or . . ."

"You're all done." Gladys wipes her forehead with the back of her hand.

"Wait, what? Done as in . . . I'm not a Guardian?"

"You're a Guardian for sure. If you've got another Bent, Devon will find it, don't you worry."

My shoulders slump. I know I'm a Seer. If Awakened can only have two Bents at most, and Gladys is certain I'm a Guardian, then there's no way I could be a Blade as well. That fact only solidifies my plans to keep my mouth shut about being a Seer until I can train with Blades. Unless I do, I won't learn how to kill the beasts and avenge Jess's death. I don't know how long before Devon will have me meet with his Seer grandfather, who is bound to detect my true Bent. Or worse, I'll have another vision.

I head toward Maddox's booth. He doesn't look up as I approach, and I don't want to interrupt him, so I set the plate down on the corner of the table and sneak away.

"Hey," he calls out after me. As I turn around, he sits up. "Thanks."

"It's from Gladys." I wave at Gladys as she watches us from the counter.

"Oh." Maddox looks as if he's about to say something more when Harper's voice comes down the hall.

"I need a few more herbs to finish the serum." She turns the corner, walking into the room, and stops as soon as she sees me.

Her eyes flicker at Maddox sitting in the booth, then back to me. "You look . . . cleaner."

Despite Harper's half compliment, Gladys's words about connecting and family linger. "Thanks for your help yesterday. I'm a whole lot—"

"Hey, Maddox." Harper blows right past me and heads straight for him with an exaggerated sway of her hips. She slides into his booth. "Whatcha working on?"

Maddox flips the paper over. "Nothing much." He slides the blueberry muffin in front of him.

Tightness wells in my chest. What is her problem? Is she looking for a fight? 'Cause if she is, I'd be happy to—

"Cera, there you are." Devon turns the corner. His smile fades when he sees Harper nestled against Maddox.

"Yup. Here I am." I throw my hands in the air. "Still stuck in here instead of on the streets with Blades." The anger in my voice carries through the café. Gladys is wiping the counter, but it must be super clean by now, and I know she heard me. Devon frowns at my outburst. When he walks off, I race after him. How could I be so dumb? "Devon, wait. I'm sorry. Can I work with the Blades now?"

"No."

"No? I already met with Gladys. You said after meeting with her, I could." When he stops midstep, I slam into his back, nearly face-planting into his faded red T-shirt.

He turns to face me. "You'll have to wait until Kellan is available. Might be as early as tomorrow."

"Tomorrow? You're joking, right?"

Devon scowls. "Cera, we've got others here that need tending to also, you're not the only one. Spend time getting to know people and stop being in such a rush to gain knowledge. This is a community. Not a training camp."

"Maybe I'm in the wrong place." Who knows how long before I have another vision. They'll find out I'm a Seer and lock me up.

"You're not in the wrong place. You're just too focused on the wrong thing. You need a day to rest and heal. Why don't you try working with Harper later today?"

The idea puts a bad taste in my mouth, but to placate Devon so he won't go back on his word, I acquiesce. "Sure," I lie, because there's no way I'm working with her.

Maddox approaches and he looks concerned. "Devon, can I talk to you?"

"Something wrong?"

Maddox pulls Devon toward the staircase to what he thinks is out of earshot. "You're not going to have Cera train with the Blades—with Kellan—are you?"

Devon lifts an eyebrow. "Her training isn't your problem."

"It's just that . . ." Maddox looks over at me. He turns back before I can read his expression.

"Kellan's a strong Blade and a good trainer," Devon says.

"Let me train with them." Maddox is completely serious.

"As a Blade?" Devon laughs. "No way. Orders are clear. Any training you get comes from Gray alone."

Devon marches off. So does Maddox—in the opposite direction. I'm not sure what's up with Maddox, but it's not my concern.

Devon's words rattle me. Maybe he's right about one thing. What makes me think my needs are more important than anyone else around here? That would make me no different than Harper. I shudder at the thought. Maybe being part of a group means not always stirring things up.

Being an only child who moved all the time, I had Mom's full attention—albeit too much attention—and I could usually get what I wanted, when I wanted it. Maybe there are times when you have to take a back seat and wait your turn. I sigh, finally understanding why Mom preferred to be alone. Being part of a community isn't easy. In fact, it looks as if it will be one of the hardest things I've ever had to do.

16

CHANGEOVER

As I wait for Kellan, I spend the rest of the afternoon as far from Harper as possible and test out different art forms. I rule out those I know I'm bad at and test a few new ones. I try pottery, but the clay keeps collapsing between my fingers like pie dough. It doesn't help that Claire's masterpieces sit on the window ledge, gawking at my inept talent.

She's really into twisting bodies into whatever elongated shapes she can, backbends, high kicks . . . you name it. I also try my hand at painting, but splats and squiggles are the best I can do.

After getting a quick bite for dinner, I settle in one of the wingback chairs near the hallway to the cellar. I pick up a pencil and spare notebook in the supply basket and scribble: "I'm awful at this." Well, there's a truth, and for some reason, writing it out makes me feel a little . . . less burdened. I want to pour out how I couldn't protect Jess, but that's classified information I can't leak out onto the page. At least not outright.

> *Failing.*
> *Falling.*
> *Life now ending.*
> *Burning in the flames.*

I lower the pencil. Each word is stuffed with meaning no one would understand except me. I strike through the words, flip to a new page, and start again. This time I let the words seep out without holding back. I snuggle deeper into the chair and draw up my knees. My muscles relax with a deep release as I write.

Melodic notes from a strumming guitar float up from Maddox's sunken alcove under the stairs. The soulful music drifts across the café, finding me. I can't concentrate on writing because the yearning song is all I hear. Then my pencil lead breaks. Forget it. I rip the sheet from the notebook and crumple the useless paper in my fist. The soft notes beckon me to peer around the back of the chair, so I do. In the nook, Maddox sits on the corner of the wooden table, barefoot, head down and lost in his own world as his nimble fingers dance over the strings. He stops then starts again, perfecting a chord. He'll have a pen I can borrow. I get up and go down the steps to meet him.

He stops playing as soon as I enter. "Sorry," I say when he looks up. "I didn't mean to interrupt."

"I could use a break. It's just not flowing today. The lyrics in my head don't go with the melody." He casually rests his arms on the guitar and welcomes me with a smile. "Do you play? Maybe you'll know what I should change."

"Me? No." I hold the wadded paper in my fist. "I tried on my own, once. I think my fingers are too short." I set the paper on the corner of the table and spread my hands wide for proof. Sure, I was five and it was my dad's guitar, but still . . .

Maddox ignores my protest. "I bet you can. Learning on your own isn't easy. C'mon. Give it another try."

I hesitate for a split second. I only came in for a pen, but this could be a good break for me too. "All right, but don't be surprised when I'm right about these mini-digits."

He laughs. "You can't start off thinking you're going to fail. Think positive." He stands and lifts the guitar strap over his head.

"I believe you're gonna crush it."

"I'm gonna crush it. Right," I say, taking the guitar. "Hopefully not literally." I glance at the stone floor, hoping his guitar doesn't accidentally slip from my clumsy hands.

He pulls the wooden bench away from the table. "It's easier if you sit down. Table or bench. It's your call, but that way you can rest it on your knees."

I sit down and slide the strap over my shoulders. The woven blue nylon carries a trace of his scent. I let out a deep, shaky breath. "Promise you won't laugh."

"I won't. Remember, everyone's had a first time."

"Second time," I'm quick to remind him.

"Not everyone gives it a second shot." He watches as I tug a lock of my hair out from under the strap, letting the strands fall over my shoulders.

I feel awkward, but I set the guitar in position and look up at him for further instructions. "Okay. Now what?"

He straddles the bench. "Get a feel for the strings. Just run your finger across like this." He gently wipes his calloused thumb across the strings the way he'd probably stroke a girl's cheek. Swooning notes fill the air. "You try." He leans back. I run my fingers over the metal strings, but not quite as smooth and melodic. "That's a good start."

"Anyone can do that." I turn, suddenly aware of how close he is.

Underneath that shaggy hair, he studies my fingers on the strings. "Maybe. But not everyone has a connection with the strings and the sound. If you don't feel what you play, then the notes won't resonate the way they should. Relax and try playing a chord." He reaches behind me and takes my left hand, placing it on the neck of the guitar. He positions my thumb and curls my fingers, guiding them onto different strings, pressing lightly. His hands are much bigger than mine and his nails are cut short and clean. "Hold it gently and relax, or else the strings will feel the tension."

How can I not be tense right now? His hand holds my fingers in place, and he is leaning against my back. His ocean scent is all I breathe. "Now strum the C chord. One long, smooth stroke."

I watch my fingers slide over the strings. The soft notes glide through the room, sounding—not half bad, actually. I want to look at Maddox and see if I did it right, but with him this close, my face would no doubt turn full-blown scarlet and he'll think I'm into him. Truthfully, I'm not used to being this close to anyone.

His breath brushes near my ear. "That's good."

My stomach flutters. I pull away and lift the strap over my head. "You proved me wrong about my fingers, but I'm quitting while I'm ahead." I hand him the guitar, putting a safe distance between us. I don't want anyone getting the wrong idea. Especially Harper. "Thanks for the lesson."

"You should keep playing." He hesitates to take the guitar back until I laugh out loud.

"I wish I could think in melody." I slide to the edge of the bench and tuck my hands between my knees. "I'm more of a word girl. But there's not much I can do to change the world with mere words. Poets are a dying breed."

His eyes spark. "You're a poet?"

My face burns hot. Why did I just say that? "I'm not—no. I'm just constantly walking around with phrases in my head. Thoughts, ideas."

"A philosopher then? Even better. Philosophers have a unique way of looking at the world."

"Hardly my story."

He sets the guitar at his feet. "Were you working on something?" He motions to the crumpled piece of paper.

"I was waiting for Blades to get back and thought maybe if I slapped down the words, they'd get out of my head and I'd be able to think more clearly about everything I've been learning."

"Can I read it?" Maddox reaches for the paper.

I jump off the bench. "No. It's not worth reading—just scrambled words."

My heart races as Maddox takes the paper and unfolds the wadded ball. Instead of reading my scribbled handwriting, he walks over and hands me the sheet. "Sharing makes your work stronger. Read it out loud. That way you can hear the rhythm." I take my wrinkled poem. "That's what we do at Hesperian, express ourselves through our art. There's no judgment here. You just heard me play a few chords earlier. It wasn't anything special, but the more I play, the more music opens up in my head. Art needs an audience to thrive. That's how we grow and strengthen our Bent. So, why not give it a try? Turn your back or pretend I'm not here, if that helps."

He stands in front of me, honest, open, and encouraging. Wow. This must be what Devon meant when he said "get to know people." I tuck my hair behind my ear. It's not my dream to be a poet, so I'm not risking much except total embarrassment. And I embarrass myself daily, so it's not like this would be something new. Plus, the words aren't anything life-changing. I guess since all my other artistic talents have been abysmal failures, I should give it a go. I want to find a way to prove I belong here, especially since he told Devon there's something different about me, and guitar isn't the answer. "Okay. You're my first audience, so . . . no judgment, right?"

He sits, resting his arms on the table. "Never."

I walk to the back of the room. There's less chance someone passing by the stairs will hear me if I read back here. I rest my shoulder against the back wall and start reading aloud, working hard to ignore Maddox as he leans forward. I focus on the words alone, feeling each one rumble inside before springing out of my mouth.

I was born the colliding line
Where shadows wrestle light
Alone, unseen
Heart breaking
Soul scraping
Trapped between the war.

My voice sounds shaky. I glance up. Maddox nods, encouraging me to go on.

Never bright enough
Not bold enough
Just a hidden marking line
Balanced on the ebb and flow
Of light and shadow's throne.

My words float back into my ears, shutting everything out as I read on.

Guiding eyes, taking sides, lining each one's shore
I'm drowning in the endless wake
Straining for the sun
Yearning for the rising dawn
Until—

I bite my lip and stare at the words. "That's all I've got. The rhythm doesn't work. That last part about the drowning doesn't transition right. The throne part feels contrived, and my imagery isn't clear." I pull away from the brick wall with the sudden urge to find a pen. Not finding one, I focus back on my words. "I wanted to finish the piece by writing about how light doesn't fall over something by accident. It's always revealing something. If everything were bathed in light, nothing would be a focal point.

Just like in a painting, the shadows are needed to help guide the eye to what matters, but—" I pull my eyes from the page and look at Maddox. He sits there with this dumfounded, entranced look as if he's never heard someone read out loud before. "You said no judgment, remember?"

"No, it was . . ." Maddox has trouble getting to his feet, as if the world's axis shifted one degree. He clears his throat. "It was great."

I clearly bored him. "Quit being nice." I wad up the paper. "It's trite and doesn't follow any traditional iambic meter. I'd get slaughtered if I ever turned something like this in for a grade. I never meant to show—or read it to anyone. I keep trying to capture what I feel, but my emotions never make it on the page the way I want."

"I felt every word." His voice is quiet. I stiffen when he looks at me as if seeing me for the first time—or maybe he sees the darkest part I keep hidden. Not only does my skin suddenly feel transparent, but Maddox doesn't take his eyes off me.

"Oh." I tuck the wadded paper under my arm. If there were a fireplace in this tiny space, I'd toss my paper soul into the flames. "Perhaps it was my grand oration and perfect enunciation because I'm a Marlowe . . . a long, long, *long* and distant relative to the playwright. At least I like to imagine so." I grin. "Alas." I let out a dramatic sigh and an extravagant curtsy to lighten the thickened air. "Reading out loud doesn't change the world."

At that moment, Harper calls Maddox's name from somewhere across the room. I'm glad, because I don't know what to do, or how to be around Maddox right now. "I'd better go," I say, heading out of the suffocating space.

Maddox blocks my way up the steps. "Come by later and I'll give you another guitar lesson." He's way too serious, or intense, or . . . something. I can't place what just happened to him, but his eyes have this stormy look that makes my insides feel squishy.

"Thanks for the offer, but I'm done with guitar."

"Cera. Your words are lyrical." When he touches my arm, I look up at him. Something about the way he looks at me makes all the air feel sucked out of the room. The Current kicks up as our eyes meet. His voice is almost a whisper as he says, "Write songs with me."

"Do *what* with her?" Harper stands at the top of the steps with her arms crossed and a heated death glare aimed right at me.

"Nothing." I'd be stupid to deny the connection between us, but I step away from Maddox. Maybe it's the Current, maybe it's something more, but he's with Harper. I might not have a tribe of friends, but I'm smart enough to know that going after someone else's guy—or even their crush—is violating a sacred "girl code." Even with someone as unlikable as Harper. "He was . . . I'm not talented at anything, and he was trying to make me feel better."

Harper marches down the steps with a plastic smile that belies the fury in her eyes. "Isn't that sweet of you, Maddox." She hooks her arm through his, smothering the space between them. "I'm beginning to think I can't leave the two of you alone." She forces a tinkling laugh.

I throw my hands out as she walks Maddox up the stairs. "No, it's not like that."

Maddox doesn't say a word and he doesn't have to. His eyes, fixed on me with an "I'm serious," expression, say it all.

I slump against the table. He's out of his mind. There's no way I'm writing with him. Especially not after the way he just looked at me. Not to mention how exposed I felt when I bared my soul. He'd have to drag words out of me if I was to wax—or wane—any poetic thoughts with him. Besides, writing lyrics hits too close to home. Dad was a musician. I'm nothing like him, and I don't ever want to be.

I look up as a group of rowdy kids jostle each other, laughing as they walk through the café after dinner, Kellan being one of them. He's back? They're headed down to the cellar. I race down the steps after him, following the voices. They're not in the storeroom but in the last room on the left where the light pours into the dank hall.

"You told Gladys we were headed out, right?" Claire's voice comes out into the hall. She must have walked right past me but I was too focused on Kellan to notice. I run my hand along the wall, staying in the shadows as I approach the room.

"First things first. We're scouting." I'm not sure who that girl is, but her deep voice makes her sound like someone I don't want to mess with. "Our only job is to track Legions. There've been more sightings than usual on the edge of town. We're only seeing if they're getting close."

I stop halfway down the hall, in front of the storeroom. Did she say Legions? I thought Maddox called the beast a Cormorant. Unless she's talking about a different creature.

Milton chimes in with the verse: *"Another world / Hung o'er my realm, linked in golden chain / To that side of Heaven from whence your legions fell."*

I know about the other realm, Milton, but don't say, *"your legions,"* otherwise it sounds like I'm on their side.

"Y'all heard Tanji." With his slight country accent, I'm pretty sure that's Kellan. "Send the signal if you spot one. We're markin' their path. Not bringin' attention to ourselves."

"Can we take them down if they cross into our territory?" That's Claire.

"Not on your own. Duck out 'n head back. We'll hunker down till they pass over." Kellan's long shadow stretches over the stone floor.

"Let's move." The girl with the cold alto voice gives the instruction. Footsteps thump over a soft surface. I don't want them to call me out for eavesdropping, so I lean into the shadows against the wall as they file out of the room. Dressed in all black, they head into the dark end of the hall and turn a corner.

Kellan is the last to leave. Before he disappears around the corner, he turns around and squints in my direction. Even though I'm swallowed in darkness, he spots me. "Cera, right?"

"Yeah . . ." Feeling a little nervous, I step out of the shadows.

He slips on a set of leather gloves. "We're goin' on a routine outing. Come see how we do things. Can't learn inside these walls. If you're one of us, it'll be clear on the street." He walks my way and tosses me a knit beanie. I catch it. "There's a tub of clothes in the gym." He motions to the room they were in. "Find a jacket that fits. Then meet me outside."

I don't hesitate. I race into a room that smells like sweat and vinyl. My feet bounce on the rubber mats as I pass by punching bags and workout equipment. I find a tub of lost-and-found items in the far corner near the wall of mirrors. I sift through the contents as fast as I can and grab a thick jacket that mostly fits, sliding it on while I race out of the room.

I yank the beanie down on my head and turn the corner, stopping at a metal door. My face is blasted with cold air as soon as I step outside. An amber light from a streetlamp illuminates the steps up to the road. I jog up and join the others.

"Who's the toddler?" The girl with the deep alto voice is a thick, amazon warrior who towers over me. Her straight and sharp nose contrasts against the tight, curly black hair puffing out under a beanie and falling around her wide shoulders.

"Tanji, this is Cera." Kellan places a hand on my shoulder. "She's runnin' with us tonight."

Tanji frowns. "You got good shoes?"

I wiggle my toes, glancing at my feet. "They're a bit worn, but they'll hold up."

"They don't look solid." She turns to Kellan. "She's running with you. I don't want any whining about blisters."

I stand tall, despite the fact that I feel tiny next to her. She's probably taller than Maddox. "I'm a good runner, and I don't whine." Much.

Tanji looks me over. Each of her thighs are thicker than my waist. It's pretty clear by looking at her running tights and thermal jacket that she's solid muscle.

I plant my feet into the concrete. "Whatever it takes, I'm in."

Tanji slips on a pair of thermal gloves. "You'll need a clear head, a quiet mouth, and a strong bladder. Hope you got all three 'cause it's going to be a long night."

Kellan, removes a glove and places his fingers in his mouth for a high-pitched whistle. Everyone scatters. Footsteps tap lightly against the concrete, my own included. I run with steeled grit, keeping pace with Kellan and Tanji as frosty air fills my lungs and adrenaline powers each step. I've never felt so alive. Even though I'm part Seer, there's no doubt in my mind this is where I belong. The only risk I pose being out here is letting the enemy intercept the vision—if I happen to have one. If that's so, then there's not much I can do to hide what I really am.

17
KEEP WATCH

Ten of us zigzag through East Ridge, but no one speaks. Sparse streetlamps give enough light to guide our way around corners without bumping into parked cars or street signs. The air smells like snow, the coming of winter mixed with car exhaust and fried food. My cheeks are frozen and my lips numb. I run with my shoulders pulled back in hypervigilant mode. Barking dogs claw at the glass from behind windowpanes as we pass. Several streets over, cars thump over potholes and truck hydraulics squeak.

I glance at Kellan as he runs with his head up and eyes watching the road. His body is lithe as he breathes steadily. Devon mentioned that Blades have an instinctive sense when something's about to strike. I'm guessing Kellan will test that trait in me while we're out here. I'm on guard for any sudden movements from him or any of the others.

He slows his stride when we get about six blocks away from Hesperian. When we reach an abandoned warehouse with broken windows, he stops. "Let's split from here. Claire, Rhys, and Cera will come with me. Tanji, take your group and head west."

"We'll take the roof." Tanji motions to the fire escape ladders on the side of the building as a group assembles behind her.

"Use the clouds to signal when you've taken post." Kellan walks over and yanks on a ladder. The ladder drops to his shoulders.

Tanji flings herself on the bars with the ease of a gymnast. "We'll walk the perimeter, make camp on the west side, and head back before sunrise."

Kellan nods his approval. Tanji scales up the side of the building as if she's on solid ground. Her crew follows. One by one, they disappear across the horizon of the roof, leaving me in the dark with Kellan, Claire, and a guy with a stiff pompadour and sharp skinny jeans named Rhys.

You'd think the Cormorants would spot them more easily if they're up that high, but I shut my mouth. I get the impression that Kellan doesn't abide ignorant questions very well. I wrap my arms around my middle to keep from shivering and wait for instructions. At that moment, a verse from Milton's poem pops in my head: *"when night / darkens the streets, then wander forth the sons / Of Belial . . ."* Thanks for the warning, Milton. I search the cloudy sky for a Cormorant. The rooftops look clear. For now.

As Kellan pulls out a leather flask from inside his vested jacket, I catch a glimpse of a hunting knife tucked in the lining. At least he's armed, since I'm not. He unscrews the flask.

"Warm up and let's go." He holds the canister in front of me.

"What is it?" I smell coffee but there's something else.

Claire snatches it out of his hands. After taking a swig, she wipes her lips with her sleeve. "It's Spike, and it keeps us up for hours."

Rhys takes the flask next. When he tilts his head back, I marvel at how each hair stays in place as he pours the drink into his mouth.

"Is it alcohol?" I ask.

Rhys coughs. "We're not stupid. Alcohol affects our reflexes." He looks into the narrow spout and swirls the canteen. "It's natural. A mixture of some type of Chinese berry and mushroom, I think."

I sniff. "Made by Harper?"

Kellan takes the small canteen back and offers it to me again. "It improves mental clarity and increases stamina."

As much as I want to prove myself to be a Blade without any help from Harper, I get the feeling this is a test.

I give in and take a little sip. The warm liquid tastes woodsy, and the aftertaste is strange: salty, sweet, bitter, tangy, and acrid all at once. Not my favorite flavor. The bitterness lingers a bit too long.

Kellan tucks the flask back inside his vest jacket. "We check the perimeter 'n stand on watch. That's all."

I catch up to him and match his pace. Out of habit, I track each step as we go, mapping the way back. My face flushes, and warmth coils through my blood from the drink, but that's about the only difference I feel. "Do you normally see the creatures on outings?"

"If they're passin', then yeah, but they usually leave this part of town alone."

"Have they attacked Hesperian before?"

He shakes his head. "We don't think they know our location. And it's not the smartest thing for us to go lookin' for a fight. Since Hesperian is a safe house and not a training camp, most of the Blades, with the exception of Tanji, haven't been prepared to fight. If we think the creatures are movin' in, we pull everyone back inside and let 'em pass."

"That's stupid," I blurt. Kellan shoots me an irritated look. "I mean, if you hide back in Hesperian, then you'd be giving the creatures your location. Why don't you lead them away? Make them think that Hesperian was at a different location so if they ever decided to attack, they wouldn't know where the real hideout is?" I glance over my shoulder. Claire and Rhys follow behind us in silence.

Kellan looks at me. "You come up with all of that just now?"

"I was thinking of ways to protect—" I regret my word choice, because at the moment, I sound more like a Guardian than a Blade.

Kellan scans the road before turning the corner. "Not a bad idea, actually. We might create a few alternative locations."

"And Tanji mentioned Legions . . . Are they like the Cormorants or something else entirely?"

"The latter. In my opinion, Legions are worse than Cormorants. You never know when one will show up. One minute you don't see 'em and then next thing you know, they're torpedoing right at you. The only dead giveaway that they're around is their sound."

My ears perk, listening for anything unusual. "Which is . . . ?"

"Hornets."

"*Brushed with the hiss of rustling wings. As bees / In spring time*?" I quote Milton as the verse pops in my head. That's how Milton described the sound of the demons as they assembled in Pandemonium after their fall.

Kellan shrugs. "I guess you could say so."

We turn the corner, cross the street, and head to a chain-link fence surrounding a ten-story cell tower.

"We'll stop here and watch for Tanji's signal."

Kellan hoists himself up onto the fence. Climbing up and over, he leaps on the other side in a matter of seconds. Rhys and Claire stand back and wait for me to go next. I look for security cameras but don't find any.

Climbing isn't my strong suit, but I'm great at faking confidence. I plant the tip of my toe in the crosshatch of the bent wires, grip the fence, and scale my way up—not quite as nimble as Kellan, but at least I don't slip. It'll be getting over the top without catching one of the wire spokes that will be the tricky part. The metal freezes my palms as I grip the top of the fence. I swing one leg over, push myself up, and bring the other around when Rhys starts the climb. "Hey, new girl." He scales up fast. The whole fence shakes, but I manage to keep my balance. "Time for a test."

Adrenaline rushes through me. "Bring it." I try not to let on how terrified I am. The idea of being tested doesn't freak me out nearly as much as the dizzying sensation of being ten feet off the ground. I've decided that heights and I aren't compatible.

Rhys laughs as he meets me eye level. Even in the dark, it's easy to see his bright teeth are about as straight as his hair. "That's a gutsy statement. You don't even know what we're about to do."

I climb over. When I'm a reasonable distance from the ground, I let go of the fence and jump, landing on my feet—not as graceful as I'd hoped, but at least I didn't twist an ankle.

Rhys glances down at Kellan. "Ready?"

"Later." Kellan walks off. Not only does he sound bothered, but the way his heavy footsteps grind into the gravel as he heads to the base of the cell tower confirms it.

Rhys's bright smile fades. "Why's he being such a joy killer?" With a nimble jump, Rhys lands beside me. He tugs at his jacket, straightening his outfit as he stands.

Claire follows, coming down with an agile leap, which only highlights how ungraceful I am. She links arms with Rhys and pats his shoulder. "It's the drink. You know K. He'll come around."

"Hope so, or else it's going to be a rough night." Rhys frowns and marches to the base of the tower toward Kellan with Claire in tow.

"We're climbing a cell tower, huh?" I look up at the crossing metal beams as they shrink, disappearing into the night sky. More heights? I swallow. I agree with Rhys: it's going to be a rough night.

Kellan walks up to me. "There ain't much to block the cold, so find a way to stay warm."

"Or we could drink more Spike to warm us up," Claire says.

He ignores her request. "You take the halfway mark with Rhys and search the ground. It's warmer there. Cera and I will scout the horizon from the platform."

Kellan hoists himself up on the ladder and starts to climb. I'm a bit shorter and pulling myself up isn't going to be easy. He looks down as I wait at the base of the ladder. "Rhys, help her up."

"I've got it." I grip the cold metal and hoist myself up. I'm pretty sure I've pulled something in my shoulder, but hey, I did it on my own, and that's what matters.

I climb, keeping a few paces behind so I don't get a boot in the face. The higher we ascend, the colder the air gets. I focus on my hands as they cling to each rung and listen for the cadence of Kellan's boots above me. As I grip the metal, the ladder vibrates as the others scale the rungs below, but I don't dare look down.

After my hands freeze over and I feel as if we've climbed well over a hundred feet, I come up through a hole in the middle of a platform. I crawl up and grip a bar. Good thing there's a low wall around the ledge.

I back myself up to a metal pole and wrap the crook of my arm around a beam to hold on. There's enough light from the moon glowing behind the blue clouds to give us light. Kellan stands not far from me. He's surveying the night sky but is turned enough to where he can see me. We're hidden in the skeleton of the cell tower. Creatures won't find us here—I don't think.

As the wind kicks up, the tower sways. I turn up the collar of my jacket. My nose runs and feels numb, but at least the dizziness of being ten stories high subsides. Even though my eyes water, I search the skyline for Cormorants—or Legions, although I've never seen one face-to-face. Bright lights pepper the darkness, others extinguish like dying fireflies, but otherwise, the night seems remarkably quiet.

A thrill courses through me as I stand above the city and

overlook the train station, the surrounding narrow buildings, and empty parking lots. In the distance, on the other side of a dark expanse of trees, lies the evening glow of Wakefield's lights. Mom will have left town by now. If she was strong enough to leave. Guilt twists inside my chest. Maybe I shouldn't have changed the last digit when I gave Gladys her number.

Far in the distance, a strong laser-like beam reflects in the clouds. "Tanji's crew is in." Kellan pulls out a thin flashlight from his jacket and points the beam at the clouds, signaling back. "We'll park here for a while 'n keep watch. Look for anything unusual in the shadows." He crouches down to sit on the platform. "You stay there." He motions to the side that overlooks East Ridge. "I'll cover this side."

I squat on the platform but hang a good distance from the ledge and keep watch. The icy air ruffles the jacket and creeps down the exposed part of my neck. I shiver, and my shoulders tighten as I keep listening for the shrieking cry of a Cormorant. In this cold, Tanji was right—it's going to be a long night. But I'm determined. I'll do whatever it takes to learn how to destroy the beasts so I can take them down for good.

18

STRIKE DEEP

We stay in the tower with our backs to each other for what feels like hours. Claire and Rhys hang several stories lower to get a better view of the street. No one talks. After a while, I stand and stretch out my legs to warm up and keep awake.

I lean against the bars and stare out into the night. My mind wanders, replaying Jess's death, my mom's drawings, that horrible bird monster hunting Maddox and me. There's so much I still don't know.

A light chime of metal hitting metal, like a zipper tag, clinks somewhere behind me. The sound stops. A brush of cold wind swooshes nearby. I lean right, thrust the point of my elbow back as hard as possible, and hit something solid. Someone grunts. I turn around to find Kellan with a pained look on his face. "Your reflexes are slow."

He thought that was slow? "I made contact. How was that—"

"You waited till I was almost on you."

"I wanted to see how quick I could react the closer you got." A total lie.

"That's a stupid idea. Don't ever do that again. Next time it might not be me." Kellan rubs his side.

"Talk about a stupid idea—attacking someone on the

platform of a cell tower . . . What if I had fallen off? What if I had knocked *you* off?"

"True." Kellan tucks his hands in his pockets. "Except being a Blade means figuring things out real quick. We're intuitive."

I glance at him, unsure if "we're" includes me. "So you're saying I passed your test. Despite my 'slow' reflexes, you think I'm a Blade?"

He shakes his head. "You read as a lot of things." My stomach sinks. Can he tell I'm a Seer?

His lean, freckled face looks pale in the night. The fading Current is almost nonexistent between us. "I don't think Hesperian is where you ought to be. If you really want to learn how to get at those creatures, someone like you should be at Council, training with Gray."

Gray. That name again. "What's the big deal about him?" I bounce on my toes to keep warm.

Kellan's smile is loaded. "You'll figure that out as soon as you meet him."

"So he's a Blade."

"Best there is."

So Kellan thinks I'm good enough to train with the best Blade there is? That's saying something. "Do I have to wait until I meet Gray to find out how to kill the creatures, or can you tell me?"

"The tactic is simple." His wavy hair doesn't move with the sudden wind gust. Mine, however, tangles in my face, even under the beanie.

I wipe the loose strands away. "Oh yeah?" I try to sound casual, nonchalant. This is the answer I've been waiting for.

Kellan stares into the night. "Aim for the heart, strike deep, and pray you don't die."

"Aim . . ." I think back. I tried throwing a metal pole at the Cormorant, but that didn't do any good. "Are their hearts anatomically in the same place as ours?"

The blue glow from the moonlight clouds deepens the shadows of Kellan's expression. "I said tactic is simple. The execution isn't. Killing any creature means gettin' close enough. You'll probably die before you make contact."

Maddox was so close to the beast, he could have easily died . . . A laser of white light flickers twice against the clouds. "Looks like all's quiet. No sightings, which is good. Let's head back."

Kellan makes his way down. So do the others. About twenty feet to the ground, my frozen toes slip. I fall a few rungs, gasping before I hook my arm on the ladder, feet dangling. Stupid. My heart races, and my breath turns icy in my lungs. I find my footing and descend a lot slower this time. No surprise that I'm the last to reach the ground.

Kellan gives instructions, making no mention of my near-death fall. I'm thankful. "Rhys, you and Claire run the fourth quadrant, then meet Tanji's group at the warehouse. Cera and I will take the first."

Claire fidgets, trying to stay warm as she leans up against Rhys. "Good. I hate running long distance."

"I'll run with you," Rhys says to Kellan. "The girls can go back together."

Kellan shakes his head. "You two go on. Cera and I will meet you there."

"You sure?" Rhys's hurt gaze lingers on Kellan.

"Come on, idiot head." Claire tugs on Rhys's arm. "Let's get out of here. I'm freezing."

Rhys hooks his arm through Claire's as they walk to the wire fence.

Kellan is patient as I climb back over. Why is Maddox so opposed to Kellan? Sure, he's uptight, but he's not jerk. I reach the ground and retie my shoe. After Rhys and Claire take off, I ask Kellan, "What's your story? You don't seem like everyone else around here."

Kellan watches me pull the laces tight. "Meaning?"

"You seem to have a lot on your mind." Intense. Burdened. Those are a few of the words I want to use.

"I'm from Council. They assigned me here."

Seriously? I've been out all night with someone who's practically CIA of this second realm, and if he knew I was a Seer, he'd lock me up. I switch position and tie the other shoe. "You don't seem thrilled with the idea of being here."

"I'm not a babysitter."

"I'll try not to be insulted." I finish the knot. "Seventeen is old enough to not need a chaperone." He might be in his early twenties, like Devon, but maybe older.

Kellan takes the flask from his jacket. "I wasn't talkin' about you."

I don't ask who. The bitter look on his face, coupled with the fact that he walks off, makes it clear that discussion is over. I catch up to him. "Have you known about this world your whole life?"

Kellan takes a sip from the canteen. "Dad's side. Mom didn't know."

So he's a Legacy like me but doesn't have a dual Bent because both parents weren't Awakened. "Was it tough having one parent who knew and one who didn't?"

"Dad taught me through stories and toy sword fights. Mom didn't have a clue." Kellan holds the flask out to me as we walk.

I shake my head, refusing. "Does your mom know what you do now?"

"She thinks I'm in the army. Dad's idea."

"You still have both your parents?" I'm a little envious. "That's cool."

Kellan puts the flask away. "Sometimes." His answer is loaded, but I get the feeling I shouldn't press him.

There is a long silence before I dare to ask, "So am I Blade, or what? You didn't exactly tell me earlier."

"Jury's still out. Your Bent seems scrambled. I'm not positive that you're a Blade, even though you read like one."

There is an instant bounce in my step. "I read like one? Seriously?"

"Some aspects you do, but like I said, other parts seem . . . I don't have any other word but *scrambled*."

If that's the case, then I've got to erase any doubt in his mind. The idea of training with a Blade like Gray sounds right up my alley.

Our cadence is light as we jog along the cracked sidewalk, searching for Cormorants in this abandoned part of town. As the sky begins to lighten, sleep and exhaustion settle in. A light two-mile jog was fine but not an eight-mile run. My mouth is dry, but I don't let up.

After ten more blocks, Kellan slows his stride. "Your endurance isn't bad." Glad he thinks so because I'm dying on the inside. "Looks all clear. We'll walk it off and head to the warehouse to meet the others."

I follow his lead. We walk several blocks, venturing deeper into East Ridge. I stuff my hands in my pockets, wishing I had taken a sip of the drink to warm me up. We turn the corner and find Claire, Rhys, Tanji, and about three others I don't know warming up by a fire lit in a trash can at the edge of an abandoned warehouse. The building lacks a wall and exposes the inside. Wind whistles through the broken panes. The smoky air inside the warehouse is warmer than the street but not by much. Broken glass and splintered pallets lie around the vast, dusty space. Huddled around the fire, Blades' distorted shadows dance on the rusted rafters. For some reason, the shadows remind me of the warped trees in Mark's gallery. Wow. The gallery and seeing the picture of *The Storm* seem like a hazy dream from long ago.

Tanji's shadow dominates the ceiling in the flickering light. "We were all clear tonight."

"Good. So were we." Kellan unzips his jacket as he warms

his hands by the fire. Whatever they're burning has a faint smell of whatever sulfuric chemical Mark had in the gallery. I don't join them, because inhaling that smoke can't be good. Instead I stay outside the circle, a few feet behind Kellan. The faint hum of an industrial light bulb echoes through the cavernous space. That's odd. There aren't any lights other than the fire.

"Can we go back now?" Claire picks up a metal lid, ready to smother the fire.

I must be exhausted because deep in the warehouse where the light doesn't reach, the darkness warps. I blink. The darkness turns to a black, misty smoke.

Maybe it's the air. I blink again. No. Something's back there.

Kellan keeps talking as the humming sound grows louder. Is that humming or buzzing? "Cera came up with a good plan. Let's head back and talk about it."

Tanji looks me over with distrust. "Plans go through me."

No one else is reacting to the sound. Can they not hear it, or is something wrong with me? I glance at my hands. They're not clenching, so I know this isn't the onset of a vision. At least it doesn't feel like one.

"Calm down, Tanji," Kellan says. "No one's putting anything into action yet. It's just an idea. I'll run it by you and see what you think."

Thick smoke moves across the far end of the warehouse floor. No. I'm not seeing things. I point to the far end of the space. "There's something . . ."

Kellan turns around. "What?"

I widen my eyes, soaking in the darkness, and step toward the fog. "There's black smoke . . . or mist . . ." The sulfur stench grows stronger. Milton nudges me with the verse: *"A pitchy cloud / Of locusts, warping on the eastern wind."* Yes, it's a black cloud for sure, Milton, but you're wrong about the locust part. *"Like a black mist low creeping."* Yes, that's more like it.

Kellan comes to my side and takes hold of my elbow to keep me from going any further. "Claire, take her back. She's dehydrated. I don't want her passing out on the streets."

"I'm not . . ." The mist sways and the cloud takes form. "Now it looks like a person . . . and there's a . . . buzzing." I pull away and turn to face him. "Can't you hear that?"

He takes another look at the darkness. His body tenses as he tilts his head in the direction of the sound. Without warning, he grabs my arm and shoves me into Rhys. Everyone huddled around the crackling fire stands frozen. No one speaks. Rhys stares at the dark shadow as he slides a short knife from his jacket.

I stiffen. "Is that a—"

Claire slaps her cold hand over my mouth and whispers against my ear. "Legions hunt by sound."

From the darkness, a shadow rises. The mist evolves into a deformed human shape with elongated arms drooping lower than possible. It has flaky, ashen skin too pale to be human. The creature doesn't walk. It has a cloud of mist where feet should be. And the face, distorted and deformed with caverns for eyes. My skin prickles. I've seen this creature once before—it's the sallow man from my visions.

Kellan puts his hand inside the lining of his jacket and draws out his hunting knife as the shape creeps forward. Tanji does the same. So do all the others. Eight pointed knives sparkle in the dying firelight. Spit sticks to my dry throat. Lucky for me, the whistling wind and a loose board banging against the side of the building hide the sound of my rapid breathing.

Kellan glances at Tanji and nods. Without making a sound, Tanji inches closer while the others slip out of the warehouse. One by one, the rest of the Blades disappear around the corner. My adrenaline runs on high. We should be attacking them, not running away.

Claire grabs my arm with her free hand. She mouths, "Get

out." I shake my head. When I step back, my heel crunches on broken glass. The sound echoes through the warehouse. I freeze. The creature stops swaying. Claire's eyes widen, confirming my screwup.

The buzzing intensifies. I look at the deformed man floating midair at the back of the warehouse. The shadow contorts, unhinging a crooked jaw, and releases a piercing shriek. Over the curdling cry, Kellan turns to me and shouts, "Get out! Now!"

19
ANOTHER ONE

The creature hovers six feet above Kellan and Tanji. Claire drags me out of the warehouse. My pulse pounds. I can't leave them alone with the beast and run away to save myself. I wrestle to break free, but Claire drags me down the street.

When we're far enough away, I whisper, "Claire, we have to help them."

"No. We've got to go back to Hesperian and let the others know to wait inside."

"But that thing was too high. It would have to descend on them before they could strike it."

Claire maintains her grip as she pushes me around the corner. "You're unarmed. If you go back there, that thing will descend on *you*, suck your soul, and leave you burning in ashes. Is that what you want? You can't fight it bare-handed. If you run back there, you'll get in the way and put their lives in danger." Her angry face looks menacing under the faint light of the streetlamp pooled by insect carcasses.

"But we should fight—"

"We're not trained the way Kellan and Tanji are. They're giving us time to get back and warn the others by holding the Legion off so it won't come after us and give away our location. Don't screw it up."

I had sworn I wouldn't hide anymore and I'd face things head-on—even if it meant my own life. I hadn't thought about what it might cost someone else.

Rhys comes around the corner. "Keep your voices down. If there's one, there's a good chance there might be others." That's another thing I hadn't thought of. I glance around. No signs of creatures or mist. So far.

I cross the street and follow Rhys and Claire, despite this nagging feeling that something's not right. Our brisk footsteps are quiet, but retreating through shadows seems like a horrible idea. I drift toward the dimly lit street. If other Legions in mist form are lingering in the dark, we wouldn't see them until it was too late.

As we walk down the street, the gnawing sensation claws at me. Something terrible is about to happen. I can sense it. My insides feel about as torn up as the demolished building we pass. We're supposed to be running back to Hesperian to warn the others to stay inside and hide, but leaving Kellan and Tanji alone to fight feels reprehensible.

Rhys and Claire jog ahead of me, knives at their sides as they scan the sky. I search the ground for mist, letting my stride fall a little slower. Shops are closed with protective metal coverings; others have barred-up windows. If I have my bearings right, we're about four blocks from Hesperian. Not far.

The nagging sensation grows like a scream I can't ignore. As soon as Rhys and Claire turn the corner, I turn around and head back. With each step, the sensation gets stronger.

I listen intently as I pass the demolished building. A sound echoes from somewhere in the rubble. It could be a buzzing, like the one in the warehouse, but the sound is so faint, it's hard to tell. I search for something to use as a weapon. Broken rebar pokes out from a busted sidewalk. Another piece lies on the ground. It's longer than my arm and wouldn't have any problem digging deep into a creature's heart.

I swipe the metal shaft off the ground, feeling the weight in my palm. The cold grooves press against my skin, and my fingers pulse with a heightened sense of danger. The chemical stench of sulfur is strong. It's the same scent from the warehouse. From what I can tell, only a trash pit remains where a building once stood. The nagging rips through me. Something is down there.

I should probably run, but I can't. This is my chance to fight back. Avenge the pain those beasts inflicted on unsuspecting kids who never deserved to die. I tighten my grip on the metal bar and squeeze my way through an opening in the fence. A few remaining steps lead to the bottom. I take one step down. Then another. It's dark, but not so much that I can't see the heaping pile of trash near the bottom of the steps. Hidden under the mess of cardboard, splintered wood, and deflated trash bags, I know the creature is there. I can feel it.

Something in the trash pile moves. Maybe a rat. Maybe not. I clutch the rebar and hold it out in front of me. According to Kellan, I've got to get close enough to stab it through the heart. I inch closer.

The pile is too small to be a Cormorant. It must be a Legion. I'll lift the trash, and in one swift motion, I'll strike the beast before it can see me. If I was confident of my strength, I'd stab through the cardboard, but I won't risk the pole not penetrating through the ghastly skin of the creature. If there's skin at all. I didn't get a good enough look.

I swallow. This is it. I'll do it on three. *One.* I tighten my grip. *Two.* I reach down and place my fingers on the wet cardboard. *Three.* I fling the cardboard back and stab the darkness.

A girl screams.

I stumble. My makeshift sword punctures a trash bag. Not the girl, thankfully. She's huddled in a tight ball with her hands wrapped over her head. My hands shake. I almost killed someone. I toss the rebar as far as possible.

Landing on the concrete, the clinking metal echoes through the dark. "What are you doing out here?" Cold sweat drenches my back. "I could have killed you!"

She uncovers her hand from her face and peers at me. She's older than I thought. "I'm hiding from the"—she hesitates—"monsters."

"Monsters?" I sink to my knees. "Oh no. I'm so sorry."

She grabs hold of me. "It was hideous. The worst. His mouth was open." She bawls the rest of the words into my sleeve.

I hug her tight. "You were right to hide."

"Was it real or . . . ?"

"It's real." I sit back on my knees and repeat what Maddox said when he first found me. "You're not alone." The words stick in my throat.

"You can see them too?" she asks through another sob. "I'm not crazy, right?"

"No. You're not." Euphoric strength churns inside me. Is this what it's like for Guardians to find someone? "Come with me. There's a place that's safe, and others can tell you what's going on—what you're seeing."

I help the girl to her feet and grab a splintered wood spear in case we encounter a creature on the way. She's a foot shorter than me, has tangled curly hair and a pronounced limp. Even though she's shaking, she follows me willingly.

I keep my voice quiet. "There's a place a few blocks from here. You'll be safe there." I slide my arm around her shoulders and help her up the steps. "What's your name?" I get the name part out of the way. Maddox took way too long.

"Juniper."

"I'm Cera." This girl is compliant and follows without question. Unlike me. It's a wonder Maddox didn't leave me on the street to die. I'll thank him for it later. "What were you doing out here alone?"

"I was on the train. I got off at the wrong stop, then I started seeing these monster things that kept following me everywhere."

"Have you seen them before?" I ask. She shakes her head. "Did you just turn seventeen?"

She nods. "Yesterday."

As I hold the chain fence open for her to slide through, I notice tiny squares of paper napkins sticking to her skin. "What happened to your arms and neck?"

"Oh, that? I had a few scratches and made a salve with honey and paper napkins to keep them from getting infected."

"How'd you know to do that?"

She shrugs. "I don't know. I just did."

She's a Healer. I smile. Harper's gonna freak.

The feeling of danger still churns in me. My smile fades. I can't tell if it's the aftereffect of the adrenaline or if there really is something looming out here. Just then, Claire turns the corner. "Where did you go?" Her harsh whisper saps my momentary joy of finding Juniper.

I motion to the girl. "This is Juniper. She might be what the Legions were looking for—she's newly Awakened and a Healer."

"I'm what?" the girl asks. It's hard for me to believe she's older than me. She looks about fourteen. There's an innocent quality to her wide eyes and round face that reminds me of Jess.

"Get her to Hesperian." Claire's frown is easy to make out in the predawn light. And so is the black mist creeping down the sidewalk. "Rhys is out looking for you."

"Claire," I whisper, motioning to keep her voice down.

Claire turns around. "What?" She's way too loud. The black fog slinks in our direction, floating a foot above the ground. I grab Claire's wrist and shove her near Juniper. I point in the direction of Hesperian, then press my finger to my lips.

Back at the warehouse, the beast didn't attack while it was a mist. If I can get close, then I'll make noise to let the beast form. As soon as it does, I'll lodge this wooden plank right through its heart.

Claire squints, looking right at the cloudy mist. "There's nothing there."

The mist curls up in the middle of the road. The shadow takes the shape of the sallow man. I'm almost out of time. I quietly race around a parked car and head straight for the creature, leaving Claire and Juniper on the sidewalk. I have to kill it before anyone gets hurt.

I leap over a puddle so I don't make any splashing sounds. I'm ten feet away from the beast. It's not fully formed. His chest needs to appear so I can strike. I grip the spear, lifting the wood up near my ear. "I'm right here!"

The creature shrieks, fully forming into the disfigured man. Juniper screams. I run full force and spear the sucker deep in the heart, just as Rhys turns the corner. "Cera, no!"

My arm sizzles with the feeling of burning acid as I slice through the beast and go flying as if he were nothing but air. I drop my weapon. The wood thumps on the ground and echoes as I land on the concrete. Broken cement digs into my palms and knees.

The ground shakes beneath me as the Legion shrieks. I glance up over my shoulder. The beast floats three feet above me. What? I did exactly what Kellan said to do. It's supposed to be dead!

Rhys races in my direction. His knife is drawn. He leaps into the air as the creature descends, but the beast slaps out an octopus-like arm, knocking him back. The blade flies out of Rhys's palm and skids out of reach as he lands on his back. The creature's shriek ripples the air. Before I can push to my feet, the monster descends on Rhys engulfing him in a black fog. He screams in agony.

I scramble over and reach through the fog finding his arm. My own flesh is burning, but I tug and pull, digging my feet into the concrete to drag Rhys out of the mist.

Footsteps pound the concrete behind me. "Leave him alone!" Claire's eyes are wild as she clutches the knife out in front of her and swipes at the beast. Sparks kick off her knife as she makes contact with the fog. The monster ascends into the sky, abandoning Rhys. Juniper is left unprotected in tears on the corner.

Claire sinks to her knees next to the wounded Blade. He's unrecognizable. Black ash eats away most of his face. Half of his hair has disintegrated, and where there should be skin, blistering black-and-red sludge remains.

Don't cry, Cera. Not now.

"Stay with me, Rhys," Claire pleads. "It's gone. The Legion is gone."

He chokes and wheezes through labored breath. Claire is wrong. The creature isn't gone.

It hovers ten feet above us in mist form, searching. Searching for . . . Juniper. She's pressed up against the corner of the building with her face buried in her hands. I put my hand on Claire's shoulder. She shoves it away and shoots me a glare that sears the truth deep in my soul—this is all my fault. Despite that, I point up and place a blistered finger over my lips.

The rising sun lightens the sky. The mist drifts closer to Juniper. The creature is too high for me to attack. For anyone to attack. I don't have a weapon, and the last one I used was futile.

I curl my fist. I tried taking out the creature, and I failed. The only thing we can do now is get Rhys back to Hesperian and protect Juniper. But how? Claire can't carry him back alone. We can't leave him on the street, but if we don't run, then we'll all be dead. I'll have to distract the beast, make it follow me so Claire and Juniper can get Rhys back.

"Rhys?" Tanji races around the corner, passing Juniper.

As soon as the beast hears her voice, the mist forms into a Legion and launches at Tanji. She dodges the hit. "Nuh-uh. Not today." The creature punctures the ground, exploding into mist before slowly reforming.

The beast is way too close to Juniper, who is whimpering way too loudly. The Legion is definitely after her. Devon said Healers are one of the most vulnerable.

Kellan turns down the other end of the street. "Get out of here!"

He doesn't need to say it twice. I run over and grab Juniper by the hand. "Stay quiet and come with me."

The creature floats back and forth, ten feet off the ground, searching for its desired target. Tanji guides the creature to her location by tapping the knife on the ground with short clinks. "Yeah, I know you hear me."

Kellan lifts Rhys to his feet and wraps an arm around his shoulder, carrying him with Claire's help. Tanji keeps the Legion at bay. She taunts it and shifts, dodging another hit.

Sunrise taints the clouds red. Juniper's limp won't let her run. The Legion shrieks. I turn around in time to see the monster form into a tornado mist, twisting in our direction. Tanji screams after it, dancing wildly, demanding its attention, coercing. "Come after me, coward!" The monster shifts toward her but then spirals after us.

I push Juniper out of the way. The beast slams into my back. I choke on the stench of sulfur. Burns sizzle on my skin, even through the jacket. I'm lifted off the ground, airborne. I cover my face with my arms, but it's too late. My head slams into a light pole. Then my knees hit the ground. Nausea roils. Screams fade, and everything turns black.

20
TAKING SIDES

"Wake up!" Someone shakes me. The ground feels hard and cold beneath me. "Please, wake up!" The squealing soprano voice splits through my head.

I wince and crack open one eye. The blurry world spins. Voices shout. Dark fog swirls then explodes into a million tiny sparks.

"Get her to her feet." I smell wet clay. My head throbs as I am hoisted up.

"What happened?" My dry lips crack. I taste blood.

"She's conscious. Good." Freckles. A face so close, I can count them. A boy with a narrow chin snaps two fingers in front of me. "Cera. What's my name?"

His name? Starts with . . . my mind feels sluggish, as if wading through a swamp. "K . . . Kellan?"

His mouth is a flat line. "Get her back to Hesperian. Tanji and I will handle Rhys."

Rhys, rhymes with geese. Groggy memories creep back. Running. Black mist. Rhys. I turn my head enough to see Tanji and Kellan lifting Rhys off the ground. His head, black and singed. Missing half his hair. Rhys hangs limp. His toes drag along the cement as they carry him.

"He's still alive," the soprano voice says from behind me. It's a curly haired girl with a round face and full cheeks. Jess? I blink. No. Not Jess. Juniper.

"Barely." Claire helps me walk.

Dawn burns like firelight. The smell of wet pavement wakes my hazy mind. The buzzing sound is gone. "The . . . Legion?"

When I'm able to stand on my own, Claire loosens her grip around my waist. "Kellan destroyed it." Her derogatory tone comes through loud and clear.

Juniper steadies me when I stumble off the curb. "The monster was after you. When the guy stabbed it with a knife, the hideous thing exploded like fireworks."

That explains the spark shower. My mind registers one image. Kellan's knife. So only knives kill the monsters. No wonder my weapons proved futile.

We head back to Hesperian in silence. This time, I'm the slow one.

Hesperian is a madhouse when we arrive. Apparently the Blades that ran with Tanji made it back first and rolled out the gossip. Kids run up and down the stairs in panic as murmurs about the attack travel. Fear laces the air, thicker than the residual sulfur left in my nostrils.

Juniper is whisked away from me as soon as we enter the café. I step aside and slump against the wall, parking myself under the Milton quote.

I oft remember, when from sleep
I first awaked . . .
Much wond'ring where
And what I was.

Thanks for the reminder, Milton, but I know what I am now, and it's no fun. Watching Kellan and Tanji drag Rhys through the door makes the days of wondering seem a distant memory.

"Give us room." Tanji scowls as she and Kellan navigate Rhys down the narrow pathway of tables clotted with the newest Hesperian recruits.

Compared to Rhys, my injury is nothing more than a sunburn. He needs Harper's help—and fast. I limp through the crowd and pull back tables and chairs to widen Tanji's path. As soon as I do, others snap out of their dazes and do the same. My fingers and hands burn as I grip the furniture, but I push aside the pain. My injuries could've been a lot worse.

"Everyone's in. Lock the place down." Devon stops halfway down the stairs when he sees the trio turn down the hall. At his command, chaos spins around me. Kids scurry in ten million directions. They grab backpacks, scoop up art projects, and race up the stairs.

Maddox pushes through the mayhem. He's not but ten feet away when Claire intercepts him. He grabs her by the shoulders. "What happened out there?"

She's only too happy to tell him. "Cera ran off instead of going back to Hesperian like she was told. Rhys and I went looking for her. We found her trying to attack a Legion, and Rhys had to step in. The beast hit him before he could strike. None of this would have happened if she had followed orders."

Her voice picks up volume, and the room goes quiet. All eyes fall on me. The disgust from all of them is apparent. Except for Maddox.

"You attacked a Legion?" Maddox makes his way over. His tone is somber, but his eyes spark with excitement.

Claire crosses her arms and stands firm as the crowd behind her grows. "She's not a Blade. She shouldn't have been out there in the first place."

I hold up my burned hands. "I know I was supposed to go back, but I couldn't. That's how I found Juniper. She was hiding from the Legions. I guess they could sense she was a Healer. If someone hadn't found her . . ." I can't get the rest of the words through the giant knot in my throat.

"The Legions would have." Maddox reaches out and takes my hand, turning it over. Three claw marks rip through my palms where I gripped the rebar, but the bleeding has stopped.

Claire points an accusing finger. "That right there is proof of how dangerous she was to the rest of us. She tried to grab hold of a Legion."

I pull my hand away from Maddox. "Rhys was swallowed in the black fog. I had to do something."

"Don't pretend to be a hero. He saved *you*, and now he's back there fighting for his life!" Her eyes well with tears as her voice grows even louder. Murmurs rumble through the café.

Maddox reaches over to Claire and places a hand on her shoulder. His voice softens as he addresses Claire, as well as the gallery of those gathered around. "Rhys will pull through. He's a fighter. *Clearly*." His smile lightens the air. A wave of gratitude washes over me.

Claire's shoulders relax as she laughs through her tears. "He is, isn't he?" She wipes her eyes with her sleeve. "The idiot."

"He'll make it. You'll see." Maddox rubs Claire's arm in comfort before addressing everyone in the room. "But for now, do me a favor. Cut Cera some slack. She's still figuring all this out. She never would have gone if she knew someone would get hurt, I promise."

Maddox speaks absolute truth. The thought of anyone getting hurt rips me up inside. Maddox takes my hand again and inspects the wounds. "We've got to clean you up. A Legion's burn will fester then eat away the skin."

"Good to know." My voice is weak and shaky. Not only that, my head is throbbing. The adrenaline crash coupled with being out all night is catching up to me.

Maddox places a gentle hand on my lower back and steers me forward. The crowd steps to the side to let us through. Despite Maddox's plea, everyone avoids eye contact as he escorts me toward the hallway.

Amide stands guard at the entrance to Harper's room. "No one's allowed. Sorry."

Maddox takes his hand from my back. "Cera was burned by the Legion. We need supplies."

Amide swallows and steps aside. "Ask Devon."

Devon is pacing the room with his arms crossed. The rattan partition is shut. Agonizing moans come from the other side. I force back tears.

"No one's allowed—" Devon stops when he sees us. "Including you."

Maddox gently nudges me to extend my hands to Devon. "Cera needs to get cleaned up." Devon glances at my blisters and then quickly looks away. "Get her some swabs and solution."

Rhys lets out another moan over the sound of clanking metal and running water from the bathroom in the back, but I can't see through the screen. Maddox stops rummaging through the cabinets and looks in the same direction. "Hold him still." Harper's voice is firm.

"Where else were you hit?" Devon asks me, but he avoids glancing at my raw hands as he looks over the rest of me.

"In the back. The beast slammed into me and my head hit a pole. I think I'm okay, but honestly, I'm not sure."

Devon lightly touches the top of my head with his fingertips. Pain radiates through the back of my eyes. I wince and pull away. "You hit something, that's for sure."

Maddox comes over with a fistful of cotton balls and a little jar of green liquid. "Keep me updated on Rhys," he says to Devon. "I'll take Cera over to my space—"

"Gladys will check her wounds. You and I need to talk." Devon's expression is hard.

"About?" Maddox asks as Devon firmly takes the supplies from him and tucks them in the crooks of my elbows.

"Council's been informed of the hit."

"They didn't need to know." Maddox is almost angry. "Harper can—"

"Rhys's injuries are beyond her capabilities."

Maddox's stiffens. "Does Gray know?"

Devon watches Maddox carefully. His tone and his eyes soften. "He's on his way."

Maddox clenches his jaw and then storms out of the room. I stand there with a handful of cotton balls and a jar of green liquid that looks more like sleep medicine. Rhys lets out another unnerving groan.

"Gladys is in the kitchen boiling towels," Devon informs me. "Have her check your wounds."

"Does she have a Healing Bent too?" I ask, hoping I can defer all injuries to her instead of Harper.

"No, but she's been trained to help with the less severe injuries." I'm glad he thinks my burns aren't that big of a deal, even though my fingers are throbbing.

Before I go, I have to ask, "What's the deal with Gray?"

Devon's face is unreadable. "It's nothing to concern yourself with."

"Keep him still. I can't find the vein," Harper's terse voice cuts through the air. Rhys moans in agony.

"Go on." Devon ushers me out of the room. I slip past Amide, who stares at the ground with his hands folded in front like he's saying a silent prayer. I lower my head and walk toward the café. I stop at the entrance. Taking a deep breath, I prepare for the dagger stares that will meet me inside.

After whisking me behind the wall to the back corner near the sink, Gladys sits me down on a barstool, then rubs me down with the solution. She checks all wounds and bandages my arms. When she's finished, she pats me. "All done. Should be good as new by tomorrow."

"Thank you, Gladys." She swaddled my wrists and hands in a way that looks like I'm wearing flesh-colored mittens. I can wiggle my thumb, but that's about it. "Do I have to keep my hands wrapped until tomorrow?" Eating with these lobster claws will be next to impossible.

She tosses the cotton balls in the trash and then washes her hands. "Give it a few hours. Then rinse off the solution." She smiles, but her eyes don't. Thick silence fills the narrow space between us. I've disappointed Gladys. My stomach turns hollow. As I slide off the barstool, she sets the dishrag on the counter and says, "Tell me something, dear."

I squirm at her tone. "Yes, ma'am?"

She walks around the corner, back to the stove. "The number you gave me . . ."

"Oh." I take a deep breath and follow after her. She's going to chew me out for lying. I can feel it coming, and I'm too tired to come up with a plausible excuse. I rest my shoulder against the wall as she stirs a pot of boiling towels.

"I had a bit of trouble reading the numbers clearly. These old eyes aren't what they used to be." Her tone tells me she knows the truth, but she's kind enough not to call me out. "Would you be a dear and write that number again?" She slides a piece of paper and a pen down the counter. "And maybe add your address in case your mother doesn't answer."

I hesitate. Gladys patiently stirs the steaming pot, but she's watching me out the corner of her eye. I pick up the pen and write my address and Mom's phone number. The real one. I slide the paper and pen back. I have no clue how my mother will react when Gladys calls her, but Mom deserves to know I'm all right. And honestly, I want to know she's all right as well. One thing's for sure, when Mom finds out where I am, she'll storm in and demand we leave. I won't have to worry about being locked up for being a Seer, but that also means there's a good chance I'll never see anyone from Hesperian ever again.

Gladys glances at the paper before tucking the information in her pocket. "Is there any reason why I *shouldn't* call your mama?"

I put my bandaged tong-hands across my middle. "I guess I like hanging out here. Until today, I didn't want to leave." It's the truth, not the whole truth, but enough.

Gladys takes the steaming towels out of the pot with a wooden spoon and transfers the rags into a red bowl. "Today was unfortunate, but that one incident doesn't change that fact that you're a part of this family."

"If that's so, then why is everyone whispering about the place being shut down? They're blaming me . . ." And with good cause, I have to admit.

Gladys takes my mitten hands in hers. I can't feel her touch through the bandage. "It's not you, dear. Hesperian is only a safe house until someone gets hurt. Then things have to change.

Council believes these kids need proper training."

She lets out the same resigned sigh she did when we were baking. "I can't say I disagree." She must see remorse in my eyes because she lets go of my hands. "You've been out all night and need sleep and time to heal." She brushes my hair away from my face and then reaches up to pull something out of her hair nest. She takes out a silver hairpin with a white flower and slips it behind my ear. "You're one of us, dear. Don't forget it." My throat tightens. Jess is the only other person who's ever given me a gift. "Now, let's put you in the girls' common room upstairs, away from the noise." Gladys says nothing about my watering eyes. "You rest, and then we'll see what the remainder of the day brings."

I'm not convinced sleeping will change anything. However, my body does feel heavy and my eyes won't stay open much longer. I've got no choice but to comply. Gladys carries the red bowl in the crook of her arm as she walks me through the café. I follow, hiding behind her. Gladys lifts her head, inspecting stares as we walk. Clustered teens with concerned faces half smile as she passes. Her eyes are warm but thick with warning and a reminder to love.

As we reach the stairs, Claire passes but won't look at me. Gladys touches her arm and stops her. "Take this to Harper, would you, love?" She hands Claire the bowl before she can protest. "And tell Devon I want you to check in on our boy, Rhys, and stay at his side. Bring me an update, later, will you?" Claire's lips pull into a thankful smile. She takes off down the hall.

Following Gladys up the stairs, I focus on climbing each step, one at a time, while trying not to look back because I can feel the glares—even if they are mere curiosity at this point—as I ascend. Rhys's agonizing moans play over and over in my head, haunting me.

Finally, we reach the top. The air is warmer on the second floor. The space opens to a large dance studio with pine floors and wall-to-wall mirrors. Gladys walks down the short hall that smells of oil paints and wet clay.

"Rest a while and come down when you're ready." Gladys opens the last door at the end of the hall. The air is damp in the large room. Eight cots, four on each wall, with fluffy green blankets and plush white pillows decorate the space—the only furniture in the place. Most of the cots have shoes tucked beside them or clothes hanging over the metal footrail. Two in the far back appear empty. I take the one on the right near the brick wall, kick off my shoes, and slip under the clean covers. Gladys stands at the door with her hand over the light switch. "I'll have fresh clothes ready for you in the bathroom across the hall when you wake."

Lights go out. I sink into the mattress. As Gladys shuts the door, I curl on my side and lie there, letting the darkness swallow me. The room feels too big. Too cold and empty. I pull my bandaged hands to my chest and quiver as a thick knot swells in my throat. I close my eyes and weep. Memories of the attack resurface, but, after a while, sleep wrestles them into a dream.

21

THE WHOLE TRUTH

I wake drenched in sweat with a scream on my lips and an aching helplessness. Jess. Rhys. The list keeps growing. The vivid dream retreats into darkness and slips from my mind but leaves me with a lingering rawness. Something rumbles outside the building. Motorcycle engines, not a buzzing sound. I relax somewhat. For a moment, I've forgotten where I am, until I wipe damp hair from my face with my bandaged mitten hands.

I'm groggy, but I push myself up. How long did I sleep? Light from the hall peers into the room. The bedsheets and blankets are thrashed in a heap on the ground. I kick them aside, set my feet on the rough wood floor, and sit still. Soft voices waft from down the hall. A guitar strums. I stumble through the dusky room, using the bedrails as a guide. Gladys promised clean clothes in the bathroom across the hall, and it's probably time to take off these tight bandages.

I lock the bathroom door and turn the water on the hottest setting before stripping down and taking off the bandages. My fingers are swollen and the skin looks a little red but feels relatively normal without any scars or blisters. I take off the hairpin and step into the shower. I pull the curtain and let the hot water wash over me.

After cleaning up and throwing on jeans and a tan-and-white-striped sweater, I make my way down the hall. I twist my hair into a messy knot and tuck the silver pin behind my ear, then glance up at the stained glass art that overlooks the café. The glass is dark. Did I lose an entire day? I can't tell if it's way past dinner or early in the morning. The quiet café feels somber. Instruments have been put away. Only a small number of kids I don't recognize hang out in the space below. A faint scent of tangy metal—or maybe it's blood—lingers in the air and turns my stomach. I search the room. The floor and unoccupied tables are wiped clean. If there was blood somewhere, there's no trace of it now.

I take a butterscotch scone off the counter and turn around, searching for a space as far away from everyone as possible. The booths are taken, and a few tables near Maddox's alcove are occupied, so I pull out a chair near the counter and sit alone. As I break off a piece of the scone, the girls in the booth whisper and stare at me. Some with angry scowls and others with accusing glances. The morsel turns bitter in my mouth. I'm not that hungry anymore.

I could go find Devon and see if Rhys is any better, but even if I did, Devon won't let me stay in the room. I wander through the kitchen to find Gladys to see if she's talked to my mom, but the place is empty and the counters are wiped clean and dry. Maybe she's in the cellar. I go out the back door and make my way down the stairs. The storeroom is empty, but the sound of grunting slaps and hard punches comes from the gym. As quietly as possible, I tiptoe down the hall to see who else is down here.

I stand at the doorway and peer around the threshold into the room. It's Maddox. His knuckles are bright red, cut open and bleeding. Sweat drips from his face as he punches the snot out of the leather bag. The bag sways with each hit. Over and over he attacks, making solid contact. I don't know him all that well, but contrary to his laid-back attitude, he seems to be unleashing a deep-seated fury on the unsuspecting bag.

After a while, he sinks to his knees, completely spent. He rests his head on the punching bag and sits there, still and silent. I suddenly feel like I'm trespassing. Maybe I shouldn't be here. Maybe I'm interrupting a private moment he doesn't want anyone to see. I start to move away when he pulls a piece of paper from his back pocket. He unfolds the page. It's a sketch, but from this far, I can't make it out, only that it looks to be the silhouette of a person. His hands tremble as he stares down at the drawing. After a long moment, he crumples the paper and gives the bag one final punch, but the hit lacks bite. Before he can see me, I move away. I don't want to go back upstairs, not yet, so I duck into the storeroom to hide for a while.

Earlier, Maddox stormed off when Devon said Council knew about the attack. Then Gladys confirmed the rumors about Council turning Hesperian, Maddox's dream and home, into a formal training camp. I know it's not all my fault, but I can't help but feel responsible for ruining everything Maddox cares about. Right now, I feel about as wanted in Hesperian as this room of broken chairs and forgotten, useless furniture—except for the table Gladys left unfinished.

The pieces we laid out are still in place, and the mortar has dried, but she hasn't filled in the grooves between the pieces. I open the container of grout she's left on the chair. I'll stay down here a while and work on the table of broken glass. A memorial to Jess for the paper mosaic she never finished.

I pull out a chair and sit to finish the work. If Gladys talked to Mom, it won't be long before she comes to get me. I use the trowel to slop a gray mound of grout in the center of the table, burying the pieces of soft pink glass. Gladys has left a cotton cloth next to a plastic container filled with clean water.

"Cera?" Maddox looks surprised as he slides the door wide open. His sweaty hair sticks to his face, but he doesn't brush it back. "What are you doing in here?"

I pick up the dingy rag. I'm not sure if I should say something about seeing him in the workout room or not. But it's me, so I do. "I was searching for a place to be alone for a while. I'm not exactly a hero upstairs. I saw you. You were . . . working out. I didn't want to interrupt, so I thought I'd come in here and help Gladys finish a few things." I look down and unfurl the poor rag that I've twisted into a tight cord.

Maddox steps into the room. "Don't let them get to you. It's not your fault." Even though he's the second person to say so, his words don't erase my guilt.

I let the rag drown in the water before wringing it out. "Thanks, but the fact that you just mentioned it makes it feel like maybe it is." I glance at him before wiping the grout in the crevices of the table.

"You're a Guardian. You were following your instinct. Rhys wasn't trained."

"And because of that, because he's hurt, Gladys told me Hesperian can't be a safe house anymore. Council will make it a training camp and change everything you've built here." I am a little too intense in smearing the chalky grout all over the table, clouding the vibrant glass.

Maddox tucks his hands in his jean pockets as he makes his way over. His knuckles are wrapped with thick tape. "I guess I was wrong to think we could have a place to encourage and create and not have to deal with the war the way Council says we should."

"You weren't wrong. I was." When our eyes meet, the Current races through me, again stealing my breath. I look down at the muddy table. "I messed things up. If I hadn't attacked the Legion, Rhys wouldn't have been hurt and Hesperian wouldn't be turning into a training camp, or whatever." I sigh in frustration. "I'm so sorry. I can't help but feel like all I've done is create problems since I've arrived."

Maddox pulls up a chair and sits across from me. "You belong here." He glances at the furniture stacked along the walls. "Well . . . not in *here*." He flashes the same diffusing smile he used on Claire. Somehow that smile manages to wipe away the shame smeared across my heart. "You belong with the rest of us. Council's wanted to close this place down ever since it opened. It was only a matter of time before they found a reason."

I focus on swirling the murky grout through the crevices. When I don't respond, he continues. "No one imagined you finding a Healer on a routine outing. The Legion fought hard because of that. The only thing the Legion would have fought harder for is a Seer. If Juniper had that Bent, chances are you'd all be dead. Somehow they sense and follow the strength of the Current. They'd do just about anything to get to a Seer."

I catch my breath. If what he says is true, then Gladys and Maddox are both wrong. The attack *was* my fault. I'm the reason the creatures are ramping up and getting closer. If they can sense my Current, it's no wonder Mom wanted me to stay inside and would move me when I had a vision. I'm a threat to everyone around me.

Maddox continues. "It's clear you're a Guardian. You've proven that. Maybe Devon's right and your other Bent is Caretaker, but you haven't been trained."

Maddox's voice is gentle, safe. Alone in this room of broken, discarded furniture, I want to tell him the truth. That it's my fault the Legions are circling closer. That my staying here will draw the creatures to this location and put everyone in danger, but I don't want to be smothered and locked away either. I rinse the cloth in the water and wring it out again.

When I drop the cloth on the table, Maddox takes hold of my hand, stopping me. "Cera. Talk to me."

The Current rages between us as I look at him. His soft eyes plead for the truth. Heat rises to my cheeks. I manage to pull my hand away and stare at the hurricane pattern in the table. Tell him. Just tell him the whole truth.

Even Milton agrees. He prods me with the verse: "*Let us no more contend, nor blame . . . but strive / In offices of love how we may lighten / Each other's burden in our share of woe.*"

Fine. I hear you, Milton. And yes, maybe confessing is the answer. I sit back and tuck a loose strand of hair behind my ear. "I need to tell you something, so hear me out for a minute, okay?" I twist my fingers in my lap, hiding them under the table. I take in a deep breath and fix my eyes on one yellow tile dulled by the smearing grout.

"The day my dad left, he was drunk, as usual. My parents were screaming. Bottles broke on the kitchen floor. They thought I was asleep, but I was hiding behind the wingback chair in the living room. I heard every word. He called me a monster. He said I'd destroy everyone in my life. And it's true . . ."

I swallow hard and run the tip of my finger along the edges of the honey tile, wiping it clean. "Mom has moved me every year since then. I didn't make a lot of friends, but the few I did have . . ." I bite my bottom lip to keep it from quivering. "They all died." I risk a quick glance up at Maddox. He listens, soaking in every word. "Until now, I've never felt like I belonged anywhere. Now that I'm here, learning all about this second realm and everything, and it seems like you're the only one wanting to be my friend, I'm terrified the same thing will happen to you."

Maddox leans back and presses his lips together. The spark in his eyes dims as he looks down. He's disappointed. "Maddox . . . I'm . . ."

"You're part of us, and if you give it time, you'll have more friends than me." He sits up in his seat. "I don't plan on dying soon, if that's what you're worried about." He tries to smile, but it falls flat. "I get that all that stuff happened when you and your mom were alone. It makes sense that she was worried about you being found. I'm not sure why your friends were attacked when you weren't Awakened yet . . . but that's in the past. We're all in this together now."

I glance at him as he searches me. The tepid air in the dusky room thickens. I spit out my confession. "Maddox, I'm a Seer." The words choke in my throat, but once they come out, a deep weight inside me buoys to the surface, breaking free. Maddox absorbs my words as his eyes scan back and forth across mine. I can't tell if he believes me, or what.

I squirm. I take the rag and wipe away the mud that covers the blue glass pieces. "I've known I was a Seer ever since Devon told me about the different Bents. I didn't tell anyone because . . . This is so selfish." My face turns hot. "I didn't want to get locked up. I want to learn how to fight beasts and even take down Sage, if I have to. I want to stop them from killing anyone ever again. I should have never gone out with Kellan. It was *me* those creatures were after. I didn't know it then, but I know now. And now Rhys . . ." My fingers are covered in gritty sand, and I rub them together nervously. "I can't be a part of this community and put everyone in danger. I'm aware that Council or the Alliance, or whatever, says I should be locked up, but I can't live a protected life if people are dying on account of those beasts. If I can't stop from having visions, then maybe I can change them so no one else gets hurt."

I wipe my teary eyes with the back of my clean hand. "People were hurt because I lied and kept things secret. I'm so sorry. I don't want to be a monster anymore, but I don't know how not to be . . ."

I feel raw, open and exposed. Thoughts churn behind Maddox's eyes, but he doesn't speak. I wish he'd say something. Anything. I rinse my hands along with the rag in the dirty water.

Maddox leans forward, and when he finally speaks, his voice drops low. "Council doesn't need to know about your Bent."

"What?" I drop the rag on the table. I half expected him to flip out or call for backup.

Maddox sits back, but his voice stays quiet, so much so that I have to lean in to hear him. "I know it sounds risky, but lately Council is only focused on sticking to rules and codes. They're not concerned with finding new Awakened the way they should. Kids out there are being left without a clue as to what's happening around them. Things have to change. Someone has to go find these Awakened and teach them what they are. If your second Bent can guide us to new Awakened, or better yet, show us ways to defeat the creatures, then we have to try. Maybe we can even find some way to take them down for good, but in either case, we can't do it alone."

His use of the word "we" sends my heart racing. If Maddox is right and we could change the outcome of my visions and use them as a way to save others instead of bringing harm, then maybe I won't be this destructive monster anymore. And for once in my life, I don't feel like I have to go solo. "You really want to end this too?"

"More than you know." Maddox's gaze lingers on mine a little too long.

"So . . . what do we do?" I hope he doesn't take my soft tone the wrong way. "I mean about me . . . about the fact that I'm . . ."

"I don't know how much control you have over that side of your Bent, but if you can, hang tight until I can work a few things out. We'll need to get you harnessed." He picks up on my skeptical frown because he quickly adds, "Not you. Your visions. It's a way to let others see what you do." Mom must have been harnessed to me. That's how she was able to see my visions. "I have a few people I trust who will help us out," Maddox continues. "Maybe we can't overthrow a system that's been in place for hundreds of years, but with your Bent, we can start something new."

Despite the fact that I know "hanging tight" is impossible

for me, I smile because his belief is contagious. "You sure you're not also a Blade?" His set jaw and determined eyes make him read like one.

Maddox's tone sours. "No. I'm not."

My cheeks warm. "I meant that as—"

Something moves at the doorway. It's Claire. I don't know how much she heard, but her suspicious gaze darts back and forth between Maddox and me. "Maddox? *Harper's* looking for you." Claire's emphasis on Harper's name makes her subtext clear. I know how things might look right now, but Harper's got nothing to worry about. I'm laser-locked on one thing, and one thing only—saving lives.

Maddox clears his throat and pushes away from the table. "Yeah. Be there in a few. I'm helping Cera get her artwork upstairs. It won't dry down here."

"Thank you," I say to Maddox. I work hard to ignore Claire's unbelieving eyes, even though her stare pierces through me. "Claire, how is Rhys?"

"Council transported him earlier today. Last I heard he was stable, thanks to Harper."

I try to smile. "That's good news."

Claire responds by marching off, boots clomping down the hall and up the stairs. I take a deep breath.

Maddox lays a hand on my arm. "It's not your fault." I nod, wanting to believe him. "Now, let's get your masterpiece out of this dungeon."

Maddox could carry the table on his own, but he grips one end and waits for me to grab the other side.

I hook my fingers under the rough wood. "For the record, this is Gladys's artwork."

His expression tells me he doesn't believe me. "Gladys designs with straight lines and pastels. She never creates anything this bold."

I adjust my grip because the table is a little heavier than I expected. "You mean a jagged hurricane isn't in her repertoire?"

"A hurricane?" Maddox examines the design. "I thought you created a flower in spring rain."

"Seriously? That's such a girly response." I look at the pattern again. In a weird way, he's right. "Okay, I take that back. I suppose from your angle, it does." I laugh lightly. "I'll take your interpretation, since a budding flower is a lot less destructive."

We walk the table to the door, and Maddox stops and waits so I can go through first. "Nah, I like your idea of a hurricane better. A storm that powerful can change any landscape." When he smiles, the gleam returns to his eyes. "You ready?"

22

WAITING FOR DAWN

When Maddox and I make it upstairs, most of the sconces are off, leaving only scattered pockets of muted light. We stumble through the dark. Actually, I'm the one to stumble. Maddox is steady as we maneuver the table to a space near his alcove.

The café is deserted, save for a few night owls curled up in wingback chairs with the blue glow of computer screens illuminating their faces and a flirty couple hiding in the shadows of the booth near the front entrance. Their teasing laughter and hushed whispers collide with tense voices flowing from Harper's room down the hall.

Maddox grabs two chairs and sets them at the table. "Meet me here tomorrow."

"Tomorrow?" Even though I lower my voice, without a room full of bodies, the sound echoes in the vast space. "Let's do this now. I still don't know much about being . . . a Seer." I mouth the last word. "I need someone to train me."

"I've got someone who can help, but not here. I need until tomorrow to pull a group together."

I plant my feet. "What's the plan? Blind following doesn't go well for me." As in, doing so just got me in a load of trouble and Rhys almost killed.

He holds his hands out, a signal for me to keep calm. "I'll have a plan in the morning." He lowers his voice and steps closer. "If I can pull things together by tomorrow, we'll leave the following morning."

"Leave Hesperian?" The words come out way too loud.

Maddox tries to hide his downcast expression but fails. "Council's taking over in a few days. If the plan's going to work, we'll have to find someplace new."

I understand, but my heart still feels heavy at the thought of leaving. Gladys is here. The food is so good. Despite everything that's happened, I've found a home and, as par for the course, I'm being forced to flee once again. And what about Mom? For all I know, she'll be here in the morning to drag me away. "What do I tell Gladys? She was calling my mom."

"Cera? Is that you?" Juniper's soft, airy voice chimes down from the top of the stairs.

"If possible, stay out of sight until I can work things out," Maddox whispers hurriedly.

"I've been looking for you." Juniper races down to meet us. Her curly hair is somewhat corralled by a headband, and a yellow flower is tucked behind her ear. Her arms are free from honey-salve bandages. "Oh. Hi, Maddox." Juniper gives a bashful grin. It doesn't help that Maddox's warm smile lights up the dark. She can't even look directly at him.

"Oh, hey, Juniper. Take Cera upstairs and make sure she gets some rest, would you?"

"Maddox?" Harper's voice echoes from down the hall. Although I can't see her yet, the sound of her ballet flats patters across the stone floor in our direction.

He touches my arm. "We'll talk tomorrow."

When he walks away, Juniper pulls me up the stairs. I go willingly because the last thing I want is for Harper to find me anywhere near Maddox, and in the dark, no less. I have no doubt that Maddox trusts Harper and will have her come with us, and I don't need her hating me any more than she already does.

Juniper, reminding me of a little pixie with dark curls and porcelain skin, chatters happily. "This place is incredible, isn't it? I've never had food that tasted so good, and ever since I left home, I haven't had a hot shower or a bed."

She takes me into the sleeping quarters. The room, a temporary shelter, looks like an orphanage straight out of an old-time movie. Some girls sit on their beds talking, some pace the room while brushing out their hair, and others lay their clothes neatly over the rails. I've seen most of these girls around but don't know their names.

Juniper escorts me through the room, oblivious to the curious glances. "I have one sister. Older. She hasn't been around for the last few months. Being here feels like having a room full of them. Oh!" Her eyes light up and her round face smiles wide. "Speaking of . . . I get to work with Harper tomorrow." She springs to the empty cot across from mine. "They say she's the best. If it weren't for her, that boy would have died."

The cold air sits heavy on my skin. "I heard she can heal just about anything." I flicker a smile.

Juniper pulls back the corner of the sheet before jumping on her bed with a hard bounce that makes the coils squeak. "Did you know she's been through five foster homes? Maddox saved her. Found her after she'd been beaten close to death and brought her here."

"No," I say quietly. "I had no idea."

Juniper sits crisscross-style and grabs her ankles before leaning forward. "Anyway, I've been looking for you because I wanted to say thanks for doing what you did—for finding me. I guess, like Harper, I'd be dead if it weren't for you." Juniper's words warm the chill in the room as the weight of her reality takes hold.

She's right. No one was out looking for her. Blades wouldn't have found her. The Legions would have. And feasted.

"I'm glad you're here, Juniper." My smile comes naturally. Finding new Awakened and saving lives—Maddox is right, this is what we're born to do. I sit on the edge of the bed and let my finger brush over the soft green blanket.

"If you're not working with someone tomorrow and have time . . ." Juniper's voice is wistfully hesitant. "Do you want to hang out? If not, I totally understand. You've probably got others to find." Her words carry through the room that has suddenly gone quiet. I can't help but feel as if the rest of the girls are waiting for my response, despite the fact that they pretend to be occupied in fluffing pillows, arranging shoes, or scrolling through their phones.

"I won't be here much longer. Gladys is calling my mom," I say. Two facts, but not necessarily the truth when put together.

Tanji walks into the room wrapped in a towel. The room puckers at her presence. "Lights out. I've been up over twenty-four hours, and I don't want to hear a word."

As I pull the blanket to my chin, Tanji flips the switch by the door. Darkness overtakes the room. I feel awkward. Out of place lying in a room full of girls, most of whom I don't know. I can't get comfortable, and every time I shift, the springs squeak.

It doesn't take but a few seconds in the dark when a girl on the far side of the room breaks the silence. "Tanji, is it true that Council is taking over in two days?"

"I told you to shut up and go to sleep."

Another second of silence passes. This time Juniper speaks. "Is it bad if they take over?"

"Not if you like hanging out with on-duty Marine commanders." The sarcastic response comes from the girl in the bed next to mine.

"You'll get proper training in your Bent." Tanji sounds annoyed, but at least she's not angry.

Somewhere across the room, a soprano voice quivers. "Won't that mean we'll have to fight in the war?"

"Not everyone. It depends on your Bent and rank. Now shut it and go to sleep." Tanji's voice is tight with warning.

No one says another word. The damp air fills with the sound of the second hand of a ticking clock and, eventually, rhythmic breathing.

Reality sinks in heavier than my body on the mattress, despite the fact that after confessing to Maddox, the weight inside me feels lighter. I lie in the dark and feel . . . wobbly. Weak. Closing my eyes, I let Maddox's words, his smile, the flicker of his eyes on mine, sink in. He believes what he says so passionately, it's hard for me not to buy in to his ideals. But how can my Bent help save others when all I do is draw the enemy closer? I listen for any shrieks circling outside these walls. Not hearing any, I tuck my hands behind my head. All I can do is lie in the dark and wait for dawn.

The room is empty when I wake. Some beds are made, some only half made. A pile of clothes, washed and stacked neatly by Gladys, sits at the foot of my bed. I know it was her because my clothes have a faint scent of peaches and vanilla. I get dressed, brush my teeth with the kit Gladys left, and try my best to control my unruly hair. No luck, so I twist my stringy locks into their messy knot, tuck the hairpin back above my ear, and head downstairs. Why didn't anyone wake me? It's way past breakfast. Maybe even closer to lunch.

Vibrant conversation once again fills the café. Most of the tables and chairs are occupied. I jog down the stairs and blend into the crowd as quickly as I can, searching for Maddox. No one pays much attention to me, which is good.

As I pass the pastry counter, I choose a blueberry muffin from the basket.

"They're downstairs," the girl with the floral headkerchief says, keeping her back to me as she pours a cup of coffee in a ceramic mug.

I'm not sure if she's addressing me and not someone else, until she slides the coffee my way. "Thanks," I say.

She gives a slight nod and walks off. I'm only a coffee drinker out of necessity, today being one of those days. Plus, the smooth chocolate taste beats drinking one of Harper's bitter elixirs so I can stay awake later on. I take a few quick sips, thankful that it's hot enough to warm me up but not burn my tongue.

I set the cup on the counter and make my way down into the cellar with muffin in hand. Voices come from the workout room. One belongs to Maddox. Adrenaline kickstarts my pulse. I've never trusted anyone the way I've trusted him. What was I thinking? I don't even know him all that well. What if telling him the truth was a mistake? I guess I'm about to find out.

I take a deep breath and walk through the door.

Maddox stands in the middle of the room wearing black jeans torn at the knees and a fitted white T-shirt. He's surrounded by a handful of people: Amide, the ever-smiling drummer; a stocky guy wearing a denim jacket with two colliding swords on the back that belies his baby face; a biker with a buzz cut and goatee; and . . . Tanji. To my surprise, Harper isn't in the room—yet.

Maddox is brimming with excitement as he talks to Amide. "Can that happen today?"

Amide nods. He spots me at the doorway and waves. "Good late-late-morning to you." Amide's contagious smile spreads wide across his face.

I give a small finger wave. "Morning."

Maddox comes over to meet me, excited. "Amide's family has a place we can use as a temporary setup. Big house with acres of land."

"That's great." I eye the others across the room. "Do they know about . . . me?"

Maddox's excitement falls. "Not yet. I want you to train first. That way, we'll be better prepared once we hit the streets."

I've just taken a bite of muffin, and the idea of leaving makes it lodge in my throat. "So tomorrow, then?"

"Amide will set up the new safe house. I've got a few others I want to come along. I'll talk to them today."

I lick blueberry off my fingers. "What about Gladys?"

Amide must have ears that can hear through walls, or I wasn't as quiet as I thought, because he says, "You better believe we need Gladys."

Maddox turns to Amide. "I'll talk to her later. After yesterday, she might not agree. Besides, we need to create something new, not recreate Hesperian. We need a place to train and hunt while we bring in as many new Awakened as we can find. What happened to Rhys can't ever happen again."

Tanji nods in agreement. "What about weapons?"

Maddox walks me to the group clustered near the punching bags. "Gustav's got that handled." He pats the baby-faced, denim-jacket guy on the shoulder.

Gustav gives a thumbs-up. "It won't happen until after Council arrives, but I can secure a crate, maybe two."

"That's a start and more than we have now," Maddox says. "Meet in my space later this afternoon. We'll decide when to leave."

As Amide walks to the door with the others, he says, "If Gladys isn't coming, then I'm telling her today is my birthday. I want a fat meal and a big party before I leave."

The biker with the goatee lets out a deep, rumbling laugh. "I'm all for that."

"Is it your birthday?" I ask. Mine isn't too far away either. It's next week, but with everything that's happened, I forgot. Then again, I haven't looked forward to my birthday for the past ten years.

Amide's smile is as mischievous as the glint in his eye. "It could be," he says. Gustav and Goatee laugh. Everyone leaves, except for Maddox and Tanji.

"All right." Tanji walks up to me. In her sports bra and workout tights, her deep olive skin shines over her muscles. She stops in front of me and rolls out her shoulders with a fierce stare painted on her smooth face. "Time to fight."

23

DUCK AND ROLL

"You want me to fight you?" Caged in the workout room, I work hard to keep my tone casual as Tanji towers over me. Maybe she'll use this training session as payback for what happened on the streets. I'm not sure. But I am positive about one thing: my elbow maneuver won't work on her cut abs.

"Do you have any fighting skills?" Maddox rubs down the tape on his knuckles. The edges curl up, exposing the raw skin underneath.

I take a quick mental inventory of my skill set. "Nothing formal, but I've been able to break away from both you and Kellan by using my elbow—and I can run fast."

"Both useless against what we're fighting." Tanji's cutting tone makes me want to hide behind the punching bag. She shoots a quick, irritated glance at Maddox before staring me down— again. "Look, about what you did out on the street . . . finding that girl, going after the Legion, then trying to rescue Rhys? It was stupid . . . but it took guts." The hard lines on her face soften. "Ain't nobody here got what you got. Everyone can sense it. Makes most of 'em afraid. Still, that don't matter when you mess with the second realm. If you don't learn to fight, you're gonna end up dead."

In a weird way, I think that was a compliment. My lips tug into a somewhat-smile.

"Now listen. When we walk out that door, you betta' be ready." Tanji rolls up her fist. "The minute you sense something come at you, duck and roll."

"Duck and roll sounds like a gourmet dish." I laugh out of sheer nerves because with all that muscle, Tanji is absolute terror wrapped in skin and performance wear.

"You think we're playing games?" Tanji's dark lips highlight her frown. "Go on and show me how you duck and roll." Cold air whips near my face. Tanji swings her fist so fast, I almost don't dodge the hit. I grab my knees and bend over as my pulse rockets. She almost punched me! She would have if I didn't move.

Maddox, who is standing near the door watching, steps in my direction but stops himself when I recover.

"That ain't ducking *or* rolling." Tanji rolls her eyes. "You bend over like that and you'll get slammed in the back." She smashes her forearm into my spine. I collapse on the floor as all the air leaves my lungs. "Just like that. *Bam.* You'll be dead. Cormorant claw through the heart or soul sucked out by a Legion."

I lie there stunned, feeling a throb in my spine, unsure if I can even move my legs. With my cheek flat on the mat, the sweaty gym smell is so strong, I can taste it.

Maddox holds out his hands. "Tanji. That's—"

"It's okay." I wipe my mouth and push up to my knees. Gritting my teeth to hide the pain, I say, "Let me try again."

I bring myself to my feet, steady my breathing and loosen my shoulders. I can learn this maneuver if I pretend this is the same game Mom played with me when I was little. She would toss a small pillow at me, and I'd have to move out of the way so it wouldn't hit me. I'd always collapse in a fit of giggles because I wanted to get bonked by it. Tanji's iron fist is far from plush fabric, and I sure don't want to feel its punch.

I find a focal point on the wall the way Mom taught me. In this case, my focus happens to be the light switch near the door, not far from where Maddox stands. I watch for Tanji's fist out of the corner of my eye. The moment I feel the air move, I duck and not-so-gracefully roll on the ground with a hard thud. Luckily the floor mat cushions my fall, but not before I bust my lip and taste blood.

Tanji rolls out her shoulders. "Better. Your landing needs work. Use your forearm as a brace and push off your left leg, then roll. Don't land on your shoulder—or hit your head. Get up. Try again." She holds out her hand to help me up.

I nod and prepare to try again. I brush the hair out of my face and set my focus on the light switch. Tanji shifts. This time her left fist swings forward. The air splits and—

"What's going on in here?"

I turn my head. Devon's voice is nothing but a faint echo as pain explodes across my face. My feet lift off the ground, and I slam hard into the cold punching bag. The next thing I know, I'm sinking onto the floor mat.

"Cera?" Maddox pushes past Tanji and kneels beside me. He touches my chin, inspecting my jaw. "Are you okay?"

Devon's boots slap against the floor mat. "What in the world?"

Tanji shakes out her fist and wiggles her fingers. "We're working out."

I hazily look up at Devon as he towers over me with a deep frown carved across face.

"Did I at least roll?" I manage to ask. "'Cause I know I flew." I try to laugh but it hurts. "Just busted my lip a little." And maybe my jaw.

Devon motions Maddox away from me. "Go get her some ice." Devon helps me to my feet and inspects my face. "Shake it off. You'll bruise for sure, but you'll be okay."

Tanji opens a mini-refrigerator in the back corner. "I saw you about to move. Then you didn't." She takes out a cloth ice pack and hands it to Maddox.

I try not to wince as Maddox gently places the ice on my jaw. I take over holding the cold pack.

Devon glares at Tanji. "She's not a Blade. She doesn't have the same instincts you do. What were you thinking?"

Maddox answers, "We were training her as a Guardian."

Devon raises an eyebrow. "Since when did—"

"I asked them to help me out. Hope that's okay," I lie and try not to wince because it hurts to talk.

Devon looks at me. "Any training will go through me from now on."

Tanji crosses her arms. "You telling me we can't even spar without running it by you?"

Devon mirrors her stance and scowl. "Council wants an account of what we do, so whether you're warming up, working out, or you're training, yes, I need to know."

"Devon, have you—" Harper stops at the door. Her cheery expression morphs into hurt when she sees the four of us clustered together. She's wearing a lot less makeup, but the tight T-shirt remains. "Did I miss some kind of meeting?" She twists the ends of her hair around her index finger.

Devon's fleeting gaze sweeps over Harper. "No, and we're getting your stuff now. I haven't forgotten." He flashes me a terse glance. "Cera, come with me."

"Where?" I lift the ice pack. Tiny patches of blood from my lip dot the fabric. "Harper needs a few ingredients. Let's go." He turns on his heel.

"You're going outside?" Maddox's quick look is full of warning. I read his thoughts loud and clear. If the creatures are around, they will sense my Current as a Seer—and now the scent of blood from my lip. Once I step outside, they'll not only find me but all of us.

As Devon strides toward the door, I stay near the punching bag. Following Devon outside will put everyone in danger. But he'll know I'm hiding something if I give him grief about not going.

I look to Maddox for a solution, but Devon, now in full-blown military mode, barks, "I said now!"

I've got to figure a way out of going outside. There's no way I'll put everyone in danger again. As I hand Maddox the ice pack, our eyes meet with mutual understanding and a kick from that blasted Current that won't go away.

I turn to Devon. "How far do we have to go to grab the ingredients?"

"Not far." Devon waits for me at the door.

"You're taking *her*?" Harper's mouth gapes as she blocks the doorway. "You don't let anyone see what's up there."

Devon ignores Harper and brushes past her. She looks downright dejected. If I wasn't so laced with worry, I'd probably gloat.

As Devon goes up the narrow cellar stairs and makes his way back to the café, a thought hits me. He wanted me to test out all the Bents. What if he wants me to meet his grandfather, the Seer? As far as I know, I haven't tested as a Caretaker, Healer, or Seer.

I hold my throbbing jaw and jog up the steps after Devon. The warm, vanilla-scented air thaws my fingers. "Does your grandfather live here? He's not around, is he?"

"Pop?" Devon sounds surprised. "No, he's not here. We have an apartment a couple blocks away. Why?"

I relax a little. But now I'm not sure how to answer without sounding suspicious. "You wanted me to check out all Bents. Gladys told me he was a Seer."

Devon doesn't slow his pace. "You'll meet him later. If you're a Seer, he'll know."

I focus on acting nonchalant. "How so?"

Devon stops at the grand staircase and places one hand on

the thick wooden banister. He turns and waits for me to catch up. "Not only would you have had a vision by now, but you'd have a distinct ability to read messages embedded in artwork."

Like seeing Jess dying on the road in my mom's drawing? Or the number five embedded in Maddox's sketch? I bite my lip. He makes no mention of my connection with Milton, and I'm glad. "Yeah. That makes sense."

Devon jogs up the wooden staircase that leads to the second-floor dance studio and sleeping quarters. I'm not sure where we're headed, but I search for a way out. "Hey, Devon? I'm thinking maybe I should go find Gladys. She was gonna call my mom."

"Gladys isn't here."

"Oh." Strike one.

When we reach the top of the steps, Devon shoots me a questioning glance. "You all right?"

"Me? Oh . . . I just don't know how my mom will take the news of me being here."

"Gladys will work things out. Don't you worry."

Instead of taking the hall that leads to the girls' room, Devon follows the balcony rail to the left. Floorboards creak as we pass a room that smells of heated metal and aged paper. I peer into it as we pass. Looks like a semi-library, except someone's left a metal engraving plate with shavings and dentist-looking tools on a square table. Other than that, the book-filled room has a few black-and-white prints.

Devon stops in front of a metal door at the very end of the hall.

The rusty hinges screech as he opens it. A gust of icy air swooshes and swirls around me. I take a deep breath, checking for the smell of sulfur, but all I get is a whiff of Devon's earthy scent. "Want me to stay here and hold the door open?" I ask, in case the door locks automatically.

"No." Devon holds the door and waits for me to step onto a rusted fire escape platform. Strike two.

Another thought hits me. Since I failed as a Blade, he's probably testing my Bent as a Caretaker. Little does he know I'm trying to "take care" of everyone by *not* going outside, but I can't tell that to Devon. I shiver.

"Is there a problem?" Devon's probing glance tells me he knows something's up. He's frustrated that I'm stalling.

"I'm a little shell-shocked from yesterday, I guess. And I could use a jacket."

"We won't be outside for long." Devon puts a thin wood block in the door jamb to keep it cracked open. He's leaving the door cracked open? That's a horrifically bad idea. I've seen Cormorants pop doors open like soda cans. Leaving one cracked ajar is an open invitation for an all-out invasion.

I search for a weapon. I'd even take a broom or mop if one was around. The crooked painting of an ocean sunset will hardly do the trick. "Do you at least have a weapon or something if one of those things comes around?"

Devon pulls out a small dagger with an ornate handle and vine pattern etched in the blade. The metal shines even though gray clouds blanket the sun.

Strike three. I take another deep breath. Fine. I'll make this trip as quick as possible, but only because he's got a weapon on him. I wrap my arms around my middle, step into the frigid air, and scan the sky and surrounding buildings. From what I can tell, the alley below looks clear of black mist, as do the rooftops. Good.

Without checking to see if I'm following, Devon goes up narrow metal steps that zigzag up the back of the building. Cold air creeps under my shirt and coils around the back of my neck as the door closes behind me, with only the fingertip space cracking the door open. We scale about three stories. I am alert for any buzzing or shrieking, but other than the train and a few cars in the distance, the late-morning sounds are uneventful.

Even though I'm determined to get this test over with as

quickly as possible and get back inside, I have to admit I'm a little curious as to what Devon keeps so private. "Are we going to the roof?" Which would be a colossally bad idea for both of us.

"No." Devon stops on a platform just shy of the roof and waits for me to catch up. A thick silver tarp tents the entire balcony and covers the side of the building like a construction zone.

My eyes widen at the size of this plastic cage. "What is *that*?"

As soon as Devon unzips an opening in the tarp, the hard lines on his face disappear. His eyes gleam. "Come take a look."

24

SACRED SPACE

Devon pushes the heavy vinyl covering aside. As soon as we step inside, I'm cocooned with warm air that smells of rosemary and fresh soil, not unlike Devon. All around me, vibrant green leaves from plants and herbs growing in handcrafted pots crowd every inch of space, save for the ceiling, where tiny heat lamps line the enclosure.

Devon zips the tarp closed, trapping in the humid air. Small wooden shelves are packed with overflowing plants. He makes his way through them to the far end of what has to be a thirty-foot balcony.

"This garden is amazing." I push aside a thick vine of plump tomatoes growing overhead and step further into the tropical haven. "It's like being in another universe."

Devon smiles and inspects a cluster of potted herbs. He gently holds the fragile foliage in his palm and brushes his fingers over the leaves. "It helps Harper and the other Healers with what they need." He inhales the scent lingering on his fingers. "And it isn't so bad for the cooking either." He picks up a pair of pruning shears.

"It's not a bad place for hiding." Something brushes against my arm. I glance down. It's a crooked lima bean stalk, wandering away from a healthy, upright cluster, the same way they did in Jess's plastic terrarium. The sight pierces my heart. Jess couldn't wrangle in her wayward vine either. I redirect the vine, carefully entwining it with another.

Sadness taints Devon's voice as he replies, "I've got no need to hide." His large hands gently prune dead leaves off a pink flowering rose bush before checking the soil. I wander the aisle, then stop in the middle of the garden oasis and watch Devon tend his garden in silence. His posture is a soliloquy of strength, defeat, and . . . grief.

"Why don't you just tell her how you feel?" My question comes out a little blunter than I intended.

I'm not sure what reaction I was expecting from Devon, but he doesn't give one. Instead, he calmly mixes plant food in a blue watering can. "There's no point."

"How can you say that? It's so clear how you feel about her, whether you think so or not. You're not hiding anything."

"It's not clear to her." He waters the pink roses before tending to neighboring plants. "It's obvious she's focused on someone else."

"That's only because he pays attention to her. Maybe if you tried giving her attention, complimenting her instead of ordering her around, she might open her eyes to what's in front of her."

He ignores me. "She needs mint." When he cuts off a leafy branch, the tiny space fills with the smell of peppermint.

He may want to drop the topic, but I can't let it go. Despite the pain in my jaw, I push on. "Just talk to her. See her strengths and tell her. If you wait too long you may never get the chance."

Devon shakes his head. "It's good to see you're only a few days in and you're already caring for everyone around you."

The walls flap as a strong wind kicks against the tarp. I listen for any telltale sound. So far, I only hear an airplane's roaring engine and a barking dog in the distance.

"So does that mean I passed your test and we can get back now?"

"Test?" Devon looks at me, confused.

"You brought me here to test me as a Caretaker, right? You'll listen to what I say, ask a few questions. Maybe even want me to pick some special herb, and depending on which one I choose, it will somehow reveal my Bent as a Caretaker. The same way Gladys did when I handed her pieces for the mosaic . . . or maybe it was the rolling out the dough. I don't know, but somehow she knew." I wander about, searching the stacked shelves for a plant that seems different, or in need of help, or smells a certain way . . .

Devon watches me with bewilderment as I touch velvety leaves. "I'm not testing you."

I glance up and search his face. He's perplexed, but his eyes are honest. He's really not testing me? My face warms. "Oh." I release the plant. "Then why did you ask me to come up here?"

"I thought after yesterday . . . I know coming back after what happened on the street was rough. Sometimes it's hard being around people all the time. I thought you'd appreciate a moment to get away. Talk things through. That's all. And you looked to be in a bit of trouble with Tanji. Thought it best to break that down."

He's so lying. Okay, so maybe not the part about Tanji, but the way he watches Harper interact with Maddox, coupled with all the radical changes about to happen at Hesperian, I'm not the one who needed to get away. "I'll pretend I believe that for now." Maybe he's the one who needs to talk things through. I lean against the wooden table that occupies the middle of the tent. "Are you just as thrilled about Council taking over as everyone else, seeing how you run the place and now they're bringing someone else in?"

Devon's tone stiffens. "Are you always this straightforward?"

I shrug. "Yeah, kinda. Community is somewhat new for me. I don't know the rules."

I watch as Devon cuts small stalks from a purple plant and wraps the ends in a wet paper towel. When he does, the whole room fills with the fragrant scent of sweet licorice. "You've got this natural authority," I say. "Seems to me, if Council was smart, they'd use your strength to their advantage."

"Council believes I let too many things slide and have no control of what goes on around here."

I laugh out loud. "You're joking, right?"

Devon looks at me, straight-faced. "Tone it down. Lay low, I'm serious. When they get here, just do what they say." He holds out the purple flower he wrapped in the cloth.

"I get it. They're intense. I read that all over Kellan." I take the cutting and bring the flower to my nose. "What is this?"

"How did you know Kellan is from Council? That's not public knowledge." He clips another cluster of herbs. The space now smells lemony. "And that's hyssop. Be careful not to crush the stalk."

I hold the hyssop more gently and examine the fuzzy purple petals arranged like a corncob on a stick. "He told me he's here on assignment and made it clear he's not happy about it. Said he doesn't want to baby . . . sit." Suddenly it all makes sense. "Is Kellan keeping tabs on you?"

Devon clips branches with hard, fast strokes. "I won't say no, but . . ."

"But what?"

Devon points to the table beside me. "Hand me those scissors. Please."

"Don't change the subject on me." Finding the scissors, I pick them up. "I'm good at keeping things ransom. It's a talent of mine." I clutch them against my chest. "Tell me."

Devon's lips tighten. "Council's watching over someone else."

"Gladys? I couldn't imagine her doing anything Council—or anyone—wouldn't agree with."

"Not Gladys." Devon holds his palm out for the scissors.

I tuck them behind my back. "Then who?"

He motions for me to hand them over. "We've got to get back. Harper's waiting."

The only other person I can think of is . . . "Wait. Do you mean Maddox? Why would Council keep tabs on him?"

Devon takes the scissors from my dangling hand. "Council wants him trained. Maddox refuses."

Another breeze kicks at the side of the tarp. I step away from the table. Still no shrieking, but I can't smell anything on account of the lemon and licorice scents permeating the space.

"Then why did you shut down our training just now?" I again search for a weapon in case of a sneak attack while we're caged in the greenhouse. The pruning shears or scissors might work—at least they're better than nothing.

"His brother, who's on Council, wants all of Maddox's training to go through him."

"Brother. You mean . . ."

"Gray Carver." Devon wraps the lemony herbs in strips of paper towel and hands them to me.

No wonder Maddox is planning to leave Hesperian. With Council taking over, he won't have a choice but to train. My chest feels hollow. His taking off doesn't seem so different from what Mom used to do. Maddox knows I don't want to run anymore. I want to stand and fight, to change my visions when they happen. I trusted him with the deepest part of me—something I've never shared with anyone. Ever. Why didn't he trust me enough to tell me the whole truth about why he wants to leave? Maybe he's only using me—or using my Bent—as his excuse to get out.

Another heavy wind ruffles the tarp. "You're right, we'd better get back." Not only have I been out here way too long, I'm going to find Maddox and get the truth.

"Almost done." I watch as Devon waters the rose bush. Why

is he a monument of strength in so many areas—except for one?

"You're going to have to be bold and take a risk with her instead of waiting for things to change. The worst thing—"

"I don't want her pity." Devon's tone turns acidic. He sets down the watering can and brushes past me.

I follow after him, pushing away the outstretched vines grabbing my hair. "Why would she pity you? That makes no sense."

He stops at the entrance. "So you don't know."

Sarcasm bleeds through my frustration. "Apparently not, seeing that I've only been here a few days. There's a lot I still don't know. Like why I couldn't kill the beasts but Kellan could, or—"

"I lost my family, Cera." Devon turns to face me. "Mom, Dad, and Althea, my little sister, in a car wreck. Only Pop and I survived."

"Oh, I didn't know that. I'm—"

"Sorry?" He turns to unzip the tarp. "That's the response I'm talking about."

"What are you wanting me to say? Too bad?"

"It's not what anyone says. It's the look in their eyes—first the look of shock, then the look that says how devastating, how awful. But no one wants the baggage. The story I have no control over pushes people away because I'm wounded, broken." A deep, scarring pain lingers on his face. "I don't want her looking at me like that if she doesn't feel the way I do. And she deserves someone strong." He pulls the tarp open.

"Aren't we all wounded?" As I exit, the icy wind steals my breath. My teeth chatter as I wait for him to secure the greenhouse. "We all limp through life in one way or another. Just because someone sees your vulnerable side doesn't mean you're weak." I hesitate as my own words slap me in the face.

"Let's get these cuttings to Harper."

I say nothing more. I *am* sorry he lost his family, but one thing I know is that loss can make us stronger. You think you can't live through it, and yet, somehow you do. You're broken and never the same but standing, nonetheless. In that moment, life changes, and suddenly the world seems tentative, a little more precious. I wish those words would come out as I follow Devon down the stairs, but instead, I keep them inside. That conversation is done.

The air whips around me as I navigate the narrow fire escape stairs as fast as possible. There still isn't a sulfur stench or any buzzing sounds. Good.

We slip back inside and make our journey down the grand staircase, through the café, and down to Harper's room. Or at least I thought. Devon stops sooner than I expect at a door opening into an anteroom next to Harper's clinic. The room is lined with jar-filled shelves and has a thick table that takes up most of the space. The clutter resembles an ancient chemistry lab—complete with burners, beakers, and glass flasks bubbling with clear liquid—and smells just as acrid.

"You're a lucky one," Harper says as she adds a spoonful of a white cream into the bubbling liquid.

"Who, me?" I glance over my shoulder. Devon waits by the door, engrossed in checking his phone. She's clearly not talking to him.

Harper takes the clippings from my hand and sets them on the table. She carefully unwraps the cloth and says, "That's sacred space. Devon doesn't let anyone up there. *Ever.*" She shoots Devon a playful glare as he glances up. Seriously Devon, come on. That's an open invitation. Go for it. Devon drops his focus back to his phone, oblivious.

Disappointed, Harper pouts and turns her back to him. She mumbles, "What'd *you* do to get a peek?" Her words sound as disgusted as the look on her face.

As I tighten my jaw, the soreness flares. Forget trying to take the high road and forget helping Devon out. He's too good for her. I force a smile. "I guess being authentic is hot." I relish how Harper's mouth gapes. She quickly shuts it and turns away in a huff.

"Let me know when the ointment is finished," Devon says from the door.

Harper looks over her shoulder after Devon as he walks off. Her narrowed eyes turn to me with this "game on" expression written all over her face.

Does she really think I'm some sort of threat to her throne? She's out of her mind. I have no desire to be the center of attention. In fact, all this relational intensity is too much. Community doesn't seem to be working out so well for me.

"Shouldn't you be somewhere else?" Harper mashes the herbs in a wooden bowl. "Unless you're injured, this room is reserved for Healers."

There are other words I'd use to describe her, but I withhold my insult and walk out of the room. I have no idea what Devon sees in her, but he's much better off running the other way.

25

THE GLOSS

As I enter the café, a symphony of voices collides in eager anticipation and panicked dread. It's clear by the tension pulsing through the room that Council will take over tomorrow and everything is definitely going to change.

I search over the sea of people and find Devon. He's at the pastry counter having a late lunch. Maddox, however, is in the back corner of his alcove, packing. When he spots me, his concentrated expression morphs into concern. Abandoning his backpack, he hurries over to me. "Everything okay?" His voice is hushed. "You were gone a while. I wasn't sure if . . ."

"If the beasts tracked me down?" I back up against the banister, putting distance between us. "No. Not that I know of."

Maybe it's the sharp tone of my voice or my accusing expression, but Maddox seems taken aback, almost hurt. "Are you still cool with leaving in the morning or . . . did something happen?"

I study him. His eyes are an endless font of wild, impossible thoughts hidden behind a veil of shaggy blond hair, masking his scar. As the Current flares between us, Maddox swallows thick and then drops his gaze to the ground.

I had every intention of calling him out about his brother, but his reaction makes me back down. That, and something about his clean ocean scent warming the air between us softens my will. It's clear that we're both after the same thing—taking down the creatures and saving lives. Maybe our motives differ, but the goal is the same. We can work alongside each other, and that's it. Just because I offered my reasoning to him freely doesn't mean he owes me an explanation for why he wants to leave. I shouldn't have expected one.

When I step back, I bump into the mosaic table. The design is clearly a hurricane with a path of destruction headed right toward the middle of the café. Leaving might be the best thing for everyone. I rest my hand on the edge and feel the smooth glass with my fingertips. "I'm all in."

"In for what?" Devon walks up. He gives Maddox a suspicious side-eye glance.

Maddox doesn't miss a beat. "The gathering tonight. Our final night as family before Council takes over."

"It'll be a good time." Devon's smile doesn't hide his downcast tone. He places a hand on Maddox's shoulder. "As for Council, I've got your back, man. I promise, things will work out."

Maddox nods, but guilt flickers in his eyes. He hooks his thumbs on his jean pockets with a slight shrug.

Devon's phone chimes. Taking it out of his pocket, he checks the number. "It's Gladys." He walks a few paces away where it's quieter.

I pull Maddox aside. "I want Devon to come with us."

Maddox raises his eyebrows. "He's too close to Council, and he's got . . . obligations. He won't—"

"Cera!" Juniper rushes through the café to meet me but stops dead in her tracks when she sees Maddox. "Oh, hi." She tucks a strand of hair behind her ear as her cheeks turn rosy pink.

Devon is making his way back over. He looks concerned. "Juniper, take Cera. I want the two of you to train with Harper the rest of the afternoon. Sit in on what she does."

I put my hands on my hips. "I'm not a Healer, Devon, and you know it. That would be a waste of time. Give me pointers to fight instead. Or at least teach me how to protect people."

Devon glances at my swollen jaw. "Cera, remember what I said? Filter your outbursts. And have Harper give you something for the swelling and bruising."

Ugh. Why is he so insistent that I hang out with Harper when he's the one who wants to be with her? She insulted me, and now I've got to beg for healing? I don't think so.

Devon must pick up on my resistance because he takes me by the elbow. When he says, "Gladys found your mom," and walks me near the hallway, I go willingly.

"What did she say?"

He stops. "It's best to have Harper look at your bruise, see what she can do, before your mom sees you."

An image of Mom white-knuckling the steering wheel as she barrels down the road in the rental truck pops into my head. "Is she on her way?" I glance at the front hall as my insides flare with a momentary freak-out. I'm supposed to leave in the morning with Maddox. If she walks through that door, how on earth will I tell her I'm not going with her? Her coming here will ruin everything. I know for a fact she won't let me stay.

"Gladys is working out those details, but it sounds like she'll be here tomorrow."

"Tomorrow. For real? I'm not sure what Gladys told her, but that doesn't sound like Mom at all."

Devon nods. His eyes are honest and . . . somber. He's telling the truth, but I'm perplexed by his expression. Unless, like everyone else around here, the sadness has to do with Council taking over. Maybe it's because he said Council believes he has no control and lets too many things slide. In my short time here, I've done more than my share of giving him grief.

He hesitates and then says, "Your mom's not well."

"What do you mean by 'not well'? Can I call her?"

Devon shakes his head. "She's not—they're taking care of her. She has a high fever and slips in and out of consciousness. She isn't talking much. Gladys wants her to rest tonight. They'll try bringing her in the morning to see if they can figure out what's wrong."

I'm stunned and confused. "Is she . . ." I swallow. "She'll be okay, though. Right? I mean, she had a cough, but it was getting better."

"She'll be fine. Don't worry." Devon puts a hand on my shoulder. "Have Harper take care of you so your mom won't be concerned when she sees you in the morning."

I nod, despite the fact that I don't want to be anywhere near Harper-the-horrible. "Thanks for letting me know."

"It's what family does. Now head over and see Harper."

Juniper comes up and puts her arm around mine. "Ready? Maybe I can help a little."

Maddox joins us and looks at me. "Talk later?"

"I'll find you after getting this"—I motion to my face— "taken care of."

Maddox grins slightly. Devon pulls him aside as Juniper takes me off to Harper's torture lab.

As we wait in the anteroom of Harper's clinic, Juniper walks the lab, inspecting the potions. Even though her hands stay behind her back, her fingers fidget, as if wishing to touch one.

Harper saunters in and drops a book on the table with a loud *thunk* and an equally menacing frown. *Anatomy.* I swear the book is a million pages thick. "Start here."

"Are you serious?" I fan the pages, picking up a few words that sound about as foreign as some of the illustrations look.

Harper looks at me scornfully underneath her perfectly straight bangs. "How do you expect to heal someone if you don't know what's going on inside? You've got to look beyond the surface and visualize what could be happening internally. If you don't, then this isn't your Bent and you'll end up doing more damage than good."

"I'm pretty sure I'm not a Healer." I shove the book aside. Juniper pulls out a wooden bench, sits at the table, and, taking the book with eager hands, practically devours the pages. I have to be careful. I don't want to get Harper angry if she's going to heal Mom in the morning. "I'll leave that Bent to truly gifted people, like you," I say. "Devon said he wanted me to give it a try, but I only want to get something for the swelling in my jaw. I feel a click when I open it."

A smile curls in the corner of her red lips. "You're not as dumb as I thought. At least you can recognize where you don't belong."

Her subtext comes through loud and clear. For Mom's sake, and maybe Devon's too, I bite my tongue before a litany of vitriolic insults launches out of my mouth. Here I am trying to be nice, trying to build a bridge . . .

"A warm lavender and Epsom salt wrap will work." Juniper's happy voice wedges through the tense air. "I've made one before and can try if you want." She studies my jawline. "I'd have to wrap your head with a bandage to keep the salt pack secure. It's also best if you lie down awhile. You know, to reduce swelling and all . . ." She clasps her hands together as she eyes me with an almost pleading expression.

I sigh. "I'll only lie down for a few minutes. I've got things to take care of."

Juniper jumps off the bench. "You're meeting with Maddox later, I know."

Harper gives me a suspicious glance. "Give her some of this." She takes a small cup and pours a teaspoon of the pink liquid. "It'll take away the bruise."

Juniper sniffs the liquid. "It smells like pineapple." Her eyes grow wide, as if she's uncovered a secret. "Is it bromelain?"

"Only part of it," Harper replies. "That mix is called Gloss."

"You made this?" Juniper is in awe as she hands me the cup. "Can you teach me?"

"Get through the book. When you're ready, then maybe I will."

Harper watches as I swig the pineapple-flavored liquid in one gulp. It tastes sweet and bitter all at once. When I set the cup on the table, she tells me, "Go next door and lie down so Juniper can wrap your head."

I do as she says and plop myself onto the cot near the door. Juniper doctors me up and then says, "Lie here a while. The wrap should take no more than thirty minutes, and the swelling will be gone. Promise." She rushes back to Harper, shutting the door behind her. Alone in the room, I lie on the cot, waiting. I hate waiting. It accomplishes nothing, and endless thoughts just ricochet through my brain.

I stare at the stucco ceiling. What am I going to tell Mom when her fever breaks and she comes in the morning? If I'm even still here. Maddox didn't say what time we'd leave. I can just see Mom totally lose it if she gets here and I'm gone. Plus, she's not well. Guilt floods my chest at the thought of leaving her behind. At least I'm not abandoning Mom the same way Dad did. I'm giving her freedom. Harper will heal her, and then she can live wherever she wants and not worry about me. Maybe she'll even meet someone new, and if I'm not around, she won't have to bother explaining me. I can go to the new safe house with Maddox and then let her know I'm all right.

The way I see things, right now, I've got three choices: I could wait around for Mom in the morning and spend the rest of my life tethered to her side as we uproot and flee, knowing others will die. Or I can stay here under Council's thumb, learn all there is about my Bent—which frankly sounds ridiculously unappealing because I know being a Seer means being locked up and never fighting the enemy. No. The only option that feels right is leaving with Maddox. I know I'll attract the beasts wherever I go, but if we can plan an ambush and use my Bent to lure and destroy them, then I'll take it.

I can't get back any of the innocent lives lost from my past visions, but I can try to stop more from being affected. I can't imagine doing anything other than finding other Awakened, saving lives, and annihilating those hideous creatures of death. Maybe it won't change the world, but maybe it will change one life. That is enough.

26

SLAMMED

Bursts of laughter exploding from the café startle me awake. No, no, no. I fell asleep? I sit up on the cot. My feet find the floor as I stumble through the dark to the bathroom in the back room. I slide the door shut and find the light switch.

After a moment of adjusting to the assaulting light, I dare myself to peer at the mirror. The wrap is gone and the bruise is slowly fading. I open my jaw with ease. It's amazing that I healed so fast. I just wish I didn't feel like my veins were flowing with plutonium. Maybe the side effect of one of the herbs in the Gloss—or whatever it was Harper gave me—causes grogginess. Don't get me wrong, I'm thankful the nasty bruise is gone and I can eat again, but Harper could have at least warned me that I'd fall asleep. I was supposed to meet Maddox. We haven't discussed when everyone is leaving. I have no idea what time it is. Only that the hall outside Harper's room is dark, which means it's probably night.

I rinse out my mouth, do my best to tame my hair, and trudge to the café. Down the hall, pulsing guitars race alongside the steady beat of a bass drum. I follow the scent of warm bread. It's the final celebration here at Hesperian. I've slept for eight hours. At least.

I can't make my way through the room without bumping into people. Tables and chairs have been pushed along the wall near Maddox's alcove to create an overcrowded buffet, stacked with every kind of food and dessert imaginable.

Eighty or more people crowd the café as they face the makeshift stage set up behind the entry hall. The audience taps their feet, singing an upbeat song I don't recognize. With this many bodies in the room, the air feels warmer than usual. I take a dinner roll off the top of a pyramid-stacked platter and work my way through the crowd to find Maddox.

"Finally woke up?" Devon is beside me holding a plastic cup.

"No one warned me I'd be knocked out for a while. That's super unnerving and frankly a bit psychopathic."

Devon smiles. "You're less trouble asleep."

I glare at him. "That was *your* idea?"

"No!" Devon laughs. "But it wasn't a bad one."

Someone's elbow jabs me in the back. My body tightens. I turn to see who it was. Everyone around me is deep in animated conversation, arms flailing, oblivious to the fact that we're standing in such a tight space.

"You've never been to this big of a party, huh?" Devon asks over the steady drumbeat.

I've never been to any parties. "Is it that obvious?"

"You look like you're about to unleash on anything that comes your way. It's a crowd, just relax."

"Relax. In a crowd. Yeah, right. That's a total oxymoron." Not only that, I'm still in a drug stupor, and it's making me super crabby.

"Who's the moron?" Kellan appears beside me, flask in hand. He holds it out, offering a sip.

I shake my head and push his hand away. "You're the moron if you think I'm having any more of Harper's Spike, or Gloss, or whatever other voodoo concoctions she mixes."

Kellan nearly spits out his drink. It's the first time I've ever seen him smile. He wipes the smirk and the Spike off his lips with the back of his sleeve. "Wow. That's quite a bite you've got tonight."

"She's probably hungry." Devon eyes the dinner roll I'm holding. Even though I don't want to give him the satisfaction of knowing he's right, I rip off a bite of the bread anyway.

Over the steady beat and crooning guitar, a girl's voice, as smooth as melting honey, serenades the room with a wistful tune. The entranced audience sways to give me a clear shot of the singer. And it's Harper. Of course it is.

Devon stands transfixed as she soaks up the spotlight. Next to her, Maddox rests on a stool in a casual stance, playing guitar. As he sings, the anthem flows from some deep part within him, oblivious to the crowd. When his smooth tenor voice sings a line about belonging, a restless ache rises within me. Guilt? Possibly, since I know I'm leaving Hesperian, leaving this community, and Mom behind.

Harper joins at the chorus, her voice a perfect handhold to Maddox's tenor. The way they sing, the two of them seem right together. I glance at Devon. He swirls the drink in his hand as if it's suddenly lost flavor. No doubt he feels it too.

I glance back at the stage as Amide pounds out the beat on the drums.

Maddox's gaze finds me in the crowd and lingers before he glances back at his fingers during a complicated riff. Has to be my imagination. I'm hidden in the swarming mass. But on the next verse, his eyes lock on mine as he belts out a line about his whole world changing. Maddox is no longer singing as if he's alone in the room. I don't grasp the exact words because, not only does he finish the song without taking his eyes off of me, but I can feel the crowd follow his line of sight. I step back, hoping to hide in Devon's shadow.

I'm not a fan of being put on the spot. I know Maddox is speaking to me about leaving and starting over, but that's not how it's coming across. He shouldn't look at me that way . . . all hopeful but somehow lost. Now a thousand pinwheels flutter in my stomach. What's worse is that Harper realizes Maddox's stormy look is fixed in my direction. She flings her hair over her shoulder with a menacing stare. As the audience applauds, I look down and pretend to study the grooves in the stone floor.

Kellan nudges me with his elbow. "Wanna grab something t'eat?"

"Mm, yeah. That'd be great." I spin around to follow Kellan as he cuts through the crowd, making a path to the back of the room.

I haven't taken two steps when Harper calls me out from the stage. "Cera, why don't you come up and read some of your work?" The microphone squeals. I stop dead in my tracks. My heart punches my throat as the crowd parts around me.

"Come on, don't be shy. Read us one of your poems. Is that what they are?" Harper's syrupy tone drips, too sticky sweet. She clutches the microphone stand two-handed, and a fake smile is on her glossy lips. If her eyes were daggers, she'd be carving out my soul. "No? Why don't I read one, since you're too shy?"

Maddox sets his guitar down. "Harper, don't."

Harper frowns and turns her back to Maddox as she pulls a sheet of crinkled notebook paper out of her pocket. Unfolding the scrap, she clears her throat before affecting a dramatic voice. "I'm awful at this . . ."

Laughter rumbles through the audience. She found my notes? I want to die. My face burns hot, and my cemented legs won't let me run.

"Harper." Maddox reaches for the microphone, but Harper pulls away.

She continues mocking me. "Failing . . . Falling. Life now ending."

My hands shake, spreading the tremble throughout my body. Images of Jess dying on the concrete flash across my mind. My eyes well with tears. Keep it together, Cera.

Harper raises one eyebrow. "That's a little morbid." Laughter rolls through the audience.

She holds up one finger, silencing the crowd, before reading the last line. "Burning in the flames." Harper lowers the paper. "Sounds cryptic. Something you want to share?"

"That's enough." Maddox grabs the microphone away from Harper.

I can barely hear the nervous laughter rippling through the café over the thrumming pulse inside my head. I feel slammed, smashed to pieces without enough oxygen in the room to fill my lungs and scream.

Maddox's voice is sharp. "Amide, play your new song." Maddox covers his hand over the microphone and says something to Harper that makes her frown. He pulls her offstage, but it's too late.

I loathe her. I hate her to the core. She mocks my pain, taking words that weren't meant to see the light of day and tossing them around like cheap Mardi Gras beads trampled by a drunken crowd.

Devon touches my shoulder. Before he can smother me with words of comfort, or apology, or whatever is about to spew from his mouth, I push through the crowd. I need air. I need to be alone. To run. Scream.

I shove open the kitchen door and, in a blur, race past someone prepping plates. I head straight for the sink behind the wall, splash cold water on my face, and grip the edge of the metal sink. I need to go down to the cellar, punch something, and calm down.

Footsteps tap across the stone tiles behind me. I glance over my shoulder to find Kellan, holding a paper plate piled with more food than any human could eat in one sitting.

"I saved a table." He holds out the plate and looks me over. "You all good?"

"Kellan?" Claire's thick slap of combat boots pounds the stairs from the cellar. She rushes into the kitchen and stops short of plowing into him. Out of breath, she pants, "Legions are moving closer. We did a quick scan from the roof and counted five."

The hairs on the back of my neck prickle.

Kellan sets the plate on the counter. "Are they passin'?"

Her eyes are panicked. "They're hovering. Searching."

I force a swallow over the desert sand coating my throat.

"They know we're here." Kellan immediately straightens to his full height. "Keep everyone inside. I'll get Council to take 'em down from the outside. We can't slay five at once. Not till we're trained."

Claire's face turns ashen. "At least five. There could be more."

Kellan rubs a hand over his head. "Cera, guard the back door. Don't let anyone go outside." He takes off, headed back into the café with Claire at his heels.

They may be after all of us, but I know for certain those beasts are hunting me. They must have sensed I was around when I stepped outside for that brief moment with Devon. Every minute I stay behind these walls is more time for them to grow closer. I know what I have to do. I abandon the sink and search the kitchen for the largest knife I can find—the butcher knife will do. At least, I hope it will.

My heart races. I rush down and into the workout room and fumble in the dark to grab a jacket from the pile. I grip the knife and slip back out into the hall. Even if Council arrives to save the day, more Legions will come. Maddox said they'd do anything to get hold of a Seer.

Being here is the problem. Leading the creatures away is the solution. Maybe if I can somehow get back on the train, they'll fall back. Finding Mom might be an option. She's kept me hidden for the past ten years. She'll know what to do. But I forgot, Gladys, and who knows who else, is with her.

I zip up the jacket. I can't put anyone in danger. I've got to head out that door on my own. Maybe I'll run back to Mark, see if I can take that job. Hide out. My head spins with bad possibilities. I don't know where I'll go; I only know I need to leave. Milton's quiet voice affirms my choice. *"Let us descend now . . . for the hour precise / Exacts our parting hence . . . We may no longer stay."* Agreed, Milton. You brought me here. You'll lead me to where I need to go. I know that now, and I trust you.

"Cera?" Maddox calls my name from the top of the steps.

"Is she down there?" Devon's voice is tight and is followed by Harper's whine.

"Couldn't this wait until after we finished the set?"

I quietly turn the handle and open the metal door enough to slide through sideways. The last thing I need is any of them derailing my plan—or worse, following me outside.

I gasp as the frigid air slaps me across the face. I shut the door quietly behind me and go up the concrete steps to the street. One hand is tucked in my coat pocket, the other clutches the butcher knife. I walk at a brisk pace, leaning close to the brick buildings to block the biting wind. My feet twitch, wanting to bust into a full-blown sprint, but I can't run just yet. I need the creatures to sense I'm around. Once they do, then I'll run.

A faint smell of sulfur tinges the air. They're not close, but they're around. But then again, the whipping wind could be messing with the strength of the scent. I turn the corner and head down the block. As the wind blows, the sulfur stench grows stronger. My insides tighten. I'm getting close to one. I just have to wait to hear the buzzing sound. I grip the knife tighter. This time I've got the right weapon. Maybe I can tackle the creature head-on before jumping on the train. I can avenge Jess. Except that Claire said there were at least five in the area. There's no way I could take down more than one—if that.

Shadows stain the streets but it's impossible to make out any black mist in the inky dark. I perk my ears for any buzzing sounds, but instead, heavy footsteps grind into the concrete. Someone is tracking behind me.

"Cera?" Maddox grips my elbow from behind. His face is stern in the pale light. "You shouldn't be out here."

"And neither should you." I jerk my arm away. "Get back inside. Claire said at least five Legions are swarming and growing closer. It's because of me." Maddox glances at the weapon in my hand as the streetlight dances on the blade. He raises a questioning eyebrow.

Now Devon turns the corner, ushering Harper along. Great. What is this, a convention? So much for stealth. "There she is. Tell her." Devon releases Harper, sending her my way.

She stumbles but stops right in front of me. "That was totally uncool of me, sorry." She shrugs one shoulder and then turns to Devon. "There, I said it. Can we go back now?" She rubs her arms and bounces on her toes. "It's freezing out here."

"Legions are in the area." Maddox's voice and body are tight.

Devon's face goes rigid. "Everyone back inside. We'll put the place in lockdown."

Fear masks Harper's face as she rushes to Maddox's side and clings to his arm. "Take me back right now."

Devon puts a hand on my back, urging me back to Hesperian and closer to the shelter of a building. "We'll keep everyone inside until they pass."

I sidestep him. "Claire just reported that they're not passing. They're searching." I glance at Maddox, who is looking at the sky. "I'm not going back to Hesperian. I got what I came for."

"Cera, you're not a Blade." Devon towers over me. He holds out his hand, asking for the knife. "Council won't issue you—"

"I don't care about Council, don't you get that?" I step back, keeping the weapon away from him. "There's only one thing I want, and that's to destroy every single beast that could ever possibly hurt anyone ever again. But it's something I've got to do on my own." I look everywhere but at Maddox.

"You can't do it alone," Maddox says, his urgent voice rising. "You need training. Weapons."

Devon holds his hand out. "Calm down. We'll work this out, but right now, we need to get everyone back inside."

A frigid wind rocks me back on my heels. My fingers clench. Pain coils through my back.

No! No. Not now. The unwelcome but familiar burning creeps down my spine.

Maddox reaches out to me. "Cera?"

The pain has sucked all the air from my lungs. I can't speak. I can't move my feet. All I can do is reach out and find rough brick before slumping my shoulder against the cold building. My fist unfurls. The knife slips from my fingers, clanking on the concrete. Another wave of fiery pain drives down my back. I double over and cry out.

Harper gasps. "Is she having a—"

"Cera!" Devon shouts.

I lift my chin. Hair hangs in my face, but even through the dark, my gaze finds Maddox. *I'm so sorry.* Out here, in the open, with Legions around. They'll intercept the vision . . . Pain kicks me in the back. I've ruined everything—again. My knees buckle. Before I hit the ground, Maddox grabs hold to keep me upright.

The last thing I hear as the world spins black is Devon yelling, "Take her to Apartment C. Now!"

27

APARTMENT C

I shut my eyes tight against the bitter wind, and my head bounces against Maddox's shoulder as he runs. His ocean scent, magnified by the heat radiating from his body, is all I breathe. Binding pain roils inside me, and the pressure of an angry fist grips my spine. Deep. Relentless squeezing. I bury my face into Maddox's jacket. The denim is rough against my wet cheek. I wrestle a scream back down my throat.

"Hang in there, I've got you. Just another block, and we're there." Maddox's voice rumbles in his chest. His breath is labored, heavy.

After a while longer, Maddox slows. "Get the door!" he shouts to someone. Warm air stings my face. Rhythmic footsteps slap against echoing metal. Stairs. His arms hold me tighter. "We're almost there."

Keys jingle. Another door squeaks open.

"Put her on the couch. I'll get Pop," Devon says as a door slams. Heated, dry air that smells of secondhand furniture and lemon oil engulfs me. "Pop?" Devon's voice collides with a television blaring somewhere in the distant background.

I'm lowered onto scratchy, musty fabric. Maddox's arms slip out from under me. Exposing cold takes their place. A sharp pain

I sniffle, wiping my dribble with my sleeve and then pushing up to my elbows. It takes everything I have not to break out into tears when I smell bile.

"Stop that whimpering." Pop shuffles closer. "Now, listen close. When that vision comes, you let the boy see it." As if on cue, the silver fog floods my sight. "Boy, go on and hold her hand. The transfer'll be stronger that way."

"You want to harness her to . . . me?" Maddox's voice sounds shaky.

"Who else, boy? I know you're right next to her, aren't you?"

Even though Harper cleaned my hands, I wipe them on the hem of my shirt. I manage to sit upright and set my feet on the floor. Maddox's hand covers mine. When he curls his fingers into my palm, a tiny flitter whirls in my queasy stomach.

Sounding satisfied, Pop continues with the instruction. "Now Honey, you go on 'n show the boy the vision."

Show him? An aftershock slashes across my back. I gasp. Maddox clutches my hand. Right when I think my fingers will crack under his hold, the fiery ache wanes, seeping out of my palm. Maddox groans. His grip slackens.

"What's wrong?" Harper's shrill cry is not about me.

"Hush yourself." Pop shuffles even closer. Another torture session cuts through my spine. I squeeze the couch, ready to scream again, but surprisingly the pain subsides. A tiny pulse flows out from my palm. "Don't be afraid. Go on. Let the boy see."

My mind clouds with silver fog like steam on a bathroom mirror. I know what these images mean. They're not some hallucinating psychosis from a panic attack. The fragmented pictures forming in my mind foretell someone's death. They always have. I sit rigid. A lumpy pillow digs into my back.

"Don't be holdin' back."

I'm not sure what the old man means, but I exhale and do the only thing I know. I imagine Maddox next to me, the same way I first did with Mom when I was seven, both of us looking at the images together, as if put on display. Maddox's arm presses against my shoulder. I lean against him. My hand trembles under the weight of his. When he gently squeezes my hand, I take a deep breath, smelling fresh ocean air, and let Maddox see.

> *A handheld lantern shines*
> *A ray of caramel light beams*
> *A narrow path illuminates through the dark*

I feel trapped. I'm choking. I have to run. Get away.

"Don't fight it, girl." The old man's voice sounds far away. "Accept what it's givin' you." The image streaks across my mind like claws slicing through canvas.

> *A yellow glass goblet, smothered in smoke*
> *The fragile spiral stem falls over, severing the bowl*
> *Greedy fingers grasp through the fog, lapping up violet liquid*
> *Bright, piercing white light*
> *A flash of red lightning*
> *Then everything turns red.*

Everything turns red. *Blood.* Someone died. My whole body convulses. I rip my hand away from Maddox. Something solid hits the carpet near my feet, landing with a hard *thud*.

"Maddox?" Harper shrieks. "Maddox!" Her high-pitched cry hammers into the back of my eyes. "What did she do to him?"

28

UNCHANGEABLE

The wispy haze hijacks my sight. Blinded, I slide my fingers across the couch, searching for Maddox, only to find nothing but rough fabric.

"Pop, what in the—what just happened?" Devon's voice is strained. "Passing out like that . . . it's not normal, is it?"

"Hmph. Looks like he collapsed during the transfer, that's all." *That's all*? How can Pop sound unconcerned, like it's no big deal, that somehow what I saw knocked Maddox unconscious? "He'll need strengthening for next time. I reckon he'll be fine soon enough."

"But he's not fine!" Harper panics.

Voices fire from all directions. I press my heated palms over my ears and draw my knees to my chest.

"Calm yourself, Rose." Pop's tone is soothing, especially compared to Harper's. "You'll do no one any good if you can't think straight."

"You know her name is Harper," Devon says wearily.

"You call her what you want and so will I. Listen good, Rose. When the boy wakes, you give him a swig of that vine juice and he'll be fine in a matter of minutes."

I crack my eyes open. The wispy fog vaporizes enough so I

can see Harper kneeling beside Maddox. He's passed out on the worn carpet near the couch. Harper holds his wrist, checking his pulse. Guilt pangs through me.

"Keep yourself still, Honey." An old man wearing blue flannel pajamas and wraparound sunglasses hobbles into view. White hair crowns his dark, wrinkled head. His cane hits the coffee table. Four round indentions in the carpet map out where the table probably sat before Harper pushed it aside to get to Maddox.

"Sorry, Pop." Devon slides the table out of the way, resting it against the wall by a worn, green recliner with patchy scabs peeling away on the arms.

The haze fully recedes, but my lungs feel bound. I can't get enough air to breathe. I get up slowly, careful not to step on Maddox. Weakly, I force out the words, "I need to know who is going to die. I have to stop—"

The old man presses both hands on the handle of his cane and leans forward. "You're no good to anyone till you rest." His loud voice feels like cannon fire inside my head. Instinctively I cover my ears.

Harper is checking Maddox's airways. Devon hovers behind her. "Pop, we better contact Council and—"

"None of you have any idea how much pain the girl's suffered, except maybe the boy." Pop pokes at Maddox with the tip of his cane like he's checking to see if Maddox is still alive.

One look at Maddox's pale face and limp body lying on the floor near my feet, and I wrestle back a sob. I didn't mean to hurt him. I didn't even know I could.

Pop lifts a boney finger at Devon. "As soon as he wakes up, he'll know exactly how much stronger she is than the rest of you."

Pop is wrong. I'm not stronger.

"Maddox is cold." Harper stands. "I'm getting a blanket."

Devon's gaze follows her as she disappears around the corner of the hall near the front door. "Pop, it's only a matter of time before the Legions find Cera. They're circling East Ridge, searching. We've got to inform Council and arrange a transport."

"The girl's done with the vision. The boy has it now." Pop hunches over his cane. He looks like a pint-sized version of Devon—only older. A lot older. They share the same round head shape and frown lines, but Pop has bulldog-like jowls that Devon lacks. "The Legions may know she's in the area, but they won't know exactly where. Now that she's tethered, they'll stop searching. We'll move her when the time is right."

Devon gestures impatiently. "But what if—"

"What's the matter with you, son?" Pop thwacks Devon with his cane. "Didn't I teach you right? The boy's intercepting them now." Pop points to Maddox. "He's near her. There's no need to worry the vision will get taken."

"I know about transfers, Pop." Devon puts his hands in his pockets as he stares at the ground. "It's just that Council orders us—"

"Don't be lecturing me on Council. I may not be in the thick of things right now, but I was running Council before your mama was in diapers. Now let that girl rest." Pop pounds his cane on the carpet with an emphatic *thud*. It's not a suggestion. It's an order. Of course, he doesn't know that I don't follow orders very well.

"I don't need rest." My head throbs. I am totally nauseous, and I want to curl in bed until the lingering pain passes. But I can't stand around and do nothing. If Devon plans on taking me to Council, I'll run out that door and find Mom—okay, so maybe walk out the door. Running won't be possible for a few more hours.

Feeling his way to the recliner, Pop says, "Honey, you'll get about two feet out that door and those beasts will track you. They ain't gone yet. Sit yourself down until you're useful again."

I freeze. How did he know what I was thinking?

Harper hurries back into the room with a green crocheted blanket. "Has Maddox woken up yet?"

"Not yet," Devon says.

She shakes her head. "He's been out too long. I'll try and wake him."

"He's breathing, isn't he?" With a grunt, Pop lowers himself into the patchy recliner planted across from me. "Don't smother the poor boy. Let him be."

Conflict burns behind Harper's eyes as she stares at Maddox. Eventually she lets out a dramatic sigh and says, "Fine," before tossing the blanket on the couch next to me. "Then I'll fix him something to eat for when he wakes." She marches into the tiny kitchen near the front door.

I wince each time she slams a cabinet or drawer. The loud thump, followed by the angry clank of a metal pan hitting the stovetop aggravates my already pounding head. I rub my temples, trying to ease the pain, as I ask, "How can I find out who was in this vision?"

"You can't interpret your own visions?" Devon gives Pop a sideways glance.

I shake my head. Bad move. I lower myself back down on the couch. "I only see fragments. Bits and pieces at a time."

"But not a whole picture?" Devon asks.

"No."

Devon turns to Pop. "Why doesn't she receive a clear image?"

With a fluid motion, Pop rests his cane across his lap like a safety bar—or a weapon. "Honey, tell me what you saw."

Right then Maddox stirs. His arm shields his face from the light. I want to kneel down and tell him that I'm sorry a million times over, but Harper has somehow long-jumped from the kitchen and swooped to his side. "I'm right here, Maddox." She grabs the blanket and tucks it behind his head. "Does anything hurt?"

Maybe I'm being hypersensitive, but her question feels like an accusing dagger aimed right at me. Especially as Maddox groans in pain. "I've got something to help." Harper takes a small purple vial out from her front pocket, the same liquid she had me drink when she removed the glass shard. She lifts his head and sets the vial to his pale lips.

"Focus, Honey," Pop tells me. "Think on the vision, on what you saw, and not on the boy."

My cheeks burn. How could he tell I was looking at Maddox? "I wasn't—"

"Don't argue. *Think*." Pop rocks forward in emphasis.

"I saw a cup. Maybe. It didn't look like a cup. It could have been a wine glass. I don't know." Doing my best to ignore Harper, I search the room for something to focus on. A Coltrane album leans against the wall near the front door; a gold picture frame with a family photo sits on the bookshelf near Pop's recliner.

Nevertheless, I can't stay focused, so I close my eyes and rest my hands on my knees. I exhale and let the picture resurface. "There was also lightning." I open my eyes. "I saw lightning."

Pop's lips press into a slight scowl. "What color?"

Harper looks surprised at his question. Anyone might think that odd but . . . "It was red . . . or the red was blood. I'm not sure."

Pop stills the recliner. His words come out slow, careful. "Honey, when were you Awakened?"

"You mean when I started seeing things?" Out of the corner of my eye, I catch Harper placing her hands on Maddox. She's listening for any injuries. What if I hurt him internally?

"That's right." Pop's tone is calm. "How old were you when you had your first vision?"

"My first vision . . . ?" I try to think. "I was . . . uh . . ."

Devon interrupts. "Did you have visions before you turned seventeen?"

"I'll be seventeen in a few days."

"So you were Awakened at sixteen?" Devon looks surprised.

"What's the big deal?" Harper sits back on her heels and looks up at Devon. "I get she's a Seer and now she'll get all the protection, but seriously, do we have to make such a fuss about when she was Awakened? So what if she got her Bent early? That doesn't make her better than the rest of us."

Fire burns through my veins. I didn't say anything when she insulted me, accused me, *humiliated* me, but I've shut my mouth for too long. I launch myself off the couch. "I'm not better than anyone else, and I don't want to be. The *only* reason I'm here is to find out how to destroy those"—I fling out an arm—"those evil beasts. You think I wanted to start seeing and experiencing this horrible pain when I was seven? I couldn't care less when I was Awakened. The only thing I care about is keeping someone else from dying!" The whole room goes quiet.

"Seven?" Devon stares at me in disbelief. "You got your Bent at *seven*?"

Harper tosses her hair over her shoulder. "That's such a lie."

This time I'm the one glaring as I tower over her. "I don't care what you believe. Unless anyone can draw out—or better yet, *tell* me—what I've seen in my vision, then somebody *will* die. Don't you get it? It has to be stopped now. Every minute we spend arguing is nothing but wasted time. We're talking about a life! If I'd had more time to find Jess—" The rest of the words get strangled in my throat. I take a cleansing breath. "Whatever it takes. The situation has to be stopped from coming true, and I won't know what it means unless I can see it drawn out. And—"

"Cera." Devon stops me. "You can't change a vision."

"What?" His words stun me. "No. No! I almost did with Jess. I just needed more time . . . I could have—"

Devon slowly shakes his head. "Visions expose elements of the second realm. Either an event so far off in the future it won't happen in our lifetime, or an event from the past, giving hints about our history as keys to protect our power. It's like getting a puzzle piece, or mosaic tile, that fills in gaps of a greater picture we can't fully comprehend. They simply show what is. They don't reveal present-day events—or foretell deaths. And even if they did . . ." He looks at me almost apologetically. "I'm sorry to say, the situation would be unchangeable."

No. He's wrong. He *has* to be wrong. "That's not true!"

"Calm down." Devon holds a hand out, and his voice is filled with warning. "Listen to me. Interfering with a vision—it's forbidden. A lot could go wrong."

"I don't care what's forbidden! I can't stand by, knowing someone is going to die, and just let it happen. Who could? Besides, what you described as a vision is *not* what I see. My visions don't show events from the past, or some event in the distant future. Every single vision I've ever had leads to a near and impending death. My mom drew out the images and even cut out newspaper articles as proof."

"I'll draw it out." Maddox's voice is rough as he pushes himself to his knees. My heart lurches. His face is ghostly pale—not unlike Mom's the morning after I've had a vision. "I saw everything in the transfer. It's in my head. We can still find a way—"

Devon's lightning-quick glance flickers between Maddox and me. "Hold up. What do you mean by 'still'? How long have you known about her second Bent?" A combined look of disbelief, hurt, and anger sweeps his face. "You knew and kept it from me. From the group? You put everyone at Hesperian in danger. And in the workout room . . ." The swelling muscles in his arms match the rising of his voice. "You were planning on leaving, weren't you? Take off right before Council arrives and use her Bent in some way to avoid training. Was *that* what was going on?"

Maddox hangs his head, teetering a little as he stands.

"Why wasn't I included?" Harper sounds as devastated as she looks.

"I . . ." Maddox presses his fingers against the bridge of his nose and squeezes his eyes shut. I know the feeling. That's the pain of your own words echoing like fireworks inside your brain, but I also know hurting someone else feels ten times worse. But Maddox wasn't alone in this. I betrayed Devon as well.

"I didn't want to get locked up by Council," I admit, my voice shaking. "I knew what I was as soon as you told me. I'm the one who put everyone in danger, and I'm sorry. I only wanted to keep those horrid things from hurting anyone else."

Despite my honest confession, Devon is still terse. "There's a reason the Alliance has ranks and order. It's for protection. Yours and those around you. Regardless of what you want, you weren't given the Bent for fighting them off."

"But I have to try." The desperation in my voice mingles with choked tears.

Devon's scowl softens. "You can't."

"No, son." Pop clears his throat. "I believe she can."

Devon stares at his grandfather. "She's not a Blade or a Caretaker. It's been confirmed."

Confirmed. My heart sinks.

Pop gently rocks in his chair. "She's absolutely a Guardian and Seer. But she's something more. You can sense it, but you don't trust yourself enough to see it."

My gaze darts between Devon, who looks dejected, and Pop, whose expression hides behind his dark glasses. "Do I have three Bents? Is that even possible?"

Harper rises to her feet and rolls the blanket in her arm, puzzled. Maddox looks at the ground.

"It's not a Bent." Pop stops rocking. "Honey, I believe you're what we call a Blight."

Blight? A disease. Decay. Death. He's tagged me with a name that can't mean anything good.

Pop adjusts his glasses and leans forward intently. "According to some folks, you're considered the biggest threat to the Alliance there ever was. Honey, it's a wonder you're still alive."

29

BLIGHT

The grim walls of the cramped apartment seem to close in on me as everyone stands frozen with fear. "What do you mean by *still* alive?" I ask.

"Does she have a virus?" Harper's fingers twitch, ready to spring into action.

Devon studies me with scrutiny, and if I'm reading him right, a hint of disgust. "No. It's congenital. Something she was born with that can't be undone. Blights are born with a mixed, dualistic bloodline with traits from both parents, one who is Awakened and the other who is a . . . Dissenter." A rebel. Devon almost spits out that last word. If what Devon says is true, then it's no wonder Mom kept moving me. Maybe it wasn't so much about the bodies I left behind as it was her way of protecting me from the Alliance—or both.

Harper removes herself into the open kitchen as Devon continues. "Blights are considered a threat because, like Sirens, they lure the Awakened away from the Alliance so they'll dissent. With every convert, Sage's army grows and gives him more power." Devon's stern look aimed at Maddox is clear.

"Tell me, Honey," Pop asks. "Did either of your parents have a red mark around their neck? Maybe looked like a birthmark, a burn, or dry skin?"

The Dissenter isn't Mom. I swallow. "My father. I only saw the mark a few times because his shirts always covered what looked like a rope burn." I'd seen a similar blotch on someone else not too long ago. I go behind the couch to create a barrier between them and me. As I try to recall who and where, a bigger truth overtakes me. Dad knew I was a Blight when I had my first vision all those years ago. That's probably why he called me a monster and ran out on us.

My heart pangs. All this time, Mom's been by my side protecting me, enduring the pain of my visions, so no one would know . . .

"You're a Blight, sure enough," Pop says firmly. "The fact that your visions are fragmented, that there is a telltale sign that your bloodline is tainted."

Tainted. I hold on to the back of the couch to support my weakening knees. "What's so bad about having a dual bloodline? I'm not on the enemy's side."

Pop folds his hands across his lap. "Unions between Dissenters and Awakened are forbidden by the Alliance. If they're even able to have children, then their offspring—a Blight, like you"—Pop points at me—"not only dilutes the bloodline and weakens our powers, but if the conditions are right, could potentially destroy the very source of that power."

His words are making me physically ill. Not as bad as a vision, but in some way, just as awful. I'm not the enemy, but the way Maddox looks away, his face a storm of emotions I can't read, makes me believe I am. Harper listens intently as she stirs a steaming pot that smells of chicken soup.

Devon is now in full-blown military mode. "A Blight like her is beyond our scope of authority. I'll inform Region and arrange a transport." He pulls out his phone.

"Don't." Maddox looks ready to tackle Devon. "I know what Region Council does to Blights."

Devon looks straight at him. "Maddox, Blights are dangerous.

We're not equipped to handle them. We could end up putting everyone in danger."

"Stop talking like she's some impersonal Alliance concept. It's Cera!"

"Doesn't matter who it is. We can't protect her. The enemy's pull toward her will be ten times stronger than what we've ever experienced. Not only is she a Seer, but a Blight? Once Sage knows she exists, he'll stop at nothing to get to her power and siphon what's inside her head or use her to read any image renderings. He'll destroy anyone who gets in the way."

"Then we'll keep Sage from finding out—"

"At what expense?" Devon's voice rises, the two of them less than two feet apart. "How many lives are you willing to put in danger? Tanji? Amide? Everyone at Hesperian?"

The thought of anyone else dying sickens me. And there's a life on the line right now. Unless Maddox draws out my vision, I won't know who it is. "What will Council do to me?" I step away from the protection of the couch. "I don't want any more blood on my hands. Will they kill me? Lock me up forever? Tell me what happens if I turn myself in. I want to know."

"Hard to say." Devon looks at Pop, who sits quietly with his hands folded over his belly, letting it all play out.

I cross my arms. "Say it anyway."

Devon fidgets with his phone. "From what I've heard, Blights are usually . . . terminated."

Harper lets out a small gasp. She tries to cover up her distress by running water into a clanging pot. Maddox's concerned eyes fight to say what his tight lips don't speak. As far as looking to Pop for help, he might as well not be in the room. So much for having a fellow Seer on my side. I guess Blights don't get that luxury.

I absorb the weight of the word. *Terminated.* They'd kill me. Me. Someone who's on their side. No wonder Mom ran from the Alliance all these years. Maybe running is still the answer.

I search for a way out. The sliding door on my left is closer and probably leads to a balcony, but I'm pretty sure Maddox carried me up a flight of stairs—or two. Jumping off a two-story balcony isn't a great escape option. Two deadbolts secure the front door, and one requires a key. Luckily the key is in the lock. That door is my only plausible way out. Except that a swarm of Legions will probably be waiting for me as soon as I step outside.

No. If I run—do what I've always done—someone will die. Running isn't the answer. It never has been. I work hard to keep my voice steady despite my frantic heartbeat. "Devon, can we make a deal? Let Maddox draw out the vision, so I can see who's in danger, and give me the chance to save one life. Just one. Pop said I have the power to destroy the creatures. Let me try. If I die, then so be it. And if survive, then turn me in so I never hurt anyone again." The rational side of my brain tells me I didn't cause what I saw in my head, but the emotional part convicts me because I did nothing to stop it. "That's all I ask," I plead. "One life." Maybe my request is impulsive and naïve. Maybe the severity of what I'm proposing isn't registering, but there's only one thing I care about, and time is running out.

Maddox's face pales. "Going to Council . . . please don't. We'll find a—"

"Even if we agreed," Devon argues, "the visions are still unchangeable. Attempting to intervene puts others on the line and is a direct violation of Alliance code."

Pop, of course, stays mute.

Devon's allegiance is clear, but so is mine. "Then I'll do it alone. I'm not asking you to violate code, I'm only asking you to hold off informing Council until I have the chance to change this one vision. That's all. One opportunity to atone for ten years of bloodshed I didn't even know was happening. Devon, let me try. Please. *Please!*"

Devon's stance and eyes are unwavering. Panic seizes me. Why doesn't he understand that I *have* to stop the vision from coming true? "Even if you call Council and tell them I'm here, what will happen when they take me out that door? Legions are swarming East Ridge. *That* would put everyone in danger."

Devon's eyes relent—a tiny bit.

"Devon, you're not letting things slide. You'd be saving a life! And, who knows, maybe more. We're running out of time. These visions come true in less than twenty-four hours."

Without waiting for Devon's answer, Maddox rushes to the kitchen counter and hunts for paper and a pencil. "I found Cera while she was intervening on a vision before this one. Her read wasn't wrong then. I was there."

Devon frowns. "Maddox, wait."

"Would you seriously leave someone to die because of some Alliance code?" Harper still stirs the boiling pot. She sounds appalled. "If Cera wants to fight the creatures in order to save someone's life, then what's the harm? Let her."

On the surface Harper sounds like she's on my side, but we both know she wants nothing more than me out of their lives. I have to admit, I'm thankful for her backhanded endorsement because, somehow, it gets through to Devon.

He glances at Pop, who is tapping his index fingers on the armrest. "Here's what we'll do." Devon rubs the back of his neck. "Maddox will draw out the vision. Cera, with Pop's guidance, you can take a look and tell us what you see. If—and it's a big if—someone's life is *truly* in danger, and Pop agrees with your interpretation, then we'll plan how to stop it."

Maddox has found a pencil in a drawer and points it at Devon. "So you won't call Council."

Devon shifts. "I want to see what the image shows. Then I'll decide if we need additional support."

Pop grunts and resumes rocking. "You done right, son."

A smile flickers across Devon's lips. He takes several sheets of paper from the middle of a messy pile on the bookshelf and hands it to Maddox. "Get started."

30
PULLING THE THREAD

Maddox. Takes. Forever.

He hunches over the kitchen counter, drawing and erasing with a focused, intense expression. Drawing again. Slow strokes. Fast, quick ones. Crumples paper. Starts over. The soft-ticking clock by the front door tells me it's almost midnight. I pace between the couch and the dinette table. I had the vision about an hour ago, maybe more. Maybe less. I know I shouldn't rush him. Mom's drawings were always complete, so if I only see half a drawing, I might read the vision wrong. And even then, if Pop doesn't agree with me, I won't get a second chance to interpret. Devon will call Council, they'll haul me out of here, and whoever was in my vision will die.

My stomach growls as the room warms with the smell of Harper's soup. Devon leans against the wall near Pop's recliner, scrolling through his phone, but everything about him is alert.

"Done yet?" I ask Maddox. He shakes his head, crumpling another sheet. I make my way to the mound of wadded pages, ready to unfurl one. "It doesn't have to be perfect, just enough detail for me to see—"

"Let the boy draw it right," Pop interrupts me. "In the meantime, have Rose get you some clean clothes."

"She needs more than clean clothes." Harper eyes my hair while chopping carrots with chef-like precision. "More like a shower." She scrapes the carrot bits off the cutting board into the boiling pot.

In light of everything going on around me, washing up seems petty and a waste of time. Maddox erases a big section. His whole back is tense. Even his hands grip the pencil tight. Maybe if I'm not around, he'll relax and draw faster.

"Where's the bathroom?" I step around Maddox, stealing a glance at the drawing, but his arm blocks my view.

"Down the hall to the left," Devon replies. "Towels are in the hall closet."

"Your pants look okay." Harper comes out of the kitchen. "I'm sure Devon has a shirt you can borrow."

Devon looks me over. "Find her something from my closet you think will fit."

"This way." Harper sways past me. As I follow behind her, the faint sound of a television game show emanates from the back room, as if normal life goes on in some part of the world.

I step into the bathroom and look at my reflection—blotched face, no makeup, matted, tangled hair, and dark eyes.

"*Which way I fly is hell; myself am hell.*" Milton's verse sears like a branding iron on my heart. Yeah, you pretty much nailed it, Milton. Right now, nothing fits me better. The creatures, the Alliance, my visions . . . all are beyond what I ever imagined. All I wanted was to end the visions. I never expected that pulling the thread would unravel a never-ending nightmare.

And what a nightmare. I sink my head into my hands. My dad, a man I never really knew, was a Dissenter. Exchanged his Bent to the enemy for who knows what. I understand now why Mom never wanted to talk about him. And she's been keeping me hidden for seventeen years because I'm a Blight—a mixed-breed danger to the Alliance. Then there's the Alliance, a society whose Council members want me dead simply because I exist, since apparently I have the ability to kill the creatures as well as snuff out the Current, even though I don't know how. I rub out my forehead. It's way too much to take in.

One thought elbows its way through the rest. The only one that really matters: finding out who will die and how to keep it from happening. If I save someone's life, maybe then I can disprove my father's words. Even if it means I die in the process.

After washing up as quickly as possible, I slip on the green flannel button-down Harper hung on the doorknob inside the bathroom and wrap my hair in a towel that smells of clean linen, not unlike the ones at Hesperian. Except this towel lacks Gladys's scent of warm peaches and vanilla. Gladys. Sorrow cuts through my gut. What's Gladys going to say when she hears I'm a Blight? I've even lost my gift—the white flowered hairpin she gave me.

I take a deep breath. Lingering on the fact that I'm no longer a welcomed part of Hesperian's family won't do any good. I quickly towel-dry my hair, twist it in its flimsy knot, and then rinse out my mouth with the spicy mint mouthwash Devon has on the counter to burn away the acrid taste in my mouth.

Hopefully Maddox has made progress. I hurry back to the living room, checking the time as I pass the clock. It's still close to midnight? That's not possible. My stomach twists.

Something is wrong with the clock. Now I've got no idea what time it is or how much time is left. Harper hangs at Maddox's side, resting her hands on his shoulder as he draws. Pop and Devon aren't around.

"Is that supposed to be a hand?" Harper reaches out to touch the paper, but Maddox brushes her away and covers the sketch.

I don't want her or any of them seeing the gruesome details of my vision. That's my own private nightmare, not something I want to share with the world. "What time is it?" I ask.

Harper checks her watch. "It's almost two." She stifles a yawn.

What? Time is slipping away. I rush over to Maddox. "Let me see what you've got so far."

Maddox lifts his head to me. "I've tried drawing each part. It's putting them together, making a whole picture, that's hard."

I look at the sketch. All I can make out is a warped stick and a splashing puddle. "I don't know if it's any good to see it in fragments. It'll be too much like what's in my head. I was only able to understand them by looking at a fully detailed scene."

Maddox glances back down. "I'm close, I think. I just need more time."

"Did Pop tell you how to transfer the broken image on the page? Or maybe I need to show it to you again, somehow?" I quickly hold my palm open. For a split second, Maddox's fingers stretch to take hold, but then pull back. Maybe it's my imagination that he did want to grasp my hand, or maybe touching a Blight is forbidden. I suppose it doesn't help that Harper's standing watch right behind him.

"Pop said Seers have a whole scene." Maddox rubs his temples. "But yours is like a photograph torn into tiny pieces. Actually, it's harder because it's not a static image. It's a scene in motion. Since this is my first time, the whole picture isn't coming in clear, and the details are hard to make out. That's why I keep starting over."

This isn't good. "How long will it take?"

Maddox shrugs with an apologetic look in his bloodshot eyes. "Don't know. If my head didn't hurt so much, I might be able to draw faster."

My vision is causing him pain. Mom likely suffered as well. No wonder she was so weak after I had an attack.

Harper rests her hand on Maddox's shoulder again, probably listening to make sure he's okay. "Get it as close as you can. I don't care how rough it is. Then let me take a look," I say as Harper pulls the purple vial from her pocket.

With a deep breath, I turn and pace the room, working hard not to let my frustration come through. Maddox is trying. It's not his fault the image is hard to draw, but still . . .

I pass the family picture on the bookshelf. There is Devon, in a royal-blue cap and gown and a beaming smile, squinting in the afternoon sun while standing between two people I assume are his parents. His mom, a fierce woman in a fitted yellow dress and perfect black curls, wraps an arm around his waist. The tall, handsome man in a brown suit next to him has a smile that matches Devon's. Standing in front is a little girl, probably around Jess's age, wearing a cornflower-blue dress with two puffy ponytails on top of her head and a mischievous grin. His little sister, Althea. My throat swells.

They looked happy. Nothing like my own messed-up family and fear-ridden mother. Mom. My pulse heats with a warning flare. What if Mom is the one in danger?

The people who died were always those I knew, even if just in passing. I squeeze my eyes shut and try to replay the recent images, hoping to piece them together for something that might show me if it's her. White flashing light and blood puddled on the ground come to mind. Nothing distinct. I open my eyes and tuck my trembling hands under my arms. Calm down. Gladys is with Mom. She's going to be all right. The best thing I can do right now is prepare. Get ready to stop whatever there is to come.

I look down. This long-sleeved shirt will help against a Legion's burn but not a Cormorant claw. But after seeing what Cormorants are capable of, I know not much will. And I need a weapon. Apparently, as I learned with Rhys, only a knife will do.

I head to the kitchen to find exactly that. Harper is behind the stove again, mixing the pot. "Soup's done if you're hungry."

Even though my stomach growls, I don't have much of an appetite. "Thanks. Maybe later." I scan the counter for a knife—or even a phone to call Mom and check on her. From what I can tell, all utensils, except the wooden spoon near the bubbling pot, have been put away and there isn't a phone in sight. The more I think about Mom, the more I need to call her. I want to know she's safe and getting better and let her know that I'm all right. And maybe even say goodbye.

At that moment, Devon steps in from the balcony door. The hard lines on his face and tense shoulders carry a weight nonexistent in the family photo. I hurry to the living room, stopping him from going further. "Can I use your phone?"

Devon raises a suspicious eyebrow. "For?"

"I want to call my mom. The last time I tried to intervene on a vision . . ." I rub my hands over my face, wiping away the memory. "I need to hear her voice."

Devon hands it over, reluctant. "Make it quick."

I walk into the hall, stopping near the bathroom, and dial. The phone rings. And rings. Until it doesn't. The automated voice repeats her number. I wait for the long beep.

I swallow. "Mom. It's me. I need to know you're okay, so please call back when you get this. It's a . . . friend's phone." I lean against the wall and lower my voice. "Mom, I don't know what anyone's told you, but I know about . . . I know I'm a Blight. I understand why you didn't tell me. And please don't be mad, but . . . I can't come home. I'll only put you in danger, so please, listen to me. Let Gladys help you. Get strong enough and then go to—to the place you had planned. Hide there. I'm going to try and make things right for us. If I can . . . I'll come find you." My voice trembles. I swallow back the tears. "And Mom? I love you. Bye."

I end the call, keeping my head pressed against the rough wall. Please let her be all right. Let her not be the one in the vision. I take a deep breath and head back to the living room.

When I turn the corner, Maddox's eyes soften as he looks at me. Despite keeping my voice low, I can tell he heard everything.

"Any closer?" I push through the tremble in my voice.

"Almost." His gaze lingers before returning to the sketch.

I go over to Devon and hand back the phone. "Thanks. If you get a call back, can you let me know?"

Devon checks his phone, saving Mom's number. "I'm headed to Hesperian to meet Council."

I shoot him a hard look.

"I'm not notifying them—yet. I'm taking Harper back. And if I get an update on your mother, I'll let you know."

Harper walks out from the kitchen. "I should stay here." She glances at Maddox. "I mean . . . if those creatures are around . . ."

"The Legions in this part of town were neutralized, but there were a few minor injuries in the fight," Devon says. "They need your help treating the burns. Both Kellan and Tanji were hit."

I stiffen. "How bad?"

"Minor, but they need more ointment." Devon shoves the phone in his pocket.

Harper switches into her focused medic mode. "Then let's go."

Devon goes over to Maddox and leans next to him. "Call me when you finish," he says quietly.

Harper takes one last, conflicted look at Maddox and then at me. Instead of shooting her usual death glare, she hooks her arm through Devon's. "We need to hurry. That poison can't settle on their skin."

Devon looks at her arm tucked in his and stands a bit taller. As soon as they shut the door, a faint click sounds in the lock. I glance at the deadbolt. Devon took the key? I rush to the front door and turn the handle. The door doesn't budge. Did he seriously just lock me up? Maddox's head is down and focused. If he finishes the drawing before Devon returns . . . My pulse flares. I won't be caged, waiting for someone to die. I'll find some other way out while Maddox finishes the sketch, even if it means scaling down two or three stories from the balcony to get free.

31

IDEA OF WAR

I head to the balcony. Devon can't lock me in the apartment and expect me to wait for him to return. Not when someone's life is at stake. As soon as Maddox finishes, I'll bolt out of here with whatever knife I can get my hands on.

I slip through the sliding door. The fifteen-foot balcony is enclosed in a thick, clear plastic, much like the greenhouse except it smells of lemony antiseptic and new plastic. Warped lights from neighboring apartments pinprick the dark, but the cold doesn't seep through the covering, which means the creatures might not be able to sense me out here. If they can, it will cause more to flood into the area. I wasn't able to fight one Legion on the street when I found Juniper, and that was at dawn. Trying to save someone with a horde of Legions swarming East Ridge in the middle of the night will be next to impossible.

"Ain't no way down from out here, Honey." Pop's voice startles me.

I turn to find Pop sitting at the shadowed end of the balcony in a plastic chair with his back to me. How did he know I was out here? I didn't make a sound.

"Don't act like you ain't standing there." He turns his ear in my direction.

"How'd you know it was me?"

He digs around for something at his side. "You smell like honeysuckle."

I find it odd he says so because my full name, Lonicera, means honeysuckle. I sniff the tips of my hair. "I smell like whatever cedar shampoo was in the shower."

Pop snorts as if he disagrees. "The boy smells like rain. The girl smells like a rose drowning in perfume." No wonder he calls her Rose. "Tell the girl she'd be a lot prettier if she didn't wear so much perfume."

I can't help it—I laugh out loud. "You have no idea what she looks like, do you?"

"Oh, I see plenty fine." Pop scolds me with a shake of his boney finger.

Even though we're tucked inside a covering, I can't help but feel as if the creatures might be lurking around. I peer through the clear plastic but can't make out anything except my own distorted reflection. I tuck my hands under my arms. "When you say, 'boy,' you mean Maddox? He smells like the ocean."

"You only think so 'cause sight clouds your ability to see. It's rain. Like after a storm."

I'm not so sure he's right about Maddox, but what does it matter? "Can you help him figure out the vision?" I move to Pop's side. "I've got less than twenty-four hours to find out who's going to die. If he can't draw it out in time—"

"Now you listen up. Rushing into things without clarity will do more harm than good. Let the boy draw it right." Pop runs his fingers over a smooth tangerine in his palm.

"I know it needs to be done right so I can read the details, but can't you help speed things up?" A slight wind pushes against the covering. My ears perk. No shrieking Cormorants or buzzing sounds. Just a muffled car engine in the distance.

"Trust the boy. He'll get it soon enough." Pop digs his

thumbnail into the tangerine. The whole space fills with a tangy orange scent.

"Is that your way of saying no?"

"Without strugglin'outta the cocoon, the butterfly won't ever fly." He tears a small piece of the peel.

He makes absolutely no sense and is avoiding my question. "So you won't help because I'm a Blight and somehow you'll violate some code, or because you have some allegiance to an Alliance that doesn't care if someone dies or not?" I throw my hands in the air. "Doesn't life matter to anyone but me?"

Pop shakes his head as if I've said all the wrong things. He tosses a piece of rind into a nearby trashcan, missing. "Sometimes, what we want costs more than we're willing to sacrifice."

What kind of answer is *that*? "The second realm has blown up my life," I inform him. "I don't have much left to sacrifice. All I know is that I can't let these massacres go on. I don't know about you, but if I have any power to stop what's happening, then I have to try."

Pop sighs. He repositions his feet on the balcony rail and sits straighter. "Honey, we've been in a long-standing battle with Sage. The fight would be easier if he was simply a man, but Sage is a wandering spirit, an ageless shapeshifter from a realm that isn't our own. He reigns over these beings, ruling in a realm only we can see, trying to gain complete control over our world."

"Gladys told me about Sage and the war. If he destroys all of the Awakened, then he wins." A cold chill prickles at the thought of the destruction of so many people. I nervously glance through the plastic again.

"He's after more than bloodshed. Even if he killed everyone in the Alliance in every part of the world, he wouldn't succeed. New bloodlines will sprout, and it would be an endless battle. But if he can eliminate the very thing that gives us our power and creates these new bloodlines . . . that's when he wins. If that day were to come, then every bit of life as we know it—as the world knows it—will be wiped away, destroyed under his control." Pop is quiet for a moment as if he sees the devastation playing out in his mind.

"Honey, we protect all the creative energy in the world—all advances and discoveries in every aspect of life. That same energy that flows creativity into the world feeds our powers. If that power is destroyed, all hope will die." A somber shadow crosses his face. "This fight is more than just stoppin' a few creatures, or savin' a few lives. It's about preserving the world's way of life by fighting a battle the Commons don't even know exists."

The idea of war is beyond me. I shake my head, even though Pop can't see, and pick up the rind off the floor, tossing it in the trash can. "All I want is to change what happens in my visions so they won't come to pass. To save each life, one at a time. I don't want to get involved in a war."

Pop purses his lips and rips the fruit into two halves. "War's in sight. We can't sit on the sidelines or be runnin' away any longer." He holds up a tiny wedge of tangerine, offering me a slice.

"No, thank you." Even though the air is warm, I shiver. "The fight is between the Alliance and Sage. According to you, I'm a free agent that doesn't belong to either side."

Pop grunts. "Honey, you belong to both sides, which gives you more power than you realize."

"Don't tell me I've got special powers because I'm some prophetic chosen one—"

"Ain't no such thing as a chosen one." Pop frowns. "But you can choose to be the one to make a change. It don't matter what you are, Blight, Awakened, Dissenter . . . even a Common, just don't go at it alone."

I rebel at the thought of more people involved in this nightmare world. "I don't want to change the world. I never did. Before I knew about the second realm, I only wanted to find out why I was having panic attacks and stop them so I could have a normal life. Now all I want is to keep what appears in my visions from coming true." My frustration grows. "What good am I if I can't save one life?"

"You've got what you need. Power from both sides—a thin line separatin' shadow from light. Just a matter of which one you gonna choose. Which one gets control."

"I choose to destroy the creatures and save lives."

Pop rests the half-eaten tangerine in his lap. "Focusin' too much on destroying might wake you to the wrong side of love."

What does *that* mean? Frankly, I'm getting irritated at his cryptic words that are far from helpful. "How can saving a life be wrong?"

"Stop gettin' all hotheaded. That ain't what I said. You only hear a small part of truth before feelings take control. If you don't like the answer, you stop listenin' and don't hear what you need."

"What I *need* is to know is who is going to die and how to stop it—or even what sort of power Blights have—"

"The war starts in here." Pop taps at his temple. "Feelings blur the lines."

Why won't he answer me directly? He's maddening and clearly not going to help me out. "I'm going to see if Maddox is almost done." I head to the door.

Before I move further, Pop says, "Honey, those creatures? They might very well be on your side."

What? A disturbing rawness gnaws at me. "Those creatures are the enemy. I'm not."

I go into the apartment, much more confused than when I went out. Pop practically said I align with the enemy, wasn't willing to help, and made no sense at all, talking about cocoons and butterflies, and how there's more important things than saving a life.

Seriously, what's wrong with everyone around here? At least

Maddox is willing to help. He's sitting at the counter . . . ripping up the sketches?

"What are you doing?" I run over and frantically collect the pieces from the floor.

"I think I've figured it out." He spins around to face me. "I couldn't draw it as one image, so I drew it in parts." He moves the paper shreds into various positions. "Maybe you can make something out if we put it together, like a puzzle. Or a mosaic." His eyes are loaded with meaning. In that moment, the Current sparks harder than ever before, catching me off guard with an intense jolt. We both quickly look away and focus on the scraps of paper.

"Let's try." I tuck my hair behind my ear, focusing on anything except how hot my face feels at the moment, or how turbulent Maddox's bright blue eyes are.

I outline the border with white scraps. Maddox's shoulder leans against mine as we move the pieces, spreading them all over the counter in silence, mapping out a broken picture. From the torn pages, images start forming.

Goosebumps rise on my skin. Maddox is brilliant. His idea might just work.

32

SINGLE-MINDED ARROW

After arranging and rearranging shreds of paper for who knows how long, the only clear items are a lantern, a cup, and a puddle. My eyes burn from staring at the pieces. Even though the clock still reads close to midnight, it has to be at least three in the morning. Devon isn't back.

"Can you pull more detail on the wine glass?" I stifle a yawn. "The goblet, or cup, or whatever—it was broken. Not shattered, but cut off somehow."

Maddox rubs his fingers over his tired face. "I think I've got the whole scene in my head. Give me a few minutes. I'll try to get that."

I won't hover. My weary legs won't let me pace the living room any longer, so I sit on the couch and close my eyes. I picture the goblet, imagining Maddox next to me, hoping he can pull out the details the way Mom somehow could.

Something scratchy rubs against my cheek. Fabric. It smells of lemon and secondhand furniture. My heart pounds as I thrust myself up on my elbows. Soft light radiates from a single light in the kitchen and pushes out the darkness in the living room. I fell asleep? No! How much time have I lost? It's dark out, the broken clock still reading just before midnight.

Pop is nowhere around, but Devon made it back. Across the cramped living room, he's asleep, snoring in the recliner. At the counter, Maddox rests his head on his arms. Also asleep.

I push off the couch, tripping over a blanket. I shake Maddox awake. "Where's the sketch?"

Maddox groans and lifts his head. "Hmm . . ."

"Did you finish? Let me see." I tug at a paper, sliding it out from under his arms as he wakes. Pieces of the torn-up sketches fall to the floor.

Maddox sits up, rubbing out his eyes. "After we laid things out and you went to take a nap, details came to me out of nowhere."

I wasn't just going off to take a nap. I was trying to picture the images in my head, hoping he could see them. I just happened to fall asleep. But none of that matters now. We might be out of time.

I place the sketch on the counter where there's more light and focus on the image. One look at his artwork and I forget to breathe. My vision, just like Mom's renderings but sketched with ten times her talent, sits right in front of me. The detailed scene looks more like a black-and-white photograph than a pencil sketch.

As my eyes fly over the page, I trace the curvy waves of the cup's stem. The goblet looks new, but fragile. The hourglass stem has been knocked over and looks like a girl diving down with her arms above her head, although her feet and arms are bound. The top is severed, cut off from the cup and half shattered on the ground. The tiny pieces of the broken basin flow on the ground like strands of . . . hair? Curly or long?

"Do you see something?" Maddox whispers. I shut him out and concentrate harder.

Liquid pours out from under the broken pieces and . . . trampled flower petals. Blood? No. In my vision the liquid was deep violet, not red. The shaded lines that hover over the liquid look like disfigured hands reaching through the fog, smearing their greedy fingers through the fluid like they're applying war paint . . . or maybe something like a tonic as if it could bring them life. Heal them somehow . . .

Then it hits me. "Oh no." I lean against the counter because my knees feel like they might buckle any minute.

Maddox stands up. "What do you see?"

Devon wakes, springing out of the recliner. "What's wrong?"

I stare at the curvy stem. "The liquid in my vision was purple like the serum. Serum. It's about healing." My shaky finger points to the drawing. "These hands in the black mist . . . they're the sallow men—the Legions. They're going to kill a Healer. There's a flower . . ." My mind races, recalling the yellow flower in Juniper's hair. "They tried to get Juniper once before . . ."

Before I know it, I bolt toward the front door.

"Whoa, hold on." Devon comes after me and takes hold of my arm. "I would have gotten a call if someone spotted more Legions."

I pull away. "Would they know to call if they saw black mist?" I ran out unprepared when I searched for Jess, and I failed. I won't make that mistake again. I need a knife. I dart to the kitchen and search the drawers.

Devon flips on a switch, filling the room with bright, assaulting light. He guards the front door, looking puzzled. "Black mist?"

That's right. He wasn't on the streets when I detected the Legion before anyone else did. Perhaps that's a unique Blight trait. "It's how Legions travel. They creep around in a black fog. Then, whenever they want, they form into Legions." I look out the patio. There's no sign of sunrise. "I don't know how much time is left before the vision comes true. I didn't get to Jess in time. I can't let that happen again."

"Before we do anything," Devon reminds me, "Pop needs to agree with your reading. That was the deal."

"We don't have time!" Opening a drawer, I pick out the sharpest knife I can find.

"Put that down," Devon demands as he pulls his own hunting knife out of his pocket. Holding the sparkling blade steady, Devon's eyes harden.

"Call Harper." Maddox comes between Devon, with his knife, and me. "Have her keep everyone at Hesperian inside—especially Juniper."

Harper. My gut twists at the sound of her name. "I'm wrong," I whisper. I set the knife on the counter and reach over to grab the sketch for a second look. At my sudden movement, Devon starts for me, but Maddox holds him back.

I focus on the drawing. The sleek stem has perfect curves. Closing my eyes, I picture the broken glass. The strands of hair in my mind were . . . blonde. "It's Harper." Her name punches me harder than Tanji's fist to my face. I know I'm right. "Harper's the one in danger."

Panic flashes through Maddox's eyes as he looks at Devon. "Call her. Make sure she's all right."

Devon is already pulling up the number. But his built-in lie detector runs high as he looks at me while placing the phone to his ear. "Maddox, wake Pop."

He thinks I'm lying? "The sleek stem." I point out. "Right here, the curves. The strands of hair. Blonde hair. And the flowers . . . petals. She'll be on the street buying flowers, or herbs, or . . ." The way the soft light falls on the glass. "It happens sometime after dawn." It's still dark outside. I shake the paper at them. "I'm telling you, it's Harper. I know it is."

"She's not answering." Devon hangs up. Fear darkens his eyes as he glances at the sketch in my hand. "How many Legions? Is that detail clear?"

I smooth the paper. The puddle of Legions. Greedy hands stretching out, smearing balm on their arms. One. Two. "Maybe three." Possibly four.

Devon tenses as he dials another number. "We can't handle three." He turns his back, putting the phone to his ear.

Maddox steps in front of him. "If you call Council, you'll only give Cera away. They'll question how you know Harper's in trouble. You'll be in violation of code. And Council won't do anything to save Harper. They won't intervene on a vision, and you know it."

"But three Legions . . ." Devon slowly drops the phone to his side. "We don't have the gear to fight and stay protected."

Maddox runs a hand through his hair, exposing the jagged red scar along his jaw. "With my Bent, I'll know how to protect Harper. Let me use your blade in case I have to fight. I'll get her back. Safe."

"You can't see the Legions in mist form. I can," I remind him as I grab the knife off the kitchen counter. "The deal was I go alone. I can't let anyone else get injured. It will happen around dawn. It's still dark. I've got time. I'll find Harper and bring her back before the Legions find her. No one has to get hurt."

"You can't chase after them." Now Maddox is the one blocking the front door. "If Sage can use you to ruin us, don't you think those Legions will do anything to get to you? Maybe they'll kill you to siphon your power, or maybe they'll alert Sage to where you are and he'll come after you. I don't know. But right now, we've still got time to keep you hidden. Get you trained to fight."

"I'm done hiding. I'm stopping this vision from coming true, Maddox. I have to. I can't let her—or anyone—die on account of what I see. And time is running out."

"Maddox is right," Devon says. "If you go out there . . ."

"That was our deal. You let me try. If I make it back, turn me in. If I don't, then—"

"Harper will die." Devon's conflicted expression is filled with despair.

"I won't let that happen," I tell him. "But standing around arguing is a waste of time. If you're not going to make a move, I will."

"Single-minded arrows, all aiming separately at the same target, will only knock one another out." Pop's shadow, cane in hand, appears at the doorway. "Goin' at it alone ain't gonna hit the mark. Aim together."

"Pop's right." Maddox turns to me. "You won't survive three Legions on your own, and neither will Harper. And kitchen knives—regular knives—for that matter, won't work against them."

I frown.

When Devon holds out his hand, the vine-etched blade glistens. "Only a particular kind of knife will work. Antique metal. Limited supply, called Paradise Steel. Named for the *Gates of Paradise,* the metal panels carved by the Renaissance sculptor, Ghiberti."

"Council doles them out," Maddox says, then frowns. "But only Caretakers and Blades are allowed to use them."

No wonder Kellan was able to kill the creatures when I couldn't. He had a similar vine-etched blade.

Devon holds the knife in his hand, as though checking the weight. "Except for now. Take this." He hands the knife to

Maddox, who looks at Devon, incredulous. "I've got my mom's as a backup."

Maddox curls his hand around the hilt as his eyes soak up the metal sparkling in the light. "You're violating code? It'll cost you—"

"It's Harper." Devon's tone is as rigid as his body. "We don't have the right gear to keep Cera safe on the street, and without a third blade, she'll have to stay," he says, dialing another number.

"No." I toss my useless knife on the counter near the scraps of paper before turning to face Devon. "Let me use the Paradise Steel. I can see the creatures before they form. If I have the right weapon, I can attack without anyone getting hurt."

"The war ain't about destroying." Pop shuffles into the light.

"Maybe yours isn't, but my war is about fighting for one life." Pieces of the sketch Maddox tore up lie on the ground near my feet. "Whatever it takes."

Maddox stands firm. "Even if we had a third weapon, you haven't been trained to use the Steel."

The sparkling etches of the deadly weapon in his hand provoke me. I rush over and grasp his forearm. "Then let me go with you. I'll be your eyes, navigate you around the Legions, or better yet, tell you where they are so you can strike them as they form so they won't have a chance to attack. I've been running from them since I was seven. I know how to survive." I force myself to look into his stormy eyes despite the fierce jolt of the Current. He glances at my hand, resting on his arm. Suddenly aware of how tight I'm gripping, I let go. I lower my voice. "In the cellar, you told me we were all in this together. You said we couldn't handle this fight alone. Together, we could start something new." His eyes lift to meet mine. "Saving one life can be the storm that changes the landscape."

Devon spins around as someone answers his call. "Claire?" He makes his way toward the balcony. "Where's Harper?"

With his jaw set and the knife in hand, Maddox steps away from the door. He gives me a sideways glance and a subtle nod, the same way he did behind the trash bin when he signaled me to run from the Cormorants.

Without hesitating, I fling the front door wide open and dart into the musty hall and then down the metal stairs. Maddox clamors right behind.

Reaching the bottom step, I race through the dark foyer. My fingers fumble along the doorframe and flip the lock. I put all my weight into opening the solid wood door. Maddox reaches over my head and helps heave the weathered blue door wide open. In that brief moment, I smell a hint of rain.

"We'll find Harper. Get her to safety. No one's going to die." He wears the same intense expression he did on the streets when he found me. "If you spot a Legion, tell me. I'll take it out. Then you hide. They'll fight harder if they sense you're around. Got that?" I look up, straight into his determined eyes. That electric Current swirls in my gut, kicking a surge of adrenaline through my blood. But I don't have time to blush.

Without another word, our feet hit the pavement in unison. Maddox guides the way with the Paradise Steel in his fist while I scan the dank streets for traces of black mist.

Together, we run down the buckled sidewalk and search for Harper.

33

SAYING GOODBYE

Maddox takes my hand to lead me as we turn another corner in the predawn light. The smell of bitter ash mixes with exhaust and chokes the soggy air. I slow to look down the darkened street. Anemic streetlights reveal overstuffed trash bags, wet cardboard, and an old recliner littering the damp curbs. Early shopkeepers roll up metal walls and unlock storefronts, but as far as I can tell, there's no sign of mist or Legions.

We jog along to the steady cadence of the city and our own breathing. Waking light blankets the violet sky. If we can find Harper before sunrise, perhaps we won't encounter any Legions. We can only hope.

One street away, a truck's squealing hydraulics break through our silence. Not the sound of hornets or bees, but I jump anyway. A cold wind taps against my back with the sulfuric smell of decay.

I stop. My heart kicks against my ribs as I squint into the dark. A hiss escapes from a decrepit building. Not the sound of hornets. Or black mist. The sound and smell come from a cracked gas pipe.

"All okay?" Maddox is barely audible, though he is close beside me.

I nod. False alarm but my pulse races just the same.

"The shop's a few blocks away." Maddox glances at the lavender sky. Darkness is lifting. We need to hurry.

I bite my chapped lips as we run in the cold shadows of the looming buildings, searching for Harper. A shiver climbs my skin. Maybe I shouldn't have come. If my presence lures the enemy, Maddox is sure to be in danger.

We jog another few blocks. As soon as we turn the corner, I inhale the sickening stench of sulfur. I come to a hard stop and turn around. Something feels wrong. Not like it did when I found Juniper. This time the creeping chill courses through me. In the dim light, shadowed shapes are hard to see. I focus on one spot and use my peripheral vision to catch any movement, the way Tanji taught me.

Not a few buildings away, something moves. "What's wrong?" Maddox whispers.

I put my finger to my lips as a signal for him to keep quiet. Pulling at his shoulder, I step up on my tiptoes and put my mouth against his ear as he leans down. "Mist is climbing up the building. Too high up for you to attack."

Maddox turns to look at me. His concerned stare, inches away, burns into me as the Current blasts between us. I swallow. That sensation keeps getting stronger when it should have faded a long time ago. I push the feeling aside and race off, following the black haze with my footsteps light and soft. With the Legion wandering that high, we can't attack. I've got no choice but to find Harper before it does.

I reach the corner and halt. Which way do I go? Maddox comes up behind me. Morning is beginning to light the sky. The mist is now easier to see, but that also means I'm running out of time. The black fog slinks along the top of a building, and Harper is nowhere in sight.

Swift footsteps sound down the pavement behind us. Before

I can turn around, Devon is at our side with sweat beading his forehead. I point to the top of the building and mouth the words, "Headed south."

"The store's the other way," he whispers skeptically, searching the roofline.

"Trust her," Maddox whispers back at him.

My gaze follows the mist creeping along the roof . . . until it doesn't. The hazy fog stops. The creature didn't hear us from this far away, did it? I scowl. Either we're too loud, or the creature senses I'm around. Both of which are not good.

In that moment, a second mist-cloud converges with the first. The black haze doubles in size before resuming the southbound course along the roof. My pulse flares. I hold up two fingers and then point again to the roof. Devon grips the short hunting knife in his fist, ready for battle. If we can find Harper before the Legions do, then there will be no need to fight.

I take off down the road in a full sprint, working hard to outrun the Legions. Maddox and Devon race after me.

I skid around the corner and trip over a garbage bag before weaving around a man carrying a paper coffee cup. "Sorry," I say, as the guy shakes his hand dry while mumbling under his breath.

As soon as I regain my balance, I see her. Down the street, near the next corner, Harper sifts through a cart parked in front of a small floral shop. She delicately picks through greenery, smelling each one, oblivious to any danger. Just like Jess.

I scan the street for the Legions. On the rooftop, directly across from her, two misted creatures rear up like onyx cobras. Right before my eyes, they shapeshift into deformed men with black vellum wings and outstretched arms. The hum of hornets' wings carries on the wind. Before I can scream and tell her to run, Devon flies past me like an all-star quarterback.

Maddox yanks me into the alcove of a vacant storefront. "We found her. Now wait here."

"No." I shift to push past him. "Move out of my way."

He slams his hand up against the display window, blocking my escape. "We know two are out there. Maybe more, and you don't have a weapon." He moves closer. So close that my heels back into the cement stair. I try to focus on anything but his warm scent of rain filling the space between us. "If the Legions find you, if they know *what* you are, they'll kill us all. The best you can do is try to outmaneuver the beasts and run."

I step up to meet him eye level, giving me distance and the ability to concentrate. "I'm not running anymore—"

"Cera." He leans in. His voice is urgent. "If anything happens to me, run back to the apartment. Hide. Pop will know what to do."

"I'm not hiding." I shove his arm aside, but he takes my shoulders, holding me so I'll look at him.

"Last time, with the truck—we almost died." His voice strains. "You have to stay safe. You can't go out there, you hear me?" A storm rages behind his eyes. In that moment, a million electric flutters take flight inside my stomach as the Current pierces through me.

I start to protest, but no words come out. Not only is he standing so close that the smell of rain fills the narrow inches separating us, but something about the way his gaze drifts to my lips as I swallow detonates a scorching fire all over my face. When his eyes rise and meet my mine, the Current explodes between us.

My heart drums so hard, he must be able to—Maddox presses his lips to mine. They're soft. Warm. Heat radiates through every part of me. My insides—along with my fight—dissolve as he holds my head in his hands. My own hands slide up and around his back. His kiss, gentle at first, turns heated and urgent, as if saying goodbye.

Without warning, the vision blasts through me:

A handheld lantern shines
A ray of caramel light beams
A narrow path illuminates through the dark
A yellow glass goblet, smothered in smoke . . .

Maddox's head snaps back. The intense, electric air between us breaks. He releases me and my hands fall to my sides. Remorse darkens the edge of his eyes, still inches from mine. "Cera . . . I . . ." He swallows the rest of his words. Taking my hand, he presses something into my palm, and then curls my fingers shut.

A shrill cry pierces the air. We both know without saying so that the cry sounds a lot like Harper. The next thing I know, he's racing out of the alcove, heading straight for battle.

I can't move. I press a hand against the cold storefront window, stunned, raw, and weightless. I open my curled fingers to find the white flower hairpin Gladys gave me. Maddox found it? My lips tingle. But as soon as glass smashes and Devon cries out in pain, the spell breaks.

I stuff the pin in my pocket and rush to find them. On the sidewalk, not far from Devon, Maddox shields Harper, urging her to run. The cart is toppled over. Flowers trampled. Smashed glass sparkles on the ground near Devon as he lies in the road, writhing in pain. The gold blade is knocked from his hand and glistens in the dawning light, too far out of his reach. Useless.

Two Legions, one a tornado of black smoke hovering two stories high, prepare for another strike. The other swirls in mist form on the rooftop across the street. My vision showed three, possibly four . . . where are the others?

I spin around searching for more, listening for the vibrating hum of hornets. Only two for now. Both misted creatures shapeshift into funneled torpedoes, simultaneous death missiles. No one can see the Legions in this form but me. Coming from opposite directions, both hazy rockets launch straight for Devon lying on the ground. At that speed, Devon won't hear the buzzing wings; he won't know to shield himself until it's too late.

I run between parked cars, scrambling to get to the street, and yell, "Devon, move to your left!"

Through the cloudy car window, I catch sight of the mist transforming into Legions a few feet before impact. Devon must have heard me—just in time too—because with great effort, he rolls to his side as the creatures explode in a plume of black smoke. And even in the explosion, they are already reforming. I slump against a red sedan, and the car alarm goes off. That was too close.

Maddox spots me. "Get out of here!" He pushes Harper toward the far corner. Instead of running away, she rushes to Devon. Hands shaking, she fumbles for the purple vial in her pocket. Both Legions retract into the sky. "Harper, no!" Maddox's yell contains the same dread in my mind: if the wretched beasts sense she has the serum, they'll attack her just like I envisioned.

I push into the wind and race toward Harper. I can make it. I can knock her away before the Legions descend. The buzzing intensifies. I hurl myself at her and shove her away as she screams. The beasts slam into my side and I'm knocked onto the concrete. I instantly cover my head. The beasts hit the pavement beside me. Devon's knife lies in the middle of the road, far beyond my reach.

"Cera, move!" Maddox's voice cuts through the horrific buzzing. Mustering strength, I push off on my elbows and shift backward as red embers burst then rain down from overhead. Maddox has taken one out. I scramble to my feet. The remaining Legion retracts three stories into the sky. A new one joins his side, both hanging in midair.

Devon, burned and holding his arm, is working hard to get up. Thankfully Harper is hidden behind a parked car, safe.

Maddox crouches behind the broken cart. But neither of them can see the vile mist billowing higher in the air, hovering in the sky, listening over the wailing alarm. The mist stops swirling and twists into two obsidian tornados.

One beast aims right for Maddox. The other kicks out toward either Devon or Harper. I don't have time to warn them all. With my heart jammed in my throat, I leap up from my crouched position and race into the middle of the street. I whisk Devon's blade off the road and shout at the vile creatures. "Leave them alone!"

Instantly the Legions stop spinning and unravel as if caught midair. An electric pulse zaps my palm where the hilt presses my flesh, but I grip tight and won't let go. The thick fog sways as though hypnotized before slowly forming into two sallow men.

I tune out all sounds around me—Maddox freaking out, the store owner's shouts, and an angry car horn—and lock in on the monsters.

"That's right," I scream at the beasts. "Follow me." Hovering over six feet in the air with outstretched vellum wings, the Legions look at me with their cavernous holes for eyes that melt down their elongated faces. I shiver when the lurid, horrible buzzing of mad hornets drowns out every other sound in the frigid air. Reason is screaming for me to run. I've never seen their sagging, ashen skin in this light or noticed the deformed claw hands that hang well below their knees. Instead of feet, the creatures rest on a black cloud that reeks of sulfuric ash.

Despite the smell burning my nose, I inhale deeply. Stay calm. Each of them was once a person. I tighten my hold on the small hunting knife. How can this possibly be the weapon to destroy the hulking mass in front of me? My feet twitch. It takes everything I have not to run. I know if I do, the Legion will only target the others again. Instead, I take a step toward the creatures. If I can get close enough, the way Kellan told me, perhaps I can stab one of them through the heart.

I'm not far from the Legion hovering near Devon. My insides

churn with each step. How could Pop say these rabid, disfigured monsters were on my side? They're nothing but ruthless, destructive, evil. They are the enemy. Not me.

I raise my weapon, ready to drive the blade through the creature's heart. As I do, the beast tilts his head as though studying me. The disfigured face shifts, revealing the outline of a square chin and pointed nose. This was once a person. A man. Someone who allowed their Bent to be siphoned and replaced with Sage's power. Someone like my father, who used to call me "ma belle," while dancing around the living room . . .

Would destroying a creature be the same as killing someone? If it is . . . My hand droops, trembling.

"To crush his head / Would be revenge indeed, which will be lost / By death brought on ourselves."

Yes, Milton. Destroying can't be the answer. I'd be no less a monster if it were. I can't cause more death than I already have. There has to be some other way.

34

IRREVOCABLE

Dawn burns like fire over the buildings. I stand in the middle of the shadowed road with a Legion ten feet in front of me and another hovering in front of Maddox a little farther away.

Maddox doesn't hesitate. He comes up behind the Legion blocking his path, and with his blade sparkling in the morning light, stabs the creature through the heart. The Legion explodes, emitting thousands of red sparks over the road like dying embers. Harper screams, and the squared-jaw Legion that was hunting Devon—the one I held captive but couldn't bring myself to slaughter—ascends into the sky with a piercing screech, its pitch cracking nearby windows.

"Cera, behind you!" Maddox gestures frantically at something looming over my shoulder.

As soon as sulfuric wind whips near me, I duck and roll into a solid crouched position that would make Tanji proud. Dodging the hit, I quickly spring to my feet. A Legion, larger than any other, implodes on the asphalt right where I had been standing. My heart races. The creature reforms. It's the fourth Legion. Two down. Two remain. So far.

Harper manages to get Devon to his feet, and they take cover. It's Maddox, hunched in the middle of the road, searching the sky, who's too exposed. And the Legions heard him call my name. Both wispy creatures, invisible to his sight, swirl twenty feet overhead, prowling like greedy vultures ready to descend.

If I can call them out again, maybe I can hold them steady until Maddox can attack. "I'm right here!" I yell, holding my weapon to the sky.

Sirens wail in the distance—police, ambulance, or both, I can't tell. But it doesn't matter. They're both equally unwelcome right now. Unless they can sense what we sense, they'll only get in our way.

I don't dare take my eyes off the beasts. I take a step away from Maddox. "It's me you want!" I shout up at the Legions. My throat tightens. The deformed beasts float in my direction as if I'm pulling hideous helium balloons on a string. I take another step on the warped asphalt, luring the creatures farther away.

But then Maddox shouts, "No, Cera, run!" The Legions break away and form into one colossal smoke bullet, aiming right toward him. No!

I scream. Maddox can't see the double assassins headed his direction. I run full force at Maddox. I crash into his side, but I'm blown back. As I'm knocked to the ground, the knife sparks against the Legion and burns my hand before flying out of my fist. My back and elbows scrape against the cement as the creature lands on top of me. My hand sizzles as I try to punch through leathery skin. Both Legions wobble for a brief moment then regain strength. Despite what they used to be, these beasts are *not* human. Suddenly the Legions retract into the sky, clearing my sight.

Maddox lies on the ground several feet away, groaning in pain with his knife nowhere around. The hair on his forehead is tainted with blood. He's too injured to get to his feet and run. Another hit and he'll be dead.

The monsters spin high above Maddox, ready for the final

blow. I can't see the blade anywhere. I stagger to my feet, weaponless.

Something uncontainable wells deep inside of me. I curl my fists tight and scream over the approaching sirens with every bit of breath I have. "Leave him alone! It's me you want. I'm a Blight."

As soon as the words escape my lips, my skin turns cold. Both vile, misted creatures stop midstrike. My stomach wrenches. I know in that moment that I've done something very wrong. Irrevocable. But I didn't know how else to protect Maddox.

He stirs on the ground, saying something about making a mistake or not listening—or both—but he's alive, and that's all I care about.

The Legions transform into two sallow men: the colossal one that attacked me, and the smaller, squared-jaw one I didn't take down when I had the chance. The smaller one fixes its hollow eyes on me. Its mouth foams with stringy saliva and opens wide, releasing a scream so shrill that windows shatter, raining glass on the shadowed sidewalks. The vile creature sails into the sky and flees to the clouds. My blood turns cold. I have no doubt he's gone to inform Sage. It's only a matter of time before it brings more beasts to the fight.

But as soon as the larger Legion torpedoes toward me, I swallow my regret and sprint away from Maddox and the others. I shift left and right, weaving through the intersection, along sidewalks, under awnings and back onto the road. The Legion hits the asphalt inches away from my heels and explodes into a cloud of black dust. But I'm not stopping, even as I race around a corner, unscathed. Not while the beast spins wildly behind me, inches out of reach, and moves farther away from Maddox. My legs pump at full speed. I'll get the Legion far enough away from everyone, and then I'll hide.

I turn another corner only to find cars backed up at a traffic light. Getting through the mess will only slow me down, so I cut through an alley instead.

I give one quick look over my shoulder. The Legion spreads over the open road like black smoke riding on an oil spill. I've gained some distance, but not enough. A train roars not too far away. I must be close to the station. As I pass a parking lot, I picture the city grid from my time in the cell tower. If I run between buildings, maybe I can ditch the Legion by jumping on the train, the same way Maddox and I did with the Cormorant. Giving everything I've got, I slap my feet hard against the asphalt and run between the narrow buildings, catching a view of the cell tower in the morning light. I'm close. The station should be four blocks down. I race across the street and duck between the next set of narrow buildings.

Halfway down, I slide to an abrupt stop before plowing into buzzing generators blocking my way out. I've made a mistake. I can't double back, and I can't climb over fast enough without being caught. Just then, soft amber headlights glow from somewhere on the other side of the generator, lighting up a path of wires against the brick wall. That's my answer. Squeeze around the side of the generator. I'm small enough to navigate through the hoses until reaching the other side. The whirring sound is loud enough to hide me. If not, then I'm trapped.

Sweat drips down my face. I suck in as much oxygen as possible, press up against the cold brick, and step over a ratty maze of wires and hoses. The space is tighter than I expected. Maybe this wasn't the best idea. I keep my head turned and watch for the Legion.

Another mistake. Now the space is too tight. I can't turn and look the other way. I'll have to blindly feel my way out.

I step over another pipe, carefully lifting one leg and then the other. I press my palms against the rough brick and take another step. When I glance at the alley entrance, my heart nearly stops. Wisps of black mist curl up, swaying and searching for prey. The mist slithers along the ground in my direction. I hold my breath and step over another mess of pipes and tubes. There's no telling how much farther I have to go. The smoke wafts back and forth, unsure of my path. Maybe the Legion can't sense my presence through the greasy air and humming motors. I can only hope.

As my foot searches for the ground, I kick a hose and trip. The sound ricochets. My heart stops. I've given myself away. The mist slinks toward the generator, following my path. Stupid me. I lift my leg higher and step over another pipe as fast as I can. The train shouldn't be more than a block or two away.

I set my foot down, ready to move again, when a tingle burns against my calf. Then I smell singed fabric. An exposed pipe sizzles into my leg. I yank my foot up, pulling away, but the damage is done. Pain blasts through my skin, eating away at my muscle.

I swallow my scream and fight to break free from the tangled wires. As I do, my shirt gets caught on a broken coil. I pull on the fabric, but my fingers won't stop shaking. I yank again, but I can't break free. The cold brick seeps through my clothes, chilling my back like a coroner's slab. My other hand searches for the edge of the generator. I'm inches from the other side. I strain, almost pulling myself out, but the shredded coils claw my shirt, keeping me trapped.

The mist snakes over the pipes, moving along the wall, inching closer. I try to step over another hose, but my throbbing leg won't cooperate. I tug harder. The shirt tears, but I can't get myself loose.

I grip the edge of the generator and pull with all my might to break free. I'm so close to getting through. But it's too late. The black mist weaves around my legs, burning through my clothes. The heated smoke slithers up my body, coiling around me. If I die, it will appear to be a natural death, like Jess. Like Silvia in the fire, or Alan drowning in a lake . . .

I'm suffocated by sulfuric ash. The burning mist cradles my cheeks like tender fingers before brushing over my lips. The feel and the sulfuric smell sickens me. I clamp my mouth shut and try not to breathe. The mist skims the side of my neck before tracing an outline around my collarbone. Burns sizzle on my skin. I writhe, struggling to break free, but the mist tightens like a noose. That's when I gasp, choking for air that now seems depleted of oxygen.

Right beside me, the mist forms into half of a sallow man. Not my father. Looks nothing like him. The beast contorts its face. His neck strains to push raspy sounds through his pulsing throat.

I open my mouth to scream, but it won't matter—no one can hear me. The generator is screaming for me. I'm light-headed, cocooned by ashen darkness. My skin burns as his arms constrict my body. I pound against the heated generator, fighting to break free, but it's no use. I'm bound. His sagging skin, sticky saliva, and vacant eye sockets hover right beside me.

The Legion has caught me.

35

SHATTERED

Blackness swirls in my vision. I'm bound by the vile creature, suffocating in bitter ash and greasy sulfuric air. I scream out the last bit of breath in my lungs. A golden flash flickers through the darkness. The Legion hisses. Frothy, rotten saliva lands on my cheek. Someone grips my elbow. Sparks fly. The next thing I know, the monster bursts into a shower of red embers, completely disappearing.

"It's okay, Cera." Maddox's voice cuts through my haze. "I've got you." He takes me out of the mess of hoses. I sputter, gasping for air. My cheek lands hard against his chest as I slump into him. I'm alive . . . Maddox . . .

I cough, finding air. Several deep breaths cleanse the burning stench of sulfur in my nose and lungs. Maddox holds me tight against him as I find the strength to stand. My leg throbs.

He wraps his arm around me and helps me limp away from the generator toward the street. I can't take two steps without wincing because the fabric of my pant leg is melted into the wound.

"Why didn't you listen to me?" His voice rumbles in his chest.

I glance up. His eyes are hard behind his tangled hair, and he won't look at me.

I wriggle out of his arms and prop myself up against the

brick wall. "I did what I had to." Pain sears through my calf as I accidentally put full weight on my leg.

"I told you to run." Maddox paces the alley in front of me. "I told you to hide. I told you not to let the Legion know who you are, and you ignored everything I said. Not only that, you ran off alone. Unprotected." He tramples over pieces of a broken beer bottle and scans the area for more Legions with the gold blade in his hand.

My own anger flares up in response. "The Legion was after you. I couldn't run. Who in their right mind could?" I bend my leg, swallowing the pain. "Not me. Especially after . . . after you . . ." I search his face for any signs that he's softening, but my words only seem to make him scowl even more.

"I messed up; I know." He exhales and runs his hands through his hair. "I shouldn't have kissed you," he mutters, pressing his palm against his forehead as if trying to block that moment from his mind.

I press my lips tight to keep them from trembling. I feel about as shattered as the glass under his feet. This must be what Harper meant when she said Maddox had a "knack for making you feel one of a kind," and I fell for it. I even kissed him back. How could I have been so stupid? Either that, or it's because he's an Elite Legacy who could never get involved with someone like me. A Blight, a tainted half-breed. "What I did kept everyone alive." I push away from the wall and hobble to the street.

Maddox follows after me. "Calling out the Legion, then running off alone so it would follow you? That was your plan?"

"And what was yours?" I shout over more sirens as they blare through the streets. Heat boils my cheeks despite the frosty air. "Have me just stand there, doing nothing, and let the Legion come after you? That was your plan, huh? Wow." Despite everything, I still scan the rooftops and under parked cars for any lingering mist.

"Yes!" Maddox ruffles his hair, exposing his jagged scar. His face turns splotchy red. "You didn't have to tell it who you were. I could have killed it. I had Devon's knife."

"I did whatever it took to keep everyone alive." I set my foot down too hard and gasp at the pain. Maddox reaches for me, but I move myself away. "To keep *you* alive! You were on the ground. That Legion was barreling right at you. If I'd stayed quiet, that Legion wouldn't have followed me, and you wouldn't be standing here screaming at me right now. You'd be dead!" I hobble away from him. "I changed a vision. I saved a life—two lives—and that's all I care about."

He grabs my arms, holding me the same way he did back in the alcove, but I won't look at him. "I can't protect you anymore." His breath is labored, and his white T-shirt is drenched with sweat.

My knees soften as the rain-scented air smothers the narrow space between us, but I lock them in place with steeled determination. Maddox doesn't have the right to toy with me ever again. "I never wanted your help in the first place." I plant my palms against his chest. His muscles tense as I try to push him away.

"Cera, listen—"

"No, you listen!" I break away. "You dragged me into this without asking and then used me as an excuse to run so you wouldn't have to train with your brother. On top of that, you kiss me as some sort of stalling tactic so I wouldn't fight the Legions. And now you have the audacity to be mad because I told it I'm a Blight just to keep everyone *alive*? Unreal." Tears threaten to erupt from the pain inside. I bite my bottom lip to keep it from trembling.

Maddox steps in front of me, blocking my path. His face turns red, or flushed, or mad. Who knows. Who cares. "It wasn't some sort of stalling tactic." He runs his hand through his hair again. "I thought—"

"Doesn't matter what you thought. Don't *ever* do that again."

As I try to step around Maddox, Devon rushes around the corner with Harper trailing a few paces behind. "Cool it, both of you. We can hear you shouting all the way down the block."

A roaring pain shoots up my calf. I crash against the wall, stifling my cry. Devon's concerned glance sweeps over me. "Cera, you did it. You stopped the vision from happening. Everyone's alive," he says. "Now let's focus on what matters and get you back inside." He looks over his shoulder as a motorcycle speeds past. "It won't be long before the cops start searching around—not to mention the threat of more Legions. We need to get out of here, fast."

"She can't run with her leg like that." Harper stays close beside Devon. Her voice quivers. Her hurt expression falls on Maddox, telling me she heard everything. "My kit. It's at Hesperian . . ." She takes the vial from her pocket and opens it. "The best I can do for now is give you some serum to numb the pain." Harper holds out the vial. "A small sip. I'm running low."

I glance at the serum then back at her. Hesitantly, I take the vial.

Devon spots the wound on my leg and then looks away. "Do it quick. Then, Harper, I want you and Maddox to head back to the apartment. Brief Pop on what happened and fetch a bag for him from the closet. Be sure to let him know that a Legion got away. There's no telling how fast the rest of them will get here. We need to have Cera long gone before they do."

Harper glances at the wound. "I've got better supplies at Hesperian to fix this."

I shiver and knock back a swig of the serum. The sweet taste of the medicine burns my mouth, erasing the lingering feeling of Maddox's lips. Good. He can't just kiss me and then call it a mistake, lie to me, then expect me to trust him.

"There's no time, we'll have to make do with what's back at

the apartment." Devon looks around at the surrounding buildings, but there isn't a trace of mist I can see.

Harper quickly inspects the burns on my neck and hands. She's wearing even less makeup than before and not only looks younger, but more vulnerable. "We'll need to clean these marks up as well. Don't want them to fester or scar." Her voice is quiet, almost kind. I hand her back the vial.

She wraps her arm around my shoulder and helps me walk as she spills a confession. "I thought it was safe to go out. I was running low on the balm and needed to make more, you know, to show Council, but I was out of lavender. Everyone said the Legions were gone. I thought I'd just run out super quick." Her eyes well with tears. "Thanks for . . . for what you did." She wipes a runaway tear with the tip of her ring finger. "I've been a total . . . I'm so sorry." She looks up at the morning sky and blinks away more tears. Her voice trembles. "You cared enough about me to stop them, even though I . . . I was so horrible." She chokes back a sob.

She didn't have to thank me. My heart swells. I lean my head against hers for a brief moment. Pop is right, her hair smells like roses spritzed with perfume, and it still overwhelms. "The vision was changed. You're alive. But it wasn't only me. Devon and Maddox"—his name gets caught in my throat—"they both sacrificed a lot for you."

She sniffles and blots her tears. Devon comes up on my other side. His eyes are sympathetic. "I know it's not what you want, but now that the Legions know you're a Blight and one got away, it's only a matter of time before Sage knows." He doesn't say what comes next and doesn't need to. I remember our deal.

Devon lifts my arm over his neck and slides his other around my waist. "Let's get moving." He holds my hand as it dangles over his shoulder and gives it a gentle squeeze. Maddox trails behind us.

Before we step across the road, Harper lifts my other arm around her neck.

Sandwiched between the both of them, I shuffle a little faster, but not by much. A bird sings a quiet melody as morning softens the clouds blanketing the gray sky. Curious cars slow at the sight of us and then speed off. Not far, a shopkeeper sweeps a storefront, while another tosses more bags onto the piles loitering on the sidewalk. Their tired faces hold the monotony of another day.

Only it's not.

Today, a life was saved. A vision changed.

At what cost? I'm not entirely sure. Maddox and I will never be the same. Battle scars are a given. But as I limp down the road, tucked safely between Devon and Harper, I don't feel so alone. And despite the throbbing in my calf, the burdened weight in my chest feels a little lighter.

"I remember our agreement," I say to Devon. With help from both Harper and Devon, I hobble over the cracked sidewalk. "You give me the chance to stop a vision from coming true, and if I survive, you turn me in."

"You don't know what you're agreeing to," Maddox says from behind us. He no longer sounds angry. It's more frustration edged with hurt. I grit my teeth and don't dare turn around. Instead, I focus on the road ahead and search for signs of Legions, breathing through every painful step.

Devon looks over his shoulder at Maddox. "You know as well as I do there's no way we can keep Sage from finding her. We don't have the manpower or the resources to do this on our own."

Maddox whips around us and charges down the sidewalk before disappearing around a corner.

Devon glances at Harper and then up at the sky. "Why don't you run after him and make sure his burns are taken care of? I've got Cera."

Harper hesitates. "You sure?"

Thunder rumbles in the distance, even though the clouds are light. Devon's face tightens. "Hurry back to the apartment."

Harper releases me. Her ballet flats patter over the pavement as she races around the corner after Maddox. "Let's get you back quickly." Devon places one hand on my back and the other down low like he's about to lift me into his arms, even though his right arm has burn marks from the Legions.

I stop him. "I don't need to be carried. Thanks to the serum, the pain isn't excruciating. I can manage."

"I don't doubt that." Devon's mouth twitches. "But we're running out of time." On cue, police sirens blip and squawk. It sounds as if they're a block away. With my leg dragging behind me, I couldn't outrun a caterpillar if I tried.

"Fine." I sigh. "Go ahead."

36

SAFE FOR NOW

After an eternity of embarrassment being bounced around in Devon's arms while he navigates through quiet streets and parked cars, I muster the courage to break his concentrated silence. "Did I really make a mistake with the Legions?" The warm feeling in my stomach turns hollow as guilt settles in, the same way it always does when I screw things up. "Maddox made that perfectly clear, but . . ."

"But nothing." Sweat dampens Devon's collar, magnifying his earthy scent. "We're all alive. Harper's alive because of you." Devon says that last part in almost a whisper. Kindness returns to his eyes. Despite my inability to walk, for the first time in my life, I don't feel that useless.

Thunder rumbles in the distance. I check the surrounding buildings for signs of mist. Nothing, so far.

Wrapping my arm tighter around Devon's neck, I hold myself upright as much as possible to lessen the burden of my weight.

"Pop knows some people on the inside. They'll see more good in you than anything else," Devon says with a confidence I wish I could believe. "When they do, we can rally their support and keep you safe."

His pace slows as he turns another corner. This road I recognize. I remember the line of parked cars, rickety buildings, and the weathered blue door to his apartment building halfway down the road.

Another round of thunder shakes the ground as we reach the building. Devon slows near a dented streetlamp. When his arms slacken, I take that as my cue to slide down and stand on my own. Once my feet touch the ground, he lets go.

The door flings open. "The girl can't help it," Pop says to the person behind him as they exit the building. He's dressed in a red flannel shirt and tan corduroys. The clothes are so sturdy, they hide how frail he really is. He adjusts his dark glasses and reaches for the rusted handrail that lines the steps to the sidewalk. "She has a pull toward Sage that she doesn't understand. You can't be telling her what to do and expect her to act like an Awakened. She's not."

Maddox follows right after him, holding the door open. Not only does he look unsettled, but he is struggling to keep a stack of flapping papers from escaping his grip. "Then how can I protect—" He cuts himself off as soon as our eyes meet and then quickly looks away. At least he's not scowling at me anymore; now he's just talking behind my back.

Devon props me up. "Pop, we're back."

"Are they here?" Harper rushes out of the door with a duffle bag in hand. As soon as she spots me, she dashes over and drops the bag on the ground. She flings my arm over her shoulder while putting her arm around my waist. "We need to get you upstairs. I've got to clean up that burn. Yours too," she says to Devon.

"We'd better move. I want to be long gone before those creatures come around." Devon picks up the bag and heads toward a white town car parked by the curb.

Pop carefully reaches the bottom step. "Devon's right. Better to patch her up en route."

"In the car?" Harper's pink lips gape open. "How good of a Healer do you think I am?"

"The best I've ever known," Devon says. At his comment, Harper's lips twist with a flirty smile. The two of them lock eyes until another round of thunder rolls overhead.

Devon clears his throat. "Did you gather supplies?"

Harper's cheeks flush. "I put them in the bag."

A cold wind whips down the sidewalk, chilling my exposed skin.

"Where are we going?" I try to suppress a shiver because the air slips through my shirt. I glance down. Claw marks from the generator coils have slashed the front.

Devon holds the car door open as Pop lowers himself into the front seat. "Honey, the Cormorants know your scent. The Legions know your voice. Both sense the feel of your Current." Pop fishes around for the seat belt. "The only place you'll be safe from Sage is The Estate."

"The Estate?" I never heard that mentioned before.

"The Gardens," Maddox mutters, more to himself than to me. He sounds bitter and looks just as repulsed.

"The Council Estate is the only place where Sage's power—including those serving him—can't reach," Devon says, putting the bag in the back seat. "They're forbidden to enter. And if they try, well, it's worse for them than Paradise Steel to the heart. We get you behind those walls, and there's no way Sage can touch you."

"Sage has been circlin' in closer," Pop says. "Even set up some shop in a town not far from here, lookin' for artwork that might lead him to someone like you."

"Wait." My heart falters. "Like a gallery?" *Elysium's Edge.* The edge of paradise. A shiver crawls over my skin. I almost brought Mom's drawings to Mark. Mark, whose strange chemical scent rivaled the Legions. Maddox was in the square not far from the gallery when I first saw him. I look over at him. Did he know? Maybe not. I can't read anything but frustration in his taut expression.

A violent wind tangles my hair. Did I come face-to-face with Sage?

No. Mark had the patch of red skin at the base of his neck, said he was part owner . . . Mark was a Dissenter. He must have sensed something in me. That must be why he offered me so much and wouldn't stop calling. And I bought right into it.

Devon looks at me. "You okay?"

"Mm-hmm." I bite my lip and hobble toward the back seat where Maddox waits, holding the door open. Had Maddox not found me . . . Sage would have. I grip the top of the car with one hand and hold the doorframe with the other, ready to lower myself. Devon places a hand on Maddox's shoulder.

"If you don't wanna go, I understand. Pop and I can take it from here."

Maddox shakes his head. "No, it's probably about time I go back." He glances my way, but only for a split second.

Booming thunder shakes the ground, rattling the car. I grip the doorframe. The wind swirls trash on the street as a low hum vibrates the ash-scented air. My hairs stand on end. The sound carried on the wind is clear. Hornets. Although I can't see them, I know they're swarming in the distance. "I hear Legions. Not two or three, but an entire hive."

Devon jerks his head up, scanning the sky. "Where are they?"

Thunder cracks. A gale-force wind smelling of ash knocks me off balance and thrashes my hair in my face. The air turns a sickish green. When I look up at the sky, I find them, and my blood turns cold.

"There." I point at a sagging raincloud stretching the entire length of East Ridge. "Rain doesn't pour out of the side of a cloud like a waterfall. Those are Legions."

Devon pushes me. "Get in the car, now!"

37

GRAY HORIZON

Hail hammers the car roof as Devon peels onto the road. We're packed in the town car, squished too close for my comfort. Pop in the front seat, and me, sandwiched between Harper and Maddox in the back. My heart pounds harder than the rain pummeling the asphalt. I can't see anything through the steamed window. I turn to get a look out the back, keeping my leg propped up so Harper can tend to the burn. But in this cramped space, I end up pressing against Maddox's arm.

A hunk of ice hurls against Harper's door. I jump. Harper gasps. Her hands tremble, but she doesn't stop slathering my burn with a cold ointment.

Devon steps on the gas, flying faster down the open road. Another round of ice bombs bullet the back window. Harper screams. My hands fly up to cover my head, anticipating shattered glass, but somehow the cracked window stays together. Although I'm not sure how much longer it will hold.

I check the front window, searching for Legions in the storm. The frantic wiper blades struggle to beat away the dumping rain. The whole window is blurry except for one peephole where the vent is aimed and blowing on high. We can't see two feet in front of us, but that doesn't slow Devon down. He races through the blinding downpour as I press my fists into the faded velour seat. There's no need for me to count the seconds in the storm. Lightning and thunder collide as one.

Maddox's jaw is clenched. Even Pop grips his cane between his knees. Harper is the only one moving, and that's because she's wrapping my leg. No one says a word. It's as if we all know we're about to die.

We're just waiting for the crash.

I search Devon's face in the rearview mirror to confirm my fear. His eyes narrow in concentration. Every now and then he flicks his gaze to the right, then the left. I can't tell if he's memorized the path and is recalling landmarks, or if he can somehow see through the bucketing rain and ice. I doubt it's the latter. His eyes briefly meet mine in the mirror before fixing back on the road. "Do you see any Legions?"

I glance out every possible window, all of them fogging in the heated air. "I can't tell." My voice quivers. For all I know there could be a Legion riding on the back of the car or right alongside us. But being unable to see a thing in this storm, I'm useless.

Pop exhales deeply while rubbing out his knee. "Don't use your eyes, Honey," he says, seeming to sense my thoughts. Though even he sounds tense.

I follow his advice and close my eyes to listen over the whacking hail, the drumming rain, and the howling wind squeezing through the cracked glass. I don't hear hornets or smell ash. Only rain. Whether the scent is coming from Maddox or from outside, I'm not sure. But I'm positive something hovers around us because my insides harden, turning cold.

"There's something—" Suddenly a wind gust shoves the car. Devon fights to regain control of a violent fishtail. The end of the car whips around and back again as Pop grabs the dashboard. Harper's shaky fingers wrap my leg faster. My heart feels caught in my throat, blocking my scream. Maddox grabs my hand and holds tight as I bury my head into the back seat and brace for impact.

By some miracle, Devon recovers.

That gust wasn't just wind. In my gut I know it was Moloch. He's stealth hunting in the torrential rain, tracking us the same way he did Jess. I pull my hand away from Maddox and grip the back of Devon's seat. "It's a Cormorant."

"Moloch?" Maddox asks, but only loud enough for me to hear. When I nod, color slowly drains from his face.

Without a word, Devon guns the engine, flying faster through the blinding rain. Pop grunts, tightening his grip on the dashboard.

Can we really outrace the Cormorant while we're caged in this tin can, unable to see through the pouring rain? We can't even find a place to hide the way Maddox and I did the last time. My insides feel as if they're about to explode, demanding I do something. We can't die. Not now. Not like this.

Strength surges from deep inside me. I pull my leg away as Harper finishes securing my bandage. "Let me out." I reach for the door. "I'll lead him away." It's an impulsive thought, with no plan, but the only one I know will keep them alive.

Maddox grabs my waist, holding me back. "You can't go out there."

"I have to do something!" I try to pull away, but Maddox won't let go. Harper blocks the door handle with her arm. The harder I fight, the tighter Maddox holds on. "Let go of me!" I wrestle against him, but he's much stronger and a better fighter. He slips his arms around me and pulls my back up against his chest, locking my arms so I can't push him off. His breath labors against my ear. "Cera, stop."

"Honey, calm yourself!" Pop yells over the pouring rain as water drips through the cracks in the windshield. "You want to help? Be on our side. Stop fighting and trust Devon to get us through." He cracks his cane on the dashboard, the sound as sharp as a slap across my face.

I slacken. I *am* on their side. Maddox's heart pounds as I slump in his arms. Pop is right. Fighting won't help us right now—but how are we supposed to trust Devon when he can't see where we're headed?

Pop's words somehow cut through my panic. If what Pop said on the balcony is true and the beasts really are on my side . . .

I think fast. The Legions followed when I told them to. I lured them, commanded them, away. Maybe I can do it again. I close my eyes and take a deep breath. I visualize Moloch flying somewhere above us and mutter, "Stay back and leave me alone." I wasn't talking to Maddox, but he releases me just the same. I lean forward between the front seats.

In that instant, the rain turns into nothing more than a light mist. We now have a clear view of the country road and the street signs marking the sharp turn ahead.

"Where's the Cormorant?" Harper's voice quivers as much as her hands.

I turn around and look through a clear spot in the rear window. A water wall spreads across the road, hiding most of East Ridge. Moloch is caught behind it. His wings beat the water as his talons scrape through the wall. He's staying back. I can't believe it. "He's not following us. He's staying inside the storm."

"Hmph," Pop grunts. "Well, good. You just go on and stay focused. Keep a lookout in case he changes his mind."

I nod and keep watch. The wet country road glistens with a honey glow as it reflects the sky. The windshield wipers slow, squeaking over the dry glass. "What about everyone at Hesperian?" I look at the dark cloud hovering over the city. "With the flood of Legions, won't they find the hideout?"

Devon glances at me in the mirror. "After last night's attack, Kellan and Tanji set up a few alternative locations around East

Ridge to throw them off. And with the team of Blades that Council sent in, they'll be all right. The backup locations will buy us some time, because once those creatures find out you're gone, they'll come after us and won't stop searching until they find you."

I say a silent thank-you to the courageous ones who left Hesperian. Not only are they protecting the others, but also the five of us as I am whisked to who knows how far away. The same way Mom would every year around my birthday.

We drive for over two hours. I continue staring out the front window, searching for the creatures. The thick silence in the cramped car makes it hard to breathe. That, and I can feel Maddox looking at me like he wants to say something. There's nothing left to say. I pull my good leg up and rest my chin on my knee, pretending to focus on the road.

When we're far enough away, and the threats seem long gone, I slouch back in the seat, scrunched between Maddox, who keeps his arms folded across his chest and stares out the window, and Harper, who reaches over and squeezes my hand before letting go.

I may have saved her life, but in doing so, I opened a door that can't be closed. Now that the Legions know I'm a Blight, and the Cormorants know my scent, I'll be forever hunted.

After driving to the other side of the world, Devon finally turns down a clearing covered with fallen leaves. I don't see anything but a forest with aspen-yellow leaves drifting like confetti announcing our arrival. A few broken logs litter the underbrush, but the woods are clear of sneaking black mist. Most of the trees stand like soldiers at attention. Only a few dare to lean.

I don't hear Cormorants, only branches scraping the top of the car, the wind whistling through the crack in the broken windshield, and pebbles from the gravel road popping under the tires. The deeper we head into the forest, the harder it is to tell that we're even on a road. Twisted tree branches seem to close behind us as drifting leaves blanket the tire tracks.

Through the quiet hum of the car engine, Milton whispers in my thoughts: *"To thee I have revealed / What might have else to human race be hid."*

Yes, I know that now, Milton. From the beginning you asked me to *"see and tell / Of things invisible to mortal sight."* I didn't know what this verse meant back then, but I understand now. You were teaching me about the visions and the second realm all along.

I stare out the window and watch the sun burn through the forest. I never wanted to change the world, let alone imagine that a world I didn't know existed would change me. But now, whether I like it or not, I'm caught in the fight. And according to Pop, only one place is safe. A garden somewhere beyond the gray horizon of barren trees where Sage's powers don't extend. These garden walls will be my sanctuary, my prison, or both—if I'm even allowed to live another day.

ACKNOWLEDGMENTS

This story would never have come to life it weren't for community. I'm grateful to so many who have walked alongside me in this journey, encouraged me, believed in the story, and sacrificed so that I could chase after an unruly idea in my imagination. I'm thankful to God for opening every door, for the people, the community, the late nights, the tears, and the joy that this journey has been.

Thank you to Steve Laube who saw the potential, encouraged me to dust off the manuscript, and gave me this opportunity to tell the story. And to Lisa Laube for being an amazing editor, making this story better than I could ever imagine. A huge thank-you to Jordan, Trissina and the fabulous Enclave team for the opportunity to bring the story into the world. And to Lindsay Franklin for the wonderful copy editing magic.

Donna Wallace for incredible guidance and helping me see the sunshine when the skies felt too dark. The Veritas Vixens Writing Community and Zena for challenging me to dig deeper and loving the story as their own. Jamie Downer for being an incredible sounding board and preliminary editor. Susan Warm for opening her home as a haven and sanctuary in the final stretch of writing.

My heart is forever grateful to my Art House Dallas community and Fort Worth Writers group for their love and support in an artist community that's as close to Hesperian as anything can get.

Mary Gammill, who opened the door that set me on this adventure. Sue Brower, who encouraged me to finish the manuscript and labored over the draft, making it a million times better. Annemieke, who listened to my crazy ideas over countless cups of coffee. Alanna, for daring to read the manuscript in its roughest form. Mary David, for being an endless font of support in the journey. Erin Turek, for being my partner-in-crime on writing research adventures. My amazing beta readers: Sarah S., Molly D., Elisabeth G., Isabelle K., and Sloane C. who pushed me to tell a better story.

My patient children Addison, Leyton, Siena, and Ethan, who endured hours and hours and hours of an absentminded mom burning dinners and forgetting lunches on account of the unruly, imagined kids wreaking havoc in her head. My mom, four sisters, and sprawling family for their ongoing love and support.

Professor John Rumrich for his unbridled brilliance that sparked my love for Milton's *Paradise Lost* when I was an undergrad at UT Austin long ago. And for the love of my life, John, who sacrificed, endured, encouraged, believed, and wouldn't ever let me quit.

ABOUT THE AUTHOR

Sandra Fernandez Rhoads is a Cuban-Colombian born in Queens, New York, but currently lives in Dallas, Texas. Her background includes an MA in her seventeenth-century crush, John Milton, and previous script-writing experience for stage and short film. She has a deep love for the artist community, whether classical or contemporary, and one day dreams of playing the theme to *Jurassic Park* on her cello, named Lysander. *Mortal Sight* is her debut novel. Visit her at sandrarhoads.com or @sfrhoads.author

WHEN WORLDS COLLIDE,
SHADOW WRESTLES LIGHT

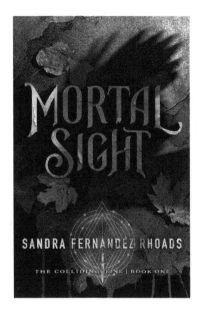
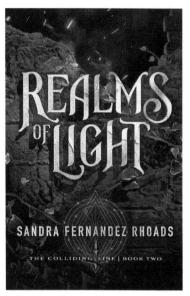

THE COLLIDING LINE SERIES

Mortal Sight

Realms of Light

Available Now!

www.enclavepublishing.com